Praise for Fel

'A dark and foreboding tale o...
of what can happen when we...
Sunda...

'Felicity has the reader gripped when she explores unhealthy
relationships based on insecurity and delusion'
Adele Parks, No. 1 bestselling author
of *Both Of You*, in *Platinum*

'Dark and gripping, this tale is perfect for snuggling up
with by the fire with a glass or two of wine'
Closer

'This was clever, relentless and utterly
recognisable. I absolutely loved it!'
Katie Fforde, No. 1 bestselling author
of *A Wedding in the Country*

'A cautionary tale of what happens when you get
caught up with the in-crowd ... I gulped it down'
Veronica Henry, bestselling author of The Beach Hut Series

'Held me in its vice-like grip from first page to last ...
A fascinating analysis of an unhealthy friendship ... and
the characters are so vividly drawn that I sympathised
with them and despaired of them in equal measure'
Sophie Hannah, bestselling author of *Haven't They Grown*

'Tense and tightly plotted'
Woman

'Excruciating yet unputdownable, this is
domestic noir at its most gripping'
Woman & Home

'I LOVED it. Such an unsettling read, with
a whole grass-is-greener vibe that makes it creepy.

Lisa H... ...*Woods*

Felicity Everett grew up in Manchester, lived, worked and raised her family of four in London and returned from a four-year spell in Melbourne, Australia to live in Gloucestershire in 2014. After an early career in children's publishing and freelance writing, she published her debut adult novel *The Story of Us* in 2011. Her second novel *The People at Number 9* was published in 2017 and her third novel *The Move* was published in 2020.

Also by Felicity Everett

The Story of Us
The People at Number 9
The Move

OLD FRIENDS

FELICITY EVERETT

ONE PLACE. MANY STORIES

HQ
An imprint of HarperCollins*Publishers* Ltd
1 London Bridge Street
London SE1 9GF

www.harpercollins.co.uk

HarperCollins*Publishers*
1st Floor, Watermarque Building, Ringsend Road
Dublin 4, Ireland

This edition 2022

1
First published in Great Britain by
HQ, an imprint of HarperCollins*Publishers* Ltd 2022

ISBN: 9780008288457

For my family

OCTOBER 2018

The hot tub was deserted now. It nestled in the corner of the dark rooftop, the thrum of its pump competing with the low moan of the wind over the nearby Pennines and the discordant hee-haw of the retreating siren. The LEDs continued to cast their psychedelic glow through the churning water, red to purple to blue to green and back to red. Rocking gently at its bubbling centre, a bottle of Moët, its neck sheared off, only the label holding together shards which had unfolded on the surface of the water like a butterfly's wings.

PART I

Down South
May 2018

1

Yvette

'Come on, Ruby love,' Yvette called upstairs, 'I said we'd be there for eleven.' She glanced in the hall mirror, one hand on the door latch. Too much make-up and her roots were showing. She looked every one of her forty-nine years.

Her daughter hurried down and grabbed a denim jacket from the newel post.

'Right, let's go get me a house!'

'Well, yeah, fingers crossed. Mark seems pretty confident there's a way.'

Yvette felt a swell of pride in her benevolent and well-connected friends – Mark and Harriet. Nice people. Classy people. Movers and shakers in a tasteful *low-key* way. She and Gary had known them forever. Bonded when the kids were little. They were an unlikely crew, but a crew nevertheless. Partners in crime; *compañeros*. It had just happened, really. All quite natural. Families like the Pendletons had been thin on the ground at Dale Road, but there were always one or two who wanted their kids to 'mix' – until it came to secondary school, anyway, when 'mixing' might hinder their prospects. Yvette wasn't complaining. They'd all four been fish out of water in their way – she and Gary, exiled Northerners, stuck in the Sarf. Mark and Harriet, blue-bloods, slumming it with the riff-raff. But the four of them had clicked from the get-go. Got on like a house on fire, which was lovely. Really, really nice. And, when it came to fixing stuff like this, useful.

So why was there a sinking feeling in the pit of Yvette's stomach? A falling away. Could it be that she secretly didn't want it fixed? Might some unworthy part of her actually prefer Ruby and Jordan's purchase to fall through, so they'd have to stay put and have the kid here, in this rickety little house? So that she could be a hands-on granny, sharing the night feeds and the nappy changes; fending off compliments when she took it out in its buggy and people mistook her for its mum.

Who was she kidding? The house was barely big enough for the four of them, let alone a son-in-law and a baby. It could all turn *Jeremy Kyle* at the drop of a hat. And as for being mistaken for its mum ... she scrutinized her reflection again ... the heart-shaped face, the turned-up nose, the blonde highlights had all looked very Drew Barrymore in the flattering light of The Clock Bar last night, but hungover in the harsh morning light, it was all a bit more ... Goldie Hawn. It was all right for Gaz – there was no age limit on picking up your guitar again. You could look like Godzilla and if the planets were aligned, still get a nostalgia tour of the smaller venues. He was in some rented studio even now, trying to 'lay down some tracks'. She was a bit peeved with Gaz, as it happened. He'd not told her he'd booked it till last thing, by which time she'd already accepted Harriet's brunch invitation, but these

6

meet-ups were never the same without Gary. The wattage always felt that bit lower. Once a rock god always a rock god ... even if he'd actually spent way longer as a music teacher in a failing comprehensive.

'Have you had something to eat, it's a longish walk?' she asked Ruby.

'Jordan made me a bit of toast first thing.'

'It's a shame Jordan couldn't come. Mark and Harriet would have loved to ... '

Ruby sighed.

'He's got a client, Mum.'

'On a Sunday?'

'Rich people want to work out at the weekend,' said Ruby with a shrug. 'He can charge twice what he gets at the gym.'

The day was overcast but mild, with an underlying humidity that threatened serious heat later on. Mother and daughter set off past their own yellow brick terrace, where SOLD signs and skips were starting to spring up almost daily, towards the scuzzier end of the street, where supermarket trolleys and abandoned mattresses languished against tumbledown walls. They crossed at the pedestrian lights, turned onto the main road and, dawdling past the estate agents, accidentally strayed too close to Budgens, prompting its automatic door to glide open. Ruby hesitated.

'Should I take them something, do you reckon?'

'What sort of something?'

'I dunno. Muffins, or ... ?'

'I don't think they're bothered about muffins,' said Yvette kindly, curious and a little sad that her daughter seemed to have inherited her own lack of entitlement. It wasn't as though the favours hadn't gone both ways over the years.

They turned into the park that marked the boundary between Yvette and Gary's affordable postcode and Mark and Harriet's more affluent one, and walked on in silence for a bit.

'What is it Mark does again?'

'PR. He's got his own business.'

'So, like, an influencer...?'

Yvette smiled.

'I suppose you could say that... except his stuff's a bit more subtle.'

They passed the graffiti-covered shelter where years ago, Yvette and Harriet had bonded over take-away coffees, while the kids played on the swings.

'D'you reckon he'd rather be rich and a nobody, or skint and famous, like Dad?' Ruby said.

'I don't know about famous,' Yvette scoffed, 'it's a while since anyone asked him for his autograph.'

'You know what I mean, though,' Ruby insisted, 'Mark's not on *Top of The Pops 2*, is he? He's not had books written about him.'

Yvette gave the question due consideration.

'I think Mark's pretty happy being Mark,' she said.

They emerged now on the other side of the park and turned the corner into Moorcroft Road.

'Ooh, look at the blossom,' said Ruby. 'Isn't it lovely?'

Yvette glanced up at the dark pink flowering cherry trees with their polished purple trunks and symmetrical clefts. Everything in Moorcroft Road was tasteful. The Edwardian semis with their well-proportioned square bays, the recycling bins in their camouflaged shacks of timber and trellis, the slatted blinds discreetly tilted to protect the expensively furnished interiors from prying eyes.

They crunched up the gravel driveway to number forty-five and Yvette rang the bell.

'Hello! Are we too early?' she said, a little defensively as Harriet flung the door open, still clutching a hand towel between damp palms. She was wearing a navy linen jumpsuit, her lovely androgynous face was make-up free and her blue-black hair was scraped into a crooked topknot. Beside her, Yvette's own outfit of skinny jeans, Converse and an oversized faux fur jacket seemed to smack of desperation.

'Any time's good, *you* know that,' said Harriet, pulling Yvette into a fond embrace. 'And as for you, stranger!' she said, relinquishing Yvette and gathering Ruby in for a hug. 'How come I never see you at the station anymore?'

'Oh yeah,' said Ruby apologetically, 'I'm going the other way now.'

'She got promoted. They've opened a posh new dental clinic in Croydon and she's Practice Manager,' said Yvette.

'It's not really posh, Mum,' Ruby corrected her. 'It's full of *Love Island* wannabees getting veneers, but the pay's all right, so ... '

'And you're buying a place with your boyfriend, your mum tells me ... ?'

'If they can raise the cash,' Yvette said breezily. 'You won't believe what a two-bed in Woolwich goes for these days.'

Yvette and Ruby followed Harriet down the hall towards an appetizing smell of coffee.

Mark bundled the newspaper to one side and stood up to welcome them. He looked, Yvette thought fondly, less like an off-duty PR executive and more like a rumpled teddy bear, the collar of his polo shirt up on one side, down on the other, a few toast crumbs still clinging to his weekend stubble. He leaned awkwardly across the table and kissed first Yvette, then Ruby on both cheeks, joggling a coffee cup in the process so that it slopped its cold remnants into the saucer. She could grow old and die in London, Yvette thought, but she would never get used to this form of greeting. A single kiss to the cheek was just about acceptable for a good friend – though if you'd tried it in Manchester in the Eighties you'd have risked a headbutt – but this showy double pucker just embarrassed her.

'Gary parking the car, is he?' Mark gathered up the various newspaper supplements into a pile and deposited them on the floor.

'Oh, no. Gary's er . . . rehearsing.'

She felt herself blushing. Gary would hate to know they were talking about his rekindled musical ambitions, but Mark had already moved on.

'You're looking well, Ruby. Feels like ages since we saw you. Or your sister come to that . . . when was it, Christmas?'

'The twins' twenty-first,' Ruby reminded him.

'O-h-h-h! Of course. Not *that* long then. Mind you . . . '

'Yes,' his wife said with a fondly admonishing tone, 'your recollection *would* be a bit hazy on that one, wouldn't it?'

She raised her eyebrows meaningfully at the visitors.

Mark had been pissed, Yvette remembered, but not in an obnoxious way. A bit of dad-dancing could be forgiven under the circumstances. And his speech had been very moving. He had held the floor effortlessly, even though glassy-eyed and semi-coherent. Only someone as comfortable in his skin as

Mark could have pulled off a car crash of a speech like that and still made everyone laugh and cry and cheer. Everyone, that is, except Ollie, the younger of the twins by forty-five minutes, in whose honour half the speech was meant to be, but who had gone AWOL as was his custom when the spotlight headed his way. It was a habit he had perfected over the course of his twenty-one years; one which, whether by design or accident gave him – the less robust, less magnificent twin – a certain power.

'Coffee?' Harriet called over her shoulder, raising her voice above the hiss of the Gaggia.

'Ooh, please,' said Yvette eagerly, although she'd have preferred a cafetière.

'Ruby?'

'Oh er ... no thanks. I'll just have a glass of water if that's OK.'

'You can have *one*, Rube,' Yvette said in an undertone.

'I know I can, Mum,' said Ruby pleasantly through gritted teeth, 'I'd rather have water.'

Harriet darted her a shrewd glance.

'Does this mean what I think it means?' she said, her tone falsely bright. Yvette hesitated and murmured to Ruby.

'Are we going public ... ?'

'I think you just did, Mum.'

'Oh Ruby, congratulations! Gosh, that's ... ' Harriet's voice cracked and she pressed the bridge of her nose, ' ... wonderful! Did you hear that, Mark? Ruby's ... '

'Yes, well, early days yet. Best not jinx it!' Yvette said briskly.

'No, quite ... ' said Mark. He darted an anxious glance at his wife, who had turned away and was rearranging the mugs on the dresser so they all faced the same way.

Yvette couldn't help feeling slightly irritated. She'd known this would be tough on Harriet, but did she always have to make it about her?

Harriet had had her own fertility issues in recent years, but they hardly compared with Ruby's. Failing to stay pregnant in your mid-forties when you already had two strapping boys just wasn't the same as having to go through IVF at thirty-three to stand a chance of a first.

'OK so, coffee's out ... what else have we got?' Harriet opened the fridge. 'Oat milk, fresh orange ... or ... how about a wheatgrass smoothie?'

Yvette suppressed a further surge of irritation. As if a cup of coffee was going to be make or break. It was this sort of attitude that was turning Ruby into a nervous wreck. The poor girl had lived a life of self-denial for the last two years – no booze, no unpasteurized cheese, folic acid coming out of her ears, and she still hadn't managed to get past the first trimester.

Ironic, considering Ruby had herself been conceived by accident after a night on the Malibu and Marlboro Lights. And what a night it had been. Miles Platting Thunderdome. Fourth of September, 1986. There had been a gang of them from school in the mosh pit, fake IDs and done up to the nines, but it was Yvette who'd caught Gary's eye; Yvette who'd got the nod, when they'd gone backstage to 'get the band's autographs', Yvette who'd hugged to herself the knowledge that the lead singer of The KMA was her boyfriend ... until he didn't call and she missed her period ...

'Water's fine,' said Ruby, giving her mother a death stare.

There was an awkward silence while Harriet coaxed ice from its plastic container, unscrewed a bottle of mineral water, rejected a perfectly clean glass for having an imaginary smear on it and finally set a drink down in front of Ruby.

'So,' Mark said briskly, retrieving his laptop from the kitchen surface, 'shall we get on to bricks and mortar?'

Mark explained that his broker (of course he had a broker) had identified several lenders who would offer a higher income multiple and a lower deposit than the high street, despite the slightly blemished credit record that Ruby had acquired. The downside was a higher interest rate, but that would only be for a few years assuming no further credit blips.

Yvette watched Ruby's face intently as she digested the significance of Mark's news. The taut, bright receptionist's mask with which her daughter had faced down her disappointment for the last eighteen months was starting to relax and crack, revealing the emotions beneath. She looked younger, softer, more vulnerable. Yvette felt a corresponding glow in herself.

2

Harriet

Harriet returned to the kitchen and stood in the doorway, watching Mark wipe down the surfaces.

'Well, I just hope it's all straightforward,' she started to say, but her voice faltered.

Mark turned around in surprise. He tossed the J-cloth back on to the draining board and came over.

'Hey... what's this? Don't upset yourself.'

'It's just... people don't realize. They take things for granted. But it's not *like* that, is it? I want to warn them. Tell them not to count their chickens, you know...? It's so fragile.'

'Oh sweetheart, come here...' He gathered her into his arms and Harriet tried to succumb to his warmth, his love, but she felt stifled, her nose full of the detergent smell of his polo shirt. She put him at arm's length and looked into his face, meeting his expression of love and concern with one as close to gratitude as she could muster.

Mark pulled her to him again and this time she didn't resist, but leaned her chin on his shoulder and let her gaze drift through the window to the garden beyond. It was starting to come into its own. Tendrils of clematis corkscrewed their way thickly through the trellis, coral-coloured peonies thrust furled buds into the spring sunshine. It was almost more than she could bear.

'It's important to keep things in perspective,' Mark told her. 'Just because you, because *we* … had … issues, doesn't mean … Ruby's situation's different. They're young. She's had trouble conceiving, I know, but now she's pregnant, there's no reason to think it won't stick.'

In the silence that followed Harriet recalled how her own last pregnancy had ended – the Heals bedspread that had to be double-bagged and taken to the dump, the mood in the house so subdued that Jack played Minecraft with the sound down for a week and Ollie barely came out of his room.

Perspective? What perspective? Had Mark forgotten how devastating it had all been? How terrifying. Had he not been there in the room with her as each contraction had picked her up like the swell of the ocean and deposited her a bit further from the shore? Did he not remember how the blood had flowed out of her, the clots getting bigger and bigger? From what possible perspective could that look OK?

A faint electronic buzz brought her back to the moment. Mark looked slightly sheepish. He patted his pocket.

'It's an alert,' he said, 'the football's on … '

Harriet smiled and rolled her eyes. Typical Mark – nothing left to chance. Everything timetabled, planned for, factored in … except the one thing that had really mattered.

'Go on then,' she said, indulgently, 'go and watch the bloody match.'

Mark squeezed her forearms gratefully and scooted.

Harriet cast an eye around the already pristine kitchen, wondering what she could usefully do. She went over to the fridge and stared unseeingly into it, as if it might contain some clue to the meaning of life. Her eyes alighted on the organic chicken that had been a bargain because its use-by-date was tomorrow. It was huge. She had inadvertently bought for a family again. Nearly three years should have been long enough to kick the habit. She wished she had thought to invite Yvette and Ruby to stay. Maybe it wasn't too late. She glanced around for her mobile phone. She could still ask them over. Gary could follow on after his rehearsal – maybe Ruby's younger sister Jade might come too, if she wasn't getting it on with her mystery man ... It would be like old times. Now Harriet remembered where her phone was. She'd left it charging in the bedroom but before she had taken two steps towards the hallway to retrieve it, her confidence in the plan had started to ebb away. There would need to be dessert. Jade was vegan. Gary would be late.

She knew already that she would cook chicken for two and they'd eat it in front of whatever Scandi noir was occupying the Sunday evening schedules at the moment.

She was on her way to her study, to console herself with her latest pet project – the conversion of a crumbling Cheshire warehouse into an eco-friendly housing co-operative on behalf of a small, forward-thinking charitable trust – when, passing the living-room door, she heard Mark talking on the phone.

'... I know, he's rubbish, but Cahill's injured ... whoa! Unlucky! Did you see that? I know. I know ... '

It was Jack. She could tell from the easy bantering tone, the effortless affection, leaking through the macho talk of team selection and tactics. She lingered in the hall, aware that she should give father and son their privacy; unable quite to do so. By now the conversation had moved on from football and Mark was having trouble staying with the detail.

'Graduation? Yeah, yeah, 'course we do... when is it? Referee! Bloody hell. July? *Yes*, both of us. Your mother'd never forgive me... *gown* hire? Are you kidding me? You pay nine grand a year in fees and they still want you to... Oh, man that was dirty! Yeah, yeah, put us down for two tickets then...'

Harriet entered the room and hovered by the door. Mark glanced up at her and she held up three fingers. Mark frowned and gestured towards the phone, asking whether she wanted to speak, but she shook her head and mouthed 'Ollie' at him. Now Mark caught on.

'Oh yeah, get three tickets, your mother says, in case your brother wants to come... I know, I know he won't, but we should give him the op... bloody *hell*! Did you see that pass? So yeah, get him one anyway. Text me the damage and I'll pay you back... Yeah, yeah. See you soon, mate. Love you.'

'I hope they don't clash,' Harriet said, chewing her lip.

'Costa and Walker?' said Mark vaguely, his eyes still fixed on the screen. 'They already did.'

Harriet couldn't tell if he was joking or not.

'Jack's and Ollie's graduation ceremonies. What if they're on the same day?'

Mark turned now and for the first time, with a martyred air, focussed his attention fully on her.

'I don't think we'll be going to Ollie's, do you?'

'What, you think Ollie's going to flunk his degree?' she

said indignantly, her mind nevertheless flitting to past parents' evenings, *behaviour issues ... disruption ... truancy ...*

"Course not,' Mark said, 'I'm sure he'll get his shit together. You have to be really fucking hopeless not to at least get a third these days. No, I just meant, it's not his style, is it? The whole mortar board thing. Going up on stage ... '

'I know what you meant ... ' said Harriet darkly but Chelsea had scored and Mark was having trouble staying on topic. 'I'm going to do some work,' she muttered and went up the two flights of stairs to the attic.

She closed the door to her study behind her and took what her yoga teacher called a cleansing breath. This room was her chapel, her place of pilgrimage. It was spartan in design and bathed in natural light, thanks to a window that took up the entire gable end and gave onto a soothing vista of treetops. The furnishings were minimal, all Harriet's files and books and plans being cleverly concealed behind almost-invisible white-painted cupboard doors, the magnetic catches of which popped open satisfyingly at the application of the slightest pressure. Only essential items of furniture – her workstation and an Eames chair – were allowed to float within the ethereal space like ideal versions of themselves. It was everything she'd want a study to be, yet the opposite of what she had intended this room to be, which was a tasteless grotto of pink chiffon and fairy lights, dress-up clothes and bean-bag chairs.

They had begun converting the attic when the twins were little, and Harriet was still studying for her architecture diploma. She had thought it a good little project to hone her skills on, but Mark hadn't been so keen. Four bedrooms were ample, he'd said. No need to tempt fate by converting a whole floor for a theoretical kid, who if he or she happened along, would be just as happy with the box room.

'*She*,' Harriet had insisted sternly, for without a 'she' of her own, how could she right her parents' wrongs? Bring up the daughter she should have been herself? Bold and messy and free. Her daughter wouldn't be forced to wear school uniform at four, cram for exams at eight, go to ballet lessons, because ice skating was 'common'. Her daughter would be a free spirit, not a photofit to meet her mother's expectations.

Not that Mark had been averse to the idea. They'd discussed names, back in the day, of course they had. But the twins' traumatic birth had shocked Mark – he'd never admit as much, but she knew he didn't *trust* her to have another child now. He thought she was too frail; the process too violent. But that sounded Victorian, so he couched it in the language of feminism – she had come this far with her studies; she might never qualify if she didn't give it her all. But Harriet couldn't let go.

Creating a bedroom for this much wanted, this *essential* child, had become an act of faith. When the phantom girl did not appear, fertility charts took over their sex life, and the act itself became a timetabled chore. As she gradually lost faith in her ability to conceive, the girly loft began to lose its lustre. Several more miscarriages followed and at some point, Harriet stopped referring to it as the baby's room, resorting instead to the more neutral 'the spare room' and then, 'the study'. Yet even as the dream receded, she still couldn't enter the room without a sense of yearning; of loss.

She sat down now, elbows perched on the arm rests of her ergonomically designed office chair, scooted herself up to the desk and turned on the computer. Just for a second, in the moment before the screen sprang to life, she thought she glimpsed, reflected in its dark gleam, a toddler playing on the rug behind her. She felt a pain in her belly like the deep drag of an impending period; closed her eyes, bit her lip... touched the mouse. A graphic appeared – the front elevation of the warehouse, bearing the legend, in a nostalgic font, 'The Button Factory. Flexible living in the heart of the community'. A pair of virtual doors slid back, splitting the image in two and hurtling the viewer into a three-dimensional plan over three floors of the layout of the warehouse.

With a few clicks of the mouse Harriet had homed in on the exterior wall of the middle floor, which at the moment featured two floor-to-ceiling sliding doors, giving onto a narrow balcony. She was wondering whether to replace them with a concertina-design more amenable to indoor-outdoor living when her phone pinged.

Fancy coming over to ours for your dinner? 🙏 Jordan wants to pick Mark's brain. Tell M I'll cook his favourite! Yx

3

Gary

Gary reversed the GTI into his resident's bay with a turbo-charged roar and opened both front windows to clear the car of cigarette smoke, forgetting that the stereo was still going full blast. The old fart from across the way glanced up disapprovingly from his hedge-cutting.

'Sorry,' called Gary cheerfully, killing the music and adding, 'you miserable cunt,' under his breath as the windows slid shut again.

He fished in his pocket for his baggy and, plucking the car manual from the driver's door, laid it across his knees. He glanced up. The old git was still eyeballing him. Probably shouldn't. He put the coke away, but couldn't resist licking his forefinger and zigzagging it back and forth across the surface of the manual, to mop up what was left from last time, before rubbing it needily around his gums. Waste not want not. He yanked the rear-view mirror down and studied his face, wiping the back of his hand across one nostril and then the other, before giving his reflection an approving nod, and pushing the mirror back into position. They'd fucking nailed the recording and he'd fucking nail it tonight. Half a term's lesson plans in one evening. Bish bash bosh. He'd do it with the football on catch-up in the background. Fuck Ofsted. He was da man.

'Gaz, is that you?' Yvette's voice called from the kitchen.

'No, it's the Dalai fucking Lama,' he called back. He could smell meat cooking, not restaurant meat – more that homey, school-dinner-y smell that went with steamed-up windows and Radio 2. Great if you were hungry but right now …

He ducked into the downstairs toilet and dry-retched a couple of times over the bowl. Lucky the lads couldn't see him. Mind you, they'd be no better – worse, if anything; specially Macca. It'd been a while.

He turned the cold tap on now and thrust his face into the narrow oblong washbasin that Harriet claimed was the only one she could find that'd fit in the space. He recoiled as the water rushed up both nostrils as well as into his open mouth, almost drowning him. He caught his breath and dived back in, gulping down mouthfuls of water until his thirst was slaked. Coming up for air, he found himself staring at his startled doppelganger in the mirror above the sink. Piss holes for eyes, cheekbones like bacon slicers, layered mod-crop plastered to his face, he looked like Munch's *Scream*. He fished for the towel and rubbed his face vigorously, then gurned into the mirror, turning his jaw this way and that. Could be worse. Could be a lot worse. He'd still got it going on. Steeling himself against the desire to retch, he sauntered into the kitchen.

'Hiya!' Yvette said, her tone sing-song and fake. She was stirring something on the stove, spray-on jeans tight over her still tasty arse, no pinny over her little fitted shirt, smudge of flour on her cheek. The sight of her made him horny; also a little lovesick. She tried so fucking hard, bless her. He went over and, seizing her by the waist, smooched her cheek.

'Gerroff us, Gaz, you're all wet.' She shrugged him off, and jerked her head meaningfully in the direction of the extension. He turned to see four pairs of eyes regarding him with expressions ranging from mild embarrassment to amused indulgence. His mind processed the information in what felt like slow motion. Ruby; fair enough. Jordan too, as per ... but Mark and Harriet? On a Sunday night? He raised his hand in a nonchalant salute and turning back to Yvette, gave her a 'what the fuck?' look.

'Little get together,' she said. 'See out the weekend.'

Her eyes tick-tocked back and forth, clocking his dilated pupils.

'Oh, Gaz you haven't ... ?' she muttered in an undertone. 'You bloody have, haven't you?' Then, sighing, 'Well, try and keep a lid on it for our Ruby's sake ... '

The smell of the food was making him gag again. He'd definitely overdone the coke, but he could handle it. He was fucked if he was going to look like a lightweight in front of these. He ducked into the big Fifties-style Smeg fridge and helped himself to a beer. Flicking the lid off on the integrated bottle opener of the island dining station, he sauntered past it towards the airy glass extension which had once comprised a side passage, scullery and outside toilet but that now accommodated two low-slung Swedish sofas either side of a coffee table in front of stylish wood-framed patio doors.

'To what do we owe this dubious fucking pleasure?' he said drolly. He could feel his scalp tingling as dopamine flooded his brain and he adjusted with a sense of frustration, then exhilaration, then a reckless God-like confidence, to the changed circumstances of the evening. What the hell. He'd be up all night anyway and these'd be fucking off to bed by eleven, latest, so there'd be plenty of time to sort his lesson plans. He was among friends. These people loved him. He loved them. Bring it on.

'Dad, mind your language, will you?' said Ruby, with an embarrassed laugh.

'Yeah man, there's ladies present,' agreed Jordan – as much, Gary could tell, to convey his easy intimacy with his soon-to-be father-in-law in front of these slightly daunting guests, as to curb Gary's behaviour. Gary fist-bumped Jordan in acknowledgement, before flumping down on the sofa and raising his bottle to the assembled company.

'Booyakasha!'

'Oh my God, Dad . . . ' Ruby closed her eyes.

'It's all right, Rubes, he thinks it's rock 'n' roll,' Mark said indulgently. 'He's been rehearsing, remember. He's the comeback kid, your old man. The Peter Pan of pop.'

'*Pop?*' Gary said. 'You cheeky cunt . . . '

Mark was a lovely bloke, no doubt about it, and a fucking clever one, but Gary had seen his vinyl collection and a man with as many Snow Patrol albums as Mark had didn't get to take the piss out of The KMA.

Mark's response was to tuck his thumbs into his lapels in the manner of a high court judge.

'Did you or did you not appear on *Top of the Pops?*' he intoned, with the emphasis on *Pops*. Gary noticed Yvette and Ruby exchange a smile, which only served to stoke his growing paranoia. Had they all just got together to rip the piss out of him or what?

'Yeah,' Gary puffed out his chest, 'and so did fucking Bowie, man, not to mention John Lennon and Nirvana and New fucking Order.'

'Please stop swearing, Dad,' said Ruby, with an awkward giggle.

Gary glanced at his daughter and felt suddenly side-swiped by shame and love and awe. Tears rushed to his eyes and he had to wipe his nose discreetly on the back of his hand. How had this happened? How had his little girl become a woman? He took a swig of beer and patted Ruby's thigh a little harder than he'd meant to.

'Sorry, mate,' he said, and she closed her eyes in what may or may not have been gratitude.

'Here, Gaz, make yourself useful and set the table, will you?' Yvette said, moving back towards the kitchen island.

'I've only just sat . . . '

'I'll do it,' Jordan sprang to his feet.

'Thanks, Jordan love. Just cutlery and red wine glasses for now. The plates are in the oven.'

'Red wine glasses?' said Gaz. 'Bloody 'ell. I was expecting summat with oven chips in front of *Antiques Roadshow*. Does someone want to tell me what's going on?'

'Does there have to be something going on for us to have our friends round for something to eat?' said Yvette, in such a way as to confirm that there was, absolutely, something going on. Gary's brain felt like a Rubik's cube, swivelling through the possibilities, trying to resolve them into a meaningful whole. Here was Jordan out to impress, cracking on like he, not Gary, was head of the household. *Yes, lad, you know where the cutlery's kept, big fucking deal.* Ruby looking all hopeful, like it was the run-up to Christmas and she didn't know if she'd been naughty or nice. Mark being Mr Smooth, like he was about to give you your annual appraisal and Harriet – hands clasped demurely around her crossed knees, smiling hopefully around the room. It was no good, he couldn't unravel it. His brain was too cooked.

'It's my fault, Gary . . . ' Jordan said, clapping him on the shoulder, 'it's just, you know, me and Rubes weren't sure if we could get the mortgage we was after? Mark's helped us out, hopefully.'

'Oh aye?' said Gary, relieved, yet also irritated. Why was it always Mark to the rescue? 'Some dodgy Ponzi scheme, it'll be, if I know that f—' Gary glanced guiltily at Ruby, ' . . . if I know 'im.'

Mark laughed and shook his head.

'Not at all. It's legit. My broker's just putting them in touch with a specialist lender.'

Jordan frowned seriously and rubbed his chin, then ruined it by breaking into a full-on smirk, like a kid who'd been told he can stay up past his bedtime. What was it with the youth today? Gary wondered. They lived at home forever, splurging all the money they saved on flat whites and Ubers, then moaned that the older generation had priced them out of the housing market. Jordan had to be thirty if he was a day. Jesus, Gary had had two careers by then. Played the GMEX a couple of times. Toured America; year or two in the wilderness, then he'd knuckled down and done teacher training. Had to, hadn't he? He'd got a fucking family to think of; a mortgage to pay.

He was a hard worker, Jordan. A good lad, if you overlooked the fact he wore a girl's hairband to keep his fucking afro out of his eyes, but honest to God it was time he grew up.

'I'm dishing up now,' called Yvette, and soon they were all perched on high upholstered stools around the dining station, knocking back Merlot and tucking into Yvette's Beef Wellington. Lips were smacked, eyes narrowed in appreciation. Luckily for Gary, Yvette was so enjoying basking in everyone's approval that he got away with eating less than half his portion and hiding the rest under a shelf of pie crust, like he used to with his school dinners back in the day. Not that it wasn't tasty, but he felt like he was on the deck of a ship in rough seas, and one more mouthful might find him heaving over the side.

'That was great, Yvette,' Mark said, aligning his knife and fork on his empty plate. 'Love a bit of beef. We're not allowed it anymore.' He pouted at Harriet like a disgruntled schoolboy and Harriet gave a weary smile.

'You are *allowed* it ... ' she said, 'I'm just trying to cook more sustainably.'

'Uh oh!' Yvette said with a comedy grimace. 'Here you go then, Mark. Best eat the evidence.' She heaped the last slice onto his plate and Mark widened his eyes appreciatively.

Gary watched the little tableau play out: Yvette, pretending not to notice Mark pretending not to notice her cleavage. His lovely wife – queen of titillation – beef, boobies, all the forbidden things. There was no threat in the frisson between them, Gary knew. Yvette fancied Mark the way she fancied the bloke off Thames News – a bit posh, a bit good-looking and a lot unattainable. Mark liked Yvette for the same reason any bloke would like Yvette – because she was fit – but he only flirted with her out of gallantry and that made Gary mad. She might dress a bit try-hard and come off a bit brassy, but she was probably the smartest out of the four of them and who knew what she might have amounted to if he'd not knocked her up at sixteen? But that was the trouble with marrying your groupie – as sound a bird as she might turn out to be, and as washed-up a twat as *you* might turn out to be, she'd always count herself lucky to have got you and, on some level, you'd always agree. She was worth two of any of 'em, as far as Gary was concerned, and yet here she was apologizing for the top-notch dinner she'd served up at a moment's notice, because she'd just found out it wasn't fucking 'sustainable'.

'It's not something I'd buy any more,' Yvette said, her well-exposed chest now a bright shade of scarlet, 'but we had this bit of silverside hanging fire in the freezer and I thought I'd best use it up while our Jade's not around.'

'Where *is* Jade anyway?' Harriet asked, pouting prettily around the room as though her sudden interest might have been enough to make the girl materialize. She couldn't take her drink, Harriet, that was the thing. Always got a bit duchess-y and shrill when she'd had a few.

'She's doing four till ten at Aldi,' Yvette replied.

'Will she be all right, walking home at ten?' said Harriet.

'Oh, *he'll* bring her back, Juris, will,' Yvette said with a nervous glance at Gary, 'the boyfriend.'

'*Boy*friend,' Gary muttered, 'stretching the fucking definition there a bit, aren't you? He's forty if he's a day.'

Yvette flashed him a pleading look.

'I don't know what she sees in him,' Gary muttered, 'brains coming out of her ears and she opts for that.'

'Oh, she'll grow out of him,' Harriet said, 'wait till she gets to uni. She'll be dating some Hooray Henry before you know it.'

'Christ, I fucking hope not!'

'There you go, you see,' Harriet said pointing her fork and wrinkling her nose, 'when it comes to your children nobody's good enough. No offence, Jordan...'

'None taken,' Jordan said, with a doubtful smile.

'So, do you reckon your Jack's in it for the long haul with... what's she called again...?' Yvette topped up their wine glasses, clearly keen to move things on from the trigger-topic of Juris.

'Maisie?' Harriet said, taking a grateful sip. 'He does seem to be, yes. She's a lovely girl. Very nice family from the sound of it. We're meeting them when we go down for graduation, next month...'

'Oh well, there you go. Practically wed.'

'One down, one to go...' said Harriet, with a jokey shrug.

'Don't hold your breath!' muttered Mark.

'Don't be like that Mar...'

'There's someone for everyone...'

The two women blurted at once, then laughed awkwardly.

Gary frowned. This, he took to be a reference to the other twin – the dodgy one. What was the kid's name again? Henry? Toby? *Ollie*, that was it. Was he finishing uni too? Or had he dropped out? Gary wasn't great at keeping up with the domestics on a good day, let alone when he was off his face. They were chalk and cheese, the two lads, that much he knew. Might as well have called them Cain and Abel and have done with it. Poor Ollie. Gary knew what it was like to be the black sheep of the family and it was no fucking fun at all. Not if his own experience was anything to go by. Three number one singles and a gold disc and his mam'd still rather he'd got his City and Guilds.

'So, did you, er . . . lay down any tracks today?' Mark said.

God love him, he was a tryer. Always papering over the cracks, making nice. No wonder he was in PR. He'd have loved the song as well, would Mark, even though it was a third-rate tune that'd need a ton of work before it even came close to a B-side from the old days. But for once, just *once*, Mark's opinion counted for nothing and he needed to know it. You forfeited your credibility when you sold yourself to the highest bidder. You couldn't be schmoozing airtime for *X-Factor* also-rans and still expect to be taken seriously as a muso, never mind how much money you earned or which fucking movers and shakers you had in your phone contacts. Gary knew this, but did any other fucker know it? Not here, it seemed; not tonight. Jordan, for one, kept looking at Mark like he was Eden Hazard and Stormzy rolled into one. It wasn't what Gary needed after a long hard day in the studio with a night of fucking lesson planning ahead of him. It wasn't fucking fair. An idea occurred to him.

'Here you go,' Gary said, clapping Mark matily on the shoulder and standing up to fish his phone out of his pocket, 'exclusive preview.'

'Yeah?' A delighted grin broke across Mark's face. Gary stabbed at his phone a few times and, when it had synched to the speakers, raised a finger to usher in a respectful silence. A long feedback-y chord faded in, followed by a chiming Rickenbacker guitar riff of such rhythmic, melodious beauty that around the table, heads began to nod and fingers to tap. Almost at once, Yvette tilted her head reproachfully and murmured, 'Gaz!'

Ruby recognized it next and Jordan had caught on by the time the vocal came in. Even Harriet looked like she might have heard the riff somewhere before, but Mark stood transfixed, mouth hanging slightly open, thumb thrust through the belt loop of his tragic chinos, fingers keeping time on his paunch.

'Not half bad for a first take,' he said.

'I should fucking think so,' Gary sneered, 'Stone Roses. "Waterfall", 1991. I'd give up sex for the rest of my life to have written that fucking tune.'

Mark's face coloured as the truth dawned. He stretched his lips into a sheepish smile.

'Yeah, very funny,' he said. Then, hopefully, 'It's not a *million* miles from your sound, though, right?'

Gary stared from face to face in amused disbelief, trying to recruit each one of them in turn to his roasting of Mark, but Harriet had gone pink, the kids were staring at their shoes and Yvette was looking daggers at him. And suddenly Gary was crying. Crying because he'd made a dick of his best mate and a cunt of himself. Crying because his band hadn't been a tenth as good as The Roses, even back in their heyday. Crying because, if this afternoon's rehearsal was anything to go by, they'd never be able to replicate the raw genius of their first album, and the absolute best they could hope for was to reprise the mediocrity of their third. Crying because the daughter who should have left home ten years ago was finally leaving home, and the daughter who was so clever she'd been offered a place at Oxford was so dumb that she was dating a hairy Latvian Uber driver twice her age who was trying to stop her going. Crying because his wife worked her socks off for peanuts and it was starting to show. Crying because he was a music teacher, not a rock god. Crying because he was coming down and he hadn't done his lesson plans and Ofsted were back in the morning. Crying because he loved all these people but he wanted them to fuck off now.

4

Mark

'Jesus!' said Mark plugging in his seatbelt. 'What was all that about?'

He checked the rear-view mirror and pulled out into the deserted street.

'Whatever he'd been snorting all day, I suppose,' muttered Harriet. 'Ecstasy? Coke? You tell me.'

'I don't know how he's got the constitution for it,' Mark shook his head, 'Sunday afternoon. Fuck me.'

'Aren't you mad at him?' Harriet said. Mark threw a perplexed glance at her.

'For pretending that was his song, you mean?'

Harriet gave him a pitying look.

'For setting you up,' she replied, 'For *humiliating* you.'

Mark frowned. *Had* he been humiliated? It seemed to him that mistaking one decent band for another decent band, especially when he'd been deliberately invited to do so, was quite a lot less humiliating than crying like a baby in front of your family, your oldest friends and your son-in-law-to-be, but what did he know.

He shrugged.

'I just hope he gets his shit together tomorrow,' he said. 'I wouldn't want to be in his shoes when the inspectors turn up.'

'Well, no, exactly. Ofsted,' Harriet agreed, darkly, as though Gary's failure to write his lesson plans was also somehow Mark's responsibility. 'I don't know what he was thinking. It wouldn't be so bad if it was only his own future he was jeopardizing, but Yvette's not going to be able to keep up the mortgage payments on a classroom assistant's wage, is she?'

'Have they still got a mortgage?' Mark did a double take. He had paid his own off some time ago – with a little help from Harriet, but not much. One point five mill their house was worth now, even after the downturn. It was a source of no little pride to him that he had managed to do that off the back of a business he had set up only ten years earlier, even if he had to sail a bit close to the wind to do it. But apparently all of that counted for nothing because he wasn't sufficiently au fait with The Stone Roses.

Harriet swivelled her face towards him. He could read her expression of cartoonish disbelief, even out of the corner of his eye.

'Of *course* they've still got a mortgage,' she said. 'They extended it to pay for the extension, remember?' She bit her lip.

Ah, so that was it. If Gary lost his job and the house was repossessed it would be his and Harriet's fault, because she'd remodelled their kitchen and he'd sorted the finance. Just like it would be their fault if Ollie flunked his degree, even though he'd wasted the entire three years watching daytime TV in a cannabis haze, and it was their fault that beef cattle

36

were destroying the planet with their farts because they once ate steak. Everything was their fault. She was such a bleeding heart, Harriet. Such an earnest, do-gooding little ... he glanced across. She was staring through the gloom with her big, grave eyes like some nocturnal creature. His heart melted.

In the dark, she didn't look much older than she had when they'd first met at a Technology in Architecture Conference in Cologne twenty-something years ago. It hadn't been the most promising location for romance, and yet it had been romantic. Mark thought back to the cavernous conference hall; the banal background chatter, the smell of pretzels. Harriet had stood on the edge of a small group, listening to his client pitch on search engine optimization. At first, she'd caught his eye for how incongruous she looked; how bohemian and strange. She was thin as a rake, with skin so pale it was almost see-through, she wore a tailored suit and her hair was cropped short like a film star of the French New Wave. Her brows were furrowed and her lips pursed in a pout of concentration so intense, you would have thought he was unravelling the mysteries of life itself, rather than extolling the virtues of digital marketing. Only later, when her colleagues had drifted away, and Harriet lingered, expressing an improbable degree of interest in domain names, did it occur to him she might be a romantic proposition and even then, it took his brain a while to catch up with his libido. Close up, there was something undeniably erotic about her crisp, clean scent; the glimpse of collarbone disappearing into the starched white V of her work shirt.

Travelling up with her in the lift after a few drinks in the bar, he must have looked like any another businessman on the make, but he had felt like an ingenue. And when they'd got to her room there had been no small talk or preamble. She had taken her clothes off, and lain on top of the burgundy bedspread, arms hooked behind her head, the look on her face neither coy nor come hither, but grave, as if this were to be truly a momentous act and it so it had proved.

If Mark had had a type, Harriet wasn't it. She wouldn't even have registered if he'd met her at uni. He'd been too busy chasing model lookalikes with waist-length hair and mile-long legs. He'd been a bit of a playboy back then and had punched well above his weight, thanks to his reputation as a heartbreaker and the fervent, if mistaken, belief of each subsequent girlfriend that she would be the one to tame him. He had swashbuckled his way, still single, into his early thirties, much to the scorn of his mother who had told him on one of his rare visits home, with a slur in her speech and a look of sly triumph in her eye, that he was running to fat and losing his looks and would never get a girl. At the time he'd assumed he'd disappointed her. Why else send him to boarding school at seven? Why play down his every achievement and undermine his confidence at every turn?

But then his mother had dropped down dead and within a year he had met and married Harriet – the opposite in every way of those high-status, arm-candy women he'd been fixated on. It was almost as though, with no further need to prove his desirability, he was finally free to be happy. Except that, however understated a beauty Harriet was, however subtle her sexual allure, the attraction Mark felt for her was intensely possessive and bordered on addiction.

'Sweetheart, their house is not going to get repossessed – believe me,' said Mark, 'and even if it was, it wouldn't be your fault, it'd be Gary's for being a dickhead. But I shouldn't worry, because if I know Gaz he'll pull it out the bag tomorrow, anyway. He'll do a *Dead Poets Society* and have the inspectors eating out of his hand.'

'I wouldn't be so sure,' Harriet replied. 'He's already on a warning from the Head. He's walking a tightrope. You've got to think it's self-sabotage, really.'

'You think he'd deliberately screw over his career?' Mark gawped.

The thought of committing such a selfish act was mind-blowing, so beyond the scope of Mark's imagination that it made his pulse race. He could never do it himself; never. Even if he hated his job, which he didn't. Bloody loved it, actually. He loved being successful, employing people, putting something back, as his dad would have seen it. When his high street travel agency had folded in the Nineties the one thing that had grieved his old man more than depriving his son of a fortune had been the laying off of nearly five hundred members of staff. It was a matter of no little pride to Mark that he was now an employer himself, albeit on a more modest scale. Even more than the putting back, though, Mark enjoyed the joining in. He loved the nuts and bolts of PR, the pitching for accounts, the deadlines, the targets, the winning and losing. He felt proud too, that he'd done so well for himself, for all of them. It was a bit disgusting how much money he earned, really. And a bit humbling when you considered that he made a lot of it piggybacking off people like Gaz – ideas people, innovators, artists of one sort or another. Not that you'd call their latest big client a visionary, exactly. Bloke who'd adapted the Edison bulb for the UK market. But thanks to

Mark's team's 'Lightbulb Moment' campaign he'd got it into all the big stores and Mark's firm were in the running for an EVCOM award off the back of it. It sometimes struck him as rather unfair that someone with such ordinary gifts as he had been blessed with – confidence, strategic thinking, people skills – should have secured such a comfortable living, while Gaz had to cross-subsidize his true vocation – playing music – with the soul-destroying job of teaching it to a bunch of disaffected schoolkids.

State education, Christ! It was a sausage factory, run on a shoestring. No wonder Gary was burned out. God alone knew what kind of company Ollie might be keeping now if he'd gone to Gary's school instead of St Bede's. He'd probably be residing at Her Majesty's Pleasure instead of about to scrape a third in Sociology from Portsmouth uni. Fingers crossed.

Mark glanced instinctively at his phone, sheathed in its holder on the dashboard. He hadn't been able to bring himself to ring Ollie in the end. It had taken him three goes even to send a text.

Oliver,
Plans for the end of term, please? Need to work out logistics.
Best wishes, Dad

Hi Ollie, Got you a ticket for J's graduation ceremony (4/7).
Up to you. Dad x

In the end he had settled for:

ET, phone home.

ET had been Ollie's favourite film when he was little. Mark could see why. Little boy who preferred an extra-terrestrial to his own family. Made all kinds of sense when you thought about it. How hard they'd tried to bond with each other. Ollie snuggling up to him on the sofa, leaning his tousled head on Mark's shoulder, sucking his thumb in that adenoidal way he had, Mark steeling every cell not to shrink from him. Oh, he'd stayed put; tolerated the intimacy, but he might as well have peeled the boy off him like an incubus, because Ollie had sensed how he'd felt. He'd known.

It had started at birth. *Before* birth, actually. Mark had made a bargain with the God he didn't believe in. The baby can die as long as Harriet lives. It had happened in slow motion and at top speed. A rush of blue offal, in a glare of white light. Harriet's body practically eviscerated. The firstborn, healthy twin wheeled away in an incubator. The monitor bleeping, the drip dripping, the midwife frowning, glancing. The consultant scrubbing up for an emergency Caesarean, Harriet's pulse dipping, Mark struck dumb, horrified, praying.

'Just get it out, for fuck's sake!' he'd heard his own voice shouting. 'Please will you just get it out? She's not doing well.'

But before the surgeon had even picked up his scalpel, Harriet had made a horrible moan and there was a slither and a stench like death and Ollie had shot out like a rejected organ. Then Harriet had haemorrhaged and everything had ramped up another notch and Mark hadn't even found out that *both* babies were alive until after the blood transfusion.

'Not deliberately, deliberately,' Harriet was saying, 'deliberately, unconsciously.'

'Sorry . . . ?'

Mark was so deep in thought that he'd forgotten they were having a conversation.

'Gary. Fucking over his career. Unconsciously. Like you're unconsciously dissing me now.'

'Dissing you?'

He pulled out onto the high street, noticing as the car slowed into a queue of traffic, a young woman, hunched in the doorway of Tesco Express. She looked like a normal middle-class girl, and at first, he thought she must be waiting for someone, but then he realized she was sitting on a sleeping bag, arms slung around her knees, paper cup in hand, face turned hopefully towards a couple who were approaching the shop. He became aware of Harriet's face, turning towards him equally expectantly.

'I was thinking I might offer Ollie an internship,' he said.

'With *you*?'

'No, with the English National Opera. Of course, with me. I mean, I'd have to OK it with Sadie and Ambrose, obviously but...'

Harriet turned face front again, her expression unreadable.

'What?'

'I just think...'

'What?'

'No, OK, if you think that's a good idea.'

'*You* obviously don't.'

'I just wonder if it... sends the right message.'

'Don't talk in riddles, just tell me what you think.'

'Well, for instance, why aren't you offering Jack an internship?'

Mark scoffed.

'Jack'll want to spread his wings. He won't need me. It'd just cramp his style.'

'But Ollie's going to need a leg-up ... ?'

'I thought you'd be pleased.'

'You see, that's why you'd be doing it. To please me, to keep him on the straight and narrow. Not because you see potential in him. If you want to know, I think it's the very worst thing you could do.'

'Blimey,' he said.

He drove on for a bit, slowed, signalled. Harriet seemed to relent.

'I mean, no harm asking around our friends for an internship for him as long as it's something he'd be into, but how's it going to look on his CV, if the only place he's worked is his dad's firm?'

'I love the idea he'll have a CV ... '

'God, Mark!'

'Look, he can stack shelves as far as I'm concerned,' snapped Mark. 'Just as long as he ... '

He shook his head in frustration, then took the turn into their street too fast and hurtled over a speed bump. There was a sound of grinding metal.

'Glad I didn't do that ... ' said Harriet.

Mark smiled grimly.

She was right, of course. Working for the firm was the last thing Ollie needed. It was the last thing Mark needed too. He'd spend his whole time making excuses for the boy, or worse – coming down harder on him than any other employee, just to prove he wasn't showing favouritism. *Favouritism*. As if.

He pulled up outside the house and they both sat in the

43

dark for a moment, staring straight ahead. Harriet turned towards him and opened her mouth as if to speak, then shut it again and peered past him through the passenger window.

'What's that?' she said frowning through the darkness towards the house. Mark turned and followed her gaze up the path towards the porch. It looked as though someone had left a pile of jumble on the front step. He got out of the car and the motion-activated light above the front door flicked on. The pile stirred.

5

Yvette

Please, God, no. It seemed she had barely closed her eyes before the opening chords of 'Coming Up' were already jangling their way into Yvette's consciousness. She should never have set The KMA's catchiest hit as her phone alarm – she had come to hate it. She associated it now, not with that first thrilling backstage fuck at The KMA gig, nor with the many subsequent loved-up all-nighters at the Haçienda but with grinding tiredness and obligation; with the relentless treadmill of work and family and servitude. She felt for her phone on the bedside table, cancelled the alarm and squinted at it in the half-light, but there was no mistake, it was 7.15 a.m.

'Gaz … ?' she mumbled patting his side of the bed but her hand met only cool, flat duvet. She sat up now, fully awake. She had left him on the sofa about ten to twelve, clutching his head in remorse, a mug of tea in front of him and a promise extracted that he would follow her up as soon as he'd finished writing last term's Key Stage 3 learning objectives. It was the least he could do, after the way he'd behaved, he'd told her, try and hang onto his job. Fuck knew, he'd need it, given the crock of shit they'd produced in the studio that day. Yvette had stopped short of reminding him that he'd once said the same thing about the first take of 'Copper Night Rate' – the gold disc for which now hung framed in the downstairs toilet.

The side of Gary they had seen last night, the blubbing man-boy undone by drug-induced paranoia and fear of failure, was just the flipside of all his machismo and narcissism, Yvette knew this. She hadn't lived with Gaz for thirty-odd years without having glimpsed this fearful inadequate wannabe from time to time, but it still shocked her when it surfaced. She was by far the stronger half of the couple, she'd come to realize. Stalwart. Good in a crisis. And boy, had last night been a crisis. She should never have asked Mark and Harriet over on a Sunday night, that much was obvious in retrospect, but there was no point beating herself up about it now. She wasn't to know Gaz would be off his face, or that he'd come down so fast and so spectacularly. This was no time to wallow in regret, someone had to keep the wheels on the wagon, and that someone was her.

If that meant dragging herself out of bed now, even though her eyes felt gritty and her limbs like lead, so be it. If it meant going downstairs, checking on Gaz, making tea for the girls and tackling last night's washing up (she couldn't *believe* she'd left the washing up) fair dos. If it meant telling Jade to tell Juris to tie a knot in it until after Gary had left for school, rather than risk a run-in on the landing, if it meant getting some Sugar Puffs down Gaz's neck so he wasn't running on empty, if it meant leaving by eight fifty, latest, so that even if the temporary traffic lights were still there, she'd get to school in time to keep an iron grip on Raymond Bennett throughout assembly, thereby denying the Deputy Head the final excuse she was looking for to suspend him, fair play.

She tiptoed along the landing and down the stairs, moving Juris's leather jacket from its conspicuous resting place on the newel post, onto a nearby coat peg where it wouldn't catch Gary's eye. It was heavy as armour and gave off a strong whiff of nicotine and some other faintly chemical smell. She was tempted to go through the pockets, but that would be looking for trouble. Gary was convinced Juris was a secret drug baron, a sideline which he seemed to take a surprisingly dim view of considering he wasn't averse to scoring the odd line himself. Like many a dissolute parent, Gary had had unfeasibly high expectations of his children's behaviour. He was often to be heard bandying about threats of the 'out on your ear if I catch you ... ' variety, which Yvette knew he would never carry through. Oh, he would kick off all right – doors would rattle, ears would be covered, eyes rolled, until the storm had passed and the threatened 'groundings' failed to materialize. That, at any rate, had been the drill in the past, when illicit stimulants of one sort or another had been discovered in the girls' rooms. But he was a proper windbag, was Gaz. Yvette's dad had been the same. 'Empty vessels make most noise,' her Mam used to mutter, rolling her eyes. But Juris was different. There was a calculation behind his quiet good manners and twinkly-eyed charm that bothered Yvette.

'Gaz ... ?' she whispered, pushing the door open but there was no sign of him. Surely, he couldn't have left for work already? She went over to the sink and filled the kettle, but as she turned the tap off again she heard a groan coming from the far end of the room.

47

'Gaz ... ?' she said, backing up until she had a view down to the French doors. She could just about see a pair of trainer-clad feet now, sticking out over the end of the leather sofa.

'Don't tell me you've slept in your ... ?' She hurried past the kitchen island, 'Oh my God, look at the state of you!'

A noxious film of orange vomit covered the keyboard of Gaz's laptop, the corner of the glass coffee table and the edge of the goatskin rug. Gaz lay on the couch, arms and legs akimbo, like a corpse tossed into a skip. Yvette edged past the coffee table, squeezed one buttock onto the corner of the sofa and shook him gently.

'Gaz,' she said, 'Gaz!'

He stirred, grunted, smacked his chops and rolled into a foetal position facing away from the room. Yvette glanced at the kitchen clock. Anxiety rose in her chest. She leaned forward and touched the mouse, her relief that the laptop was still working quickly overtaken by dismay and then anger when the webpage that sprang up proved not to be Statutory Programmes of Study for Key Stage 3 Music, but Hot Lubed-up Asian Babes.

By the time she got to school, Raymond was scuffing the already worn lino outside the Deputy Head's office while the strains of 'I Can See Clearly Now' sung in three-part agony came drifting down the corridor from the school hall.

'Morning, Raymond,' she said briskly.

'Miss,' he said, without raising his eyes.

'Want to tell me about it?'

He gave a hard-done-by shrug as though no amount of explanation could convey the avalanche of injustice that had just engulfed him.

'The thing is, Raymond . . . ' Yvette started saying, and she could feel the frustrations of the morning coming to a rolling boil inside her.

This was Gary's fault. She had got him showered and shaved and more or less respectably dressed, at the expense of her own appearance – creased trousers, hair every which way, botched mascara – had deposited him with his laptop, its search history now as clean as its keyboard, outside Beresford Academy, only narrowly avoiding a ticket from a jobsworth parking warden for stopping on the zigzags, and arrived at Dale Road Primary ten minutes too late. Gary may or may not pull it off. Yvette was fully aware of the possible consequences, not just for her and Gaz, but for the whole family, if the music department wasn't deemed 'improved' today. But for Raymond, ten years old and already on a trajectory to delinquency, the stakes were even higher. A third suspension this academic year and he'd be sent to the pupil referral unit, just like his stepbrother, who was now in a young offenders institution. She took a deep breath, crouched down and looked into his face gravely.

' . . . We've talked about this, haven't we? You're in year six now. The little kids look up to you. What were you doing to make Ms Wakefield send you out again?'

He pouted at her between beetling brows, the way fifty, or a hundred little boys must have done over the fifteen years she had worked at Dale Road. In all that time, there had only been two she hadn't warmed to. One had been a pale, dead-eyed boy who had gone on to rape his foster mother at knife point. The other had been Ollie Pendleton.

Not that anyone would have known it – Ollie least of all. Yvette prided herself on giving everyone a chance. She wasn't one of those like Deborah Wakefield who assessed a kid at five and saw either an asset or a liability, destined to raise or lower the stock of the school in the precious league tables. In any case, being from the right side of the tracks, Ollie would probably have flown straight under Ms Wakefield's radar if Yvette hadn't marked his card. 'Call me Deb' tended to overlook bad behaviour if the parents made a standing order to school funds when their little darling was registered. And if Yvette had known how fiercely Harriet would react when approached 'in confidence' to discuss her adored son's 'issues', she might have left well alone too, but thank God she hadn't, as that unpromising first encounter had led to an unlikely but devoted friendship which both women still cherished.

Yvette had been perched on a tiny plastic chair, a roll of Sellotape clamped between her teeth, about to secure the spine of *The Very Hungry Caterpillar*, when a beady-looking Harriet had poked her head around the open classroom door and said,

'Knock, knock.'

'Hello, Mrs Pendleton, come in,' Yvette had said, jumping up to welcome her visitor.

'Ms Constantine, actually,' Harriet had corrected her.

'Oh, sorry, I just assumed . . . ' Yvette stammered, suddenly hyper-aware of the tawdriness of her New Look dress beside Harriet's expensively cut jeans and blazer.

'Yes, well, we are married, but I go by my own name for professional reasons.'

'Good idea,' Yvette said. 'Have a seat . . . I say "seat" . . . ' She shrugged apologetically and pulled another diminutive chair out from under the hexagonal table. Harriet looked around the classroom as if puzzled.

'Don't we need to wait for Mr Stewart?'

Mr Stewart was the ponytailed, fresh-out-of-college class teacher, helpless as a puppy, but nominally Yvette's superior.

'Oh well, no, I mean, I could get him for you if you ... '

'I thought he had concerns about Ollie?'

'No, it was me that was wanting a chat but it's nothing to worry about ... ' Yvette lied. 'We try and check in with all the parents and carers in the first few weeks, just to get the bigger picture ... Can I get you a tea?'

'I'd rather you just told me what this is about.'

Harriet perched on the tiny chair hugging her Mulberry bag defensively.

'Ollie's got a twin in Badger class, hasn't he?' Yvette said, 'How's he settling in?'

Harriet coaxed a stray lock of hair behind her ear and pursed her lips cagily.

'Jack's fine.'

'Are they ... would you say they were ... close?'

'Yes, mainly. A few spats, you know, they're brothers, but ... '

'I just wondered whether Ollie might be ... missing him.'

'What makes you say that?'

'Only, well, we put them in different classes because that's the thinking these days, isn't it – you don't want to lump them together just 'cos they're ... '

'*Lump* them together?' Harriet looked up sharply and two spots of pink appeared on her ivory cheeks.

'No, sorry, I just mean ... we're supposed to treat them as individuals ... '

'They *are* individuals.'

God, this woman! It was like handling a piece of fine

china – one false move and you felt she could shatter. How could someone so smart and classy-looking, so far out of Yvette's league in every way, still act so brittle and defensive?

'Yeah, no, sorry, Ms Constantine, I didn't mean…' Yvette pursed her lips for a moment, 'only, what can sometimes happen… We had this one set of twins who found it quite hard at first when they were put in separate classes, because they'd been joined at the hip at home… I don't mean literally… they weren't… anyway, they were almost telepathic, these two little girls…'

'Yes, well that's just a trope. Most twins aren't telepathic. Jack and Ollie *certainly* aren't. They have their own interests and quite distinct personalities. They have their own bedrooms, their own hobbies… I've read all the literature, so if this is just one of those "this one's the extravert, that one's the introvert"…'

Right. Enough. Yvette raised her voice.

'… Only Oliver's showing symptoms of selective mutism.'

Harriet's eyes widened, the pink spots on her cheeks seemed to explode like planets and her voice, when it came, seemed fraught with tears.

'Selective…? I've never heard of… I'm sorry, I don't know what that means.'

She folded in on herself now, hugging her bag ever more tightly, plaiting her ankles and flicking the heel of one loafer on and off with the toe of the other. Now Yvette saw what it had cost her to come here today, how much she cared for her son and how vulnerable she felt on his behalf. She bit her lip, leaned forward, touched Harriet's sleeve.

'It's OK, really it is. It's not uncommon. We just need to get to the bottom of what's going on for him.'

Yvette took care to be tactful. She went at Harriet's pace, pretended to consider the possibility that Ollie was being bullied – though if anything it was him doing the bullying through his silence. He wielded it like a superpower – only had to cross his arms and jut his jaw to have all the children on his table wooing him with plasticine and clandestine handfuls of Haribo. Yvette decided against mentioning the stealing at this stage – plenty of time to tease that one out once she'd got a special educational needs co-ordinator involved, but first she needed to get Mum onside. By the end of the meeting, she had achieved her aim – Harriet was practically begging her to call round after school, to see what a clever boy Ollie was, how chatty and straightforward in his home environment. And whilst Yvette had insisted that home visits were the remit of the SENCO, not her, she nevertheless felt so gratified by Harriet's change of heart (and, if she was honest, so intoxicated by Harriet's sudden transformation from ice queen to BFF) that she found herself agreeing to pop round for a cuppa later in the week.

It had been an eye-opener, that first visit to Moorcroft Road. It wasn't as though Yvette hadn't met posh or clever people before – there'd been plenty of posh girls at Loreto, not least the unholy trinity of Caroline Braithwaite, Stephanie Henderson and Amanda Clarke on the fringe of whose golden circle Yvette had hovered for a while. Those girls had seemed the apex of sophistication at the time, with their mock-Tudor homes, their wraparound couches and their Austrian blinds. It had been a strain keeping up with them. Until she got into the grammar school, Yvette had never thought of herself as disadvantaged or her home as tasteless. But once she had seen how the other half lived, the thought of her new friends being dropped off outside her Wythenshawe council house and walking up the concrete path flanked by regiments of vulgar orange dahlias and plaster garden gnomes, made her blanch with shame. When Yvette had got pregnant and they had cut her adrift, it had almost been a relief not to have to make any more excuses as to why she couldn't invite them round to hers.

'Hiya,' Yvette had said, when Harriet appeared, 'I hope you don't mind me bringing my youngest. This is Jade.'

'Of course not!' Harriet had said. 'Hello, Jade. I don't know if you'll know my boys, Jack and Oliver? They're out in the garden if you want to … ?'

She peered vaguely through the window, 'at least, *Jack* is …'

Yvette wobbled her daughter's clasped hand by way of inquiry, but Jade shook her head. As they followed Harriet through the hallway, Yvette felt a prickle on the back of her neck. She turned around to see Ollie's face peering down at them through the balustrade at the top of the stairs. Jade looked up and saw him too. She stopped and stared beseechingly at Yvette.

'What, you want to go and play with Ollie?' Yvette said, surprised and not a little taken aback, but Jade was already freeing her fingers from her mother's grasp.

'OK,' Yvette laughed uncertainly. 'Well, come and tell us if you want some juice or …'

But her daughter was already halfway up the stairs.

6

Harriet

'Ollie! Sweetheart. Are you OK?'

Harriet squatted down beside the hunched figure on their doorstep and shook his shoulder gently. His hair was greasy and he smelled of BO. A perished bag for life, bulging with clothing and computer paraphernalia, hung off his chafed wrist. He unfolded himself from sleep with the gingery stiffness of an old man and stared blank-eyed into her face.

'How long have you been here? You should have rung!' she wailed.

'Battery died,' he said. 'What happened to keeping the spare key behind the drainpipe?'

'It's not there?' Harriet turned to Mark with a look of alarm.

'Oh shit, sorry, I moved it.'

'Thanks for telling me,' said Harriet.

As Mark stooped to unlock the door his face came within grazing distance of Ollie's cheek but they might as well have been inhabiting parallel universes.

'Hello, Ollie,' Harriet prompted him.

She saw Mark stiffen slightly in exasperation and could have kicked herself. She made it worse, she knew she did. Obediently, he gave Ollie an awkward hug.

'All right, mate?' he murmured, before breaking away again with a flurry of brisk backslaps and Harriet winced. She watched him clamber over Ollie, step into the hall and snap the light on.

'Wha' the fuck?' Ollie winced away from the brightness like a vampire and Harriet leaned down to attend to him.

'Mark, help him up, can you, he's too heavy for me,' Harriet said. 'Here, give me your bag, darling, I'll get your stuff in the wash ... '

'No, Mum, it's OK.' Ollie scrambled to his feet, suddenly energized, 'I'll sort it, there's stuff in there that can't ... '

Mark turned and eyed the bag hawkishly, the look not lost on Ollie.

'Want to check it for illegals, Dad?' he said sarcastically, opening the bag as if for a customs inspection. Mark frowned as, with great ostentation, the boy took out his computer, then tucking it under his arm, disgorged the rest of his belongings onto the hall tiles.

'Boxers, T-shirts, jeans – they're all for the wash. Charger, revision notes, they're not.'

He scooped them on top of his computer, then sneered at Mark, '*Revision* break, see?'

Mark cast Harriet a baleful glance over Ollie's shoulder and she shrugged, hardly knowing herself what the shrug was supposed to mean. Sorry you have a bad relationship with your son. Sorry we have a problem son. Sorry I try to compensate for the awkwardness between you and our son and in so doing, aggravate it. Sorry, sorry, sorry.

'Right, I'm going up now,' said Ollie with a brisk half-smile. 'Four fuckin' hours, it's been, door to door.'

'That's awful, darling,' Harriet said, gathering the dirty clothes into her arms, 'but you know you can claim compensation now if your train's delayed ... '

'Not if you've hitched, you can't.'

'Oh, Ollie,' she straightened up, appalled, 'you shouldn't do that. It's really dangerous. You never know who you're getting in a car with. I told you to tell me if you were short of cash.'

'I'm always short of cash,' Ollie said, 'I'm a student.'

'Yeah, well, some of us *worked* our way through college,' muttered Mark. 'It's sociology not medicine. I'd have thought you could fit in a few fast-food shifts.'

'Mark, he's got finals!' said Harriet turning to glare at him. By the time she'd turned back, Ollie was halfway up the stairs.

'Ollie, wait, sweetheart,' she wailed, apologetically, 'the bed's not made up ... '

'Christ all-fucking mighty!' she heard Mark mutter as he stalked off towards the kitchen.

Harriet woke the next morning to find Mark gazing at her across the expanse of pillow.

'I'm sorry,' he whispered, smoothing her hair back from her forehead.

She blinked and frowned.

'What for?'

'I was a prick last night.'

'Not to *me* you weren't ... '

'I know, I know. And I'll make it up to him, I will. I just ... ' He sighed.

'You always think the worst of him.'

'I really don't! That whole ... bag thing ... was just him being paranoid. I didn't think for a minute that he was ... '

' ... But where does the paranoia *come* from, Mark?' Harriet interrupted. 'Why d'you think he behaves like that?'

Mark bit his lip and lowered his eyes. He looked back up at her and their eyes met. Mark's face broke into a smile.

'What?' Harriet said suspiciously. '*What?*'

'No ... it's just, you're so *beautiful.*'

Harriet sighed.

He leaned across and stroked his finger back and forth over her skin.

'I love how you've got fur on your face like a hamster.'

'It's not fur,' she said with a sulky smile, 'it's down.'

'Well, it's nice.'

He leaned in and kissed her lingeringly on the lips.

'*You're* nice,' she said, but just as she grabbed his buttock and hitched her hips towards him, he shrank away.

'Easy, tiger,' he said, 'I've got to get the eight fifty-three and you'll be wanting your cuppa ... '

He threw off the duvet.

'It's Monday ... ' she protested, stretching her hand feebly after him. 'You work from home on Mondays ... '

She narrowed her eyes.

'Oh, I get it.'

'What?'

'You're avoiding him, aren't you?'

'Who, *Ollie*? Not at all. Ambrose has set up a meeting with the accountant. It's a one-off. I'll be home early.'

'I wanted us to go out for brunch.'

'I thought you'd got a deadline anyway,' said Mark. 'Aren't the Button Factory people chomping at the bit?'

'They are, yes,' she replied testily, 'but unlike you, I'm prepared to carve an hour out of the day to touch base with my son, who's just spent four hours hitching home from bloody Portsmouth and looks like he hasn't had a square meal since Easter.'

'You think he'll be up in time for brunch?'

'*Lunch* then. God, Mark. You see this is the problem.'

'What?'

'Your expectations of him are always rock bottom. Ollie won't be up in time for brunch, Ollie won't get his degree, Ollie won't be able to get a job without you greasing someone's palm. Whereas *Jack* ...'

'I never said he wouldn't get his degree.'

'Oh, for fuck's sake.'

Harriet threw her head back on the pillow and stared up at the ceiling.

'OK, OK, I'll take him a cup of tea before I go ...'

She relented and gave him a wan smile.

'And ... how about we get a takeaway tonight and find something we can all watch on Netflix?' he added.

'OK, but nothing raunchy and ideally not American. Ollie's not keen on ...'

'Jesus!'

And he was out the door.

Always. Always this atmosphere, whenever the two of them

were in the house together. She felt like a tightrope walker, trying not to put a foot wrong. It was exhausting. All the same, she hoped Mark would come up and see her before he left. He'd got her all revved up now. They hadn't had sex for weeks. The last time they had, it had been like waiting for jelly to set. She wasn't sure he had even come. He'd been like this ever since that Impactful Leadership course he'd done in Harrogate last year and the more she thought about it, the more she wondered whether he'd had a fling while he was there; she knew from the circumstances of their own first meeting that he was far from immune to the aphrodisiac qualities of the four-star hotel. But surely an affair was meant to pep things up a bit, as long as it was meaningless? Make you more, not less randy? And anyway, it didn't ring true. In all their time together, Mark had never strayed, nor looked like straying. His devotion to her had always been steadfast. It wasn't something he enacted like some women's husbands, with lavish gifts and spontaneous bouquets, it was just a given, there in the background, like air and water. A gay fling, then? Surely not. She *would* forgive it, considered herself open-minded on the matter of sexual orientation, more so perhaps than her family and friends would think, but Mark's rugger bugger heterosexuality was not the kind that encompassed the occasional locker-room shag, boarding school notwithstanding. It was as unambiguously straight as it appeared, of that she had little doubt. So, what was it then? Why had he lost his mojo on that trip? And why did his indifference make her so horny?

She slipped her hand under the duvet, closed her eyes and, frowning fiercely in concentration, began gyrating her fingertips over her vulva but it was no good, Mark had put Radio 4 on downstairs and the prospect of bringing herself off to the strains of Nick Robinson interviewing some pompous cabinet minister was too big an ask.

She sighed, scooped her phone off the bedside table instead and scanned the notifications. Nothing. She tapped on Instagram. Jack had posted a story. Bodies gyrating to techno, flashing lights, close-up of some girl's pierced belly – spaced-out faces, segueing into a morning shot of Jack peeling open a can of Red Bull. The words HANGOVER CURE pulsing in a comedic green script above the image. She started typing a comment, *Revision going well?* then deleted it. He was on for a first. Easier on Ollie if he only got a two-one. What was she like? What an attitude. Willing one of her twins to underachieve to mitigate the inadequacy of the other. She should just butt out. That's what Mark said. But she'd been so flattered that Jack had allowed her to follow his account, she couldn't help herself. If only she had such a window onto Ollie's world, she'd have been on there all the time, stalking him. Probably just as well he didn't do social media. Didn't do social anything, come to that.

Jack would get a first anyway. It was just who he was. One of those kids who'd always sailed through effortlessly. Teacher's pet, first pick for the football team, string of girl-friends stretching all the way back to year six – Ellies and Amelias and Saskias. Maisie was just the culmination of a pro-cess of natural selection that had been going on throughout Jack's teens. Clever, but not too clever. Beautiful and socially adept, she was on for a two-one in art history and a life of unearned privilege courtesy of her father's pharmaceutical fortune. She ticked every box.

'Don't s'pose you've got a twin sister for Ollie?' had been

Mark's opening gambit when they'd gone down to Brighton to help the golden couple move into their third-year flatshare. Maisie had laughed charmingly and shaken her head.

Harriet scrolled through her other Instagram contacts. Nothing from Yvette, nothing new from anyone she cared about. A thought occurred to her. She searched The KMA. A fan site came up. A patchwork of old photos she had seen before – bucket hats, smiley T-shirts, blissed-out close-ups, Gaz with a roll-up clamped between his teeth, hunched over his guitar like a superstar. A link to the documentary, a link to an old series of *I'm a Celebrity*. Nothing about a relaunch. Nothing from Gaz. No sign of the new material that had prompted his meltdown last night. She went into Facebook chat. Yvette was offline.

> Are you OK? she typed. Sorry for bailing on you, but it felt like Gaz needed space . . .

She waited in the hope her activity would prompt a response, but her phone remained inert. She started to fret. They shouldn't have left when they did. They shouldn't have gone in the first place. She should have invited Yvette and Gaz to theirs. She shouldn't have let Yvette go over-budget on the kitchen refurb; should never have shown her the reclaimed oak. She shouldn't have let Mark persuade them to remortgage. What if Gaz lost his job? What if they lost the house? Which reminded her – she must make sure Ruby and Jordan didn't over-reach themselves. They might think the house was the most important thing, but it wasn't. The baby was. Their baby. Her baby. A great surge of pain reared up from her gut, but she didn't dare open her mouth in case the noise that came out was not the polite sob of a twenty-first-century professional woman who'd got her timing wrong, but the primordial howl of a swamp creature needing to spawn.

'Hey, hey, hey!'

She heard the chink of a mug being hastily set down, and Mark's arms were around her, hugging her close, rocking her back and forth.

'What's this? What's this about? Look, I'll go in later. We'll do brunch. I know I've been useless, but I'll be better, I promise. It's not Ollie that's the problem, it's me, it's me!'

She clung to him then and sobbed silently, for Mark, for Ollie, but most of all for herself.

7

Gary

'Mornin', sir,'

'Rough night, Mr Kershaw?'

Gary shouldered his way through the teeming playground, pretending not to hear the kids' greetings. Normally he'd have given them the time of day, dispensed the odd fist bump, but not today. Today was about survival. He'd have called in sick, except Yvette hadn't given him the option. His feet hadn't touched the ground since she'd woken him – black coffee, shower, dressed and out the door before you could say Ofsted. It was the lesser of two evils, anyway – he'd had no desire to hang about and make small talk with Juris. They all thought if they kept it hush hush, Gary wouldn't notice the bloke had spent the night. Like the whole place didn't reek of his cheap aftershave. Fucking pervert. One breakfast with Juris had been more than enough. It had turned Gary's stomach having to make nice over toast and marmalade. Twat had slumped on his stool as if he owned the place, coffee mug like a thimble in his meaty paw, eyes dancing with mirth as if to say, *Yeah, I fucked your daughter, Mr Has-been Rock Star and she's a right goer. Think she's going to Oxford, do you? Well, think again, she's coming back with me to wear a headscarf and make borscht.* Gary's insides roiled with hatred at the memory. He'd had to stop slagging the bloke off in front of Yvette – she said he was being racist. He'd pointed out that he couldn't be, 'cos he didn't have a problem with Jordan and she'd said that *in itself* was racist. Work that one out. Women. He knew in his heart that his motives were pure. Chrissakes, he didn't even know any other Latvians. He didn't hate Juris because he was Latvian, he hated Juris because he was a cunt.

The staffroom was emptying as he rushed to his locker.

'Ready for the inspectors, Gaz?' Mo, Head of maths, winked at him as he gathered up a pile of freshly marked books and slurped the last of his coffee.

'Ducks in a row and heading for the abattoir, mate,' replied Gary grimly.

The bell for first period sounded and, having checked which class he was teaching, he made his way down the corridor towards the asbestos-riddled slum that was 'The Music Suite'. Crossing the vestibule, he pretended not to hear the Head Teacher call:

'Ah, Mr Kershaw, may I introduce … ?'

Gary dived into his classroom and shut the door. It was an uninspiring learning environment – dirty uPVC windows, a handful of broken music stands, an out of tune upright piano, and a cock and balls sketched on the whiteboard. His chest grew tight with anxiety. He searched his desk drawer for a cloth, and failing to find one, reached in his pocket for a crumpled tissue, spat on it and had only erased half the scrotum when the first cluster of recalcitrant fifteen-year-olds pimp-rolled their way into the classroom.

'All right, sir,' they muttered before heading for the back of the room, circling their chairs and taking out their phones.

Ever since Macca had come out of the *I'm a Celebrity* jungle triumphant, fuelling speculation that The KMA might reform, the feeble sense of vocation that had tied Gary to teaching had been stretched to breaking point. He was marking time now, and he knew it. The strategy he'd adopted since the beginning of term for 'teaching' this tricky year nine class was the cold war principle of mutually assured destruction. The kids would leave him alone if he left them alone; the consequences for all of them, should things kick off, being equally dire. Hence, Gary would put some classical music on to throw any passing busybodies off the scent and then skulk in the stockroom playing fruit ninja on his phone, while the kids treated the music room as a sort of youth club, the girls styling each other's hair and sharing selfies while the boys listened to rap music through their headphones and watched porn. He was providing a service to the community, Gary told himself. If he'd tried ramming the lacklustre music syllabus down their throats they'd only have voted with their feet, truanting en masse and getting involved in the shoplifting and turf wars that were sure to claim them the minute they left school. He had been vindicated too. Things had ticked along quite amicably and no one in authority had been any the wiser.

'Sir, isn't it the inspectors are in?'

'Are you gonna get detention, sir?'

'Stay up, sir, we ain't gonna opp you. Do you want us to do like, singin' an' that?'

'Shut up, Nathan, sir's gonna slay it. Isn't it you're going to slay it, sir?'

'Look,' Gary said, trying not to get vexed, 'I'm in a bit of a bind here, you're going to have to work with me. Just look busy while I have a root around out back, see if I can find any musical instruments...' The phrase sounded quaint and improbable to his ears, like 'holy grail'. The school had had no budget for such fripperies since 2014. Wind band had limped along thanks to the handful of middle-class kids whose parents allowed them to bring their own instruments in, though he'd stretched their indulgence at the last open day by having the band perform a medley of Metallica hits. Otherwise it was down to a lacklustre choir, some computer-aided composition and, if Gary was feeling indulgent, a virtuoso recital on his own second-best Gibson guitar. None of that was going to save his bacon here. He was less than five minutes from a – they called it a lesson observation, but show trial was nearer the mark – and he'd got nothing; *nada*; zilch. He had a vague idea where he could put his hand on a couple of tambourines and a triangle, but he was fucked if he knew where his predecessor Miss Danjuk had hidden the recorders. They'd probably got woodworm by now, anyway.

He left the stockroom door ajar so he could listen out for the inspectors and started hauling things off shelves with a growing sense of panic. A plastic storage box on the top shelf looked quite promising, but when he got it down, it contained a dozen maracas made out of yoghurt pots. He nearly sprained his wrist yanking an old keyboard from behind the photocopier, only to discover the plug had been removed. He could hear the class getting restive in the background.

Then came a hush, followed by the sound of adult voices, the most penetrating belonging to the Head, who was trying to come across friendly and authoritative, but was sounding like Simon Cowell on an off day.

Gary's chest was heaving now. He couldn't tell whether it was the exertion of moving the photocopier, or the certainty of losing his job within the next half hour, the prospect of which inspired exhilaration and shame in equal measure. He wondered if he was having a heart attack, and thought under the circumstances it might be no bad thing if he were.

8

Mark

It had been a dog of a day. Mark's brunch with Harriet and Ollie had, as predicted, run late and had been far from the bonding experience it was meant to be. Ollie had been on his phone for most of it and when Mark had made some mildly sarcastic remark about getting more change out of him if they FaceTimed, Ollie had gone into a major sulk and Harriet had – *deliberately*, he was sure, and knowing Mark was on a timetable – ordered the house special which took another twenty minutes to prepare and then looked daggers at him when he said he didn't have time for another round of coffees. They had parted on bad terms and then the Piccadilly Line was down, making Mark late for his meeting with APC Finance, which wasn't ideal as he already felt jumpy about it. It had passed off without a hitch, and he'd come away almost frustrated at how little they'd needed to know, in the end, of his almost entirely fabricated reasons for restructuring the business. But instead of emerging triumphant, he'd felt the way he used to when, as a kid, he'd managed to smuggle a giant KitKat up to bed under his mother's nose – dirty and greedy.

And now, for the purposes of relaxation, he was getting thrashed at snooker by his best mate, whose day outwitting Ofsted inspectors had evidently been an order of magnitude more gruelling, more compelling, more *heroic*, than Mark's humdrum paper-pushing could ever be.

'And I look across to see how it's going and the inspector's only fucking crying!' Gary was shaking his head and grinning. He chalked his cue and leaned over the snooker table.

Gary had the green ball nicely lined up over the pocket and the others looked easy to pick off. At this rate, Mark thought, Mr Chips here would win every game and he'd be buying the drinks, as per. That was the deal – loser picked up the tab; and loser was generally Mark, although, on the odd fluky occasion he'd actually won, he recalled Gary frisking himself for his wallet and saying, 'You'll never guess what . . . ?'

He watched now as his friend narrowed his eyes and played the shot, but too aggressively, so that the cue ball leap-frogged the green and rolled in slow motion into the corner pocket. Mark's heart leaped with joy.

'Unlucky,' he murmured. He paused, took a sip of beer, then sauntered up to the table.

'Anyway, Stiff's got his clipboard out now . . . ' Gaz continued, without missing a beat. He was usually a sore loser, but tonight, apparently, it was all about the story, 'meant to be ticking his little inspector boxes – or more likely, in this case, *not* ticking them – but when I catch him wiping away a tear I know I've fucking aced it.'

How long was it going to go on, this much-embellished

story of Gaz's? Mark wondered. Should he get his shot in now, or wait till the end?

'How d'you manage that, then?' he asked, sounding, he thought, suitably engaged. 'No, let me guess – I bet you got them doing "Somewhere Over the Rainbow" in three-part harmony with you on the banjolele?'

Gaz almost choked on his beer.

'Kidding, I'm kidding,' Mark said, giving Gaz a matey nudge, which he seemed to take as carte blanche to continue his story.

'Yeah, very funny. No. Stroke of fucking genius, if I do say so myself. I'm in the stockroom, shitting my whack because the inspectors aren't just in the building now, they're in the fucking music room and I've got nowt to show them. Not a report, not a lesson plan, not a learning outcome. So, I'm crashing around looking for something, *anything* to get me out of a hole, and then I find it.'

Here we go, thought Mark.

'Oh yeah?'

'Right at the back of the stockroom, under this mucky old sheet. It doesn't even belong to the school. Been there for years, since the last Head of Music done a joint production of *The King and I* with the local amdram. Thereby hangs a fucking tale – suffice it to say they never asked for it back – great big fuck-off gong with a proper nifty sheepskin mallet...'

Gary grinned and took two or three gulps of beer, and Mark seized his chance.

He chalked his cue, retrieved the ball and positioned it on the semi-circle, then picked off the green, brown and blue in quick succession.

'A *gong*?' he said, struggling to keep the smirk of satisfaction of his face, but Gaz was so into his story he barely seemed to notice Mark's *coup de grace*.

'You've been to Glasto, right?' said Gaz.

'Glastonbury? Yeah, 'course, we went with you guys the year Gorillaz headlined, remember?'

Gaz frowned, evidently unable to distinguish one bout of drug-fuelled hedonism from another in his dope-addled memory.

'Well, anyway, time before last or summat – I forget what year it were – they'd got this thing called a sound bath.'

Mark nodded vaguely, but he'd stopped listening. He was recalling his own Glastonbury highlights. He and Harriet had stayed at a nice little B&B. Harriet had wanted to stay on site, but Mark couldn't be doing with the toilets and she'd stopped complaining when she saw the four-poster bed. Come to think of it, that was the last time he remembered them having really good sex. She'd worn this foxy little grey satin number, they'd been a little bit high and Harriet was feeling frisky 'cos she reckoned Damon Albarn had given her the eye when she'd passed him backstage. They'd been unencumbered by the twins, having dropped them at Harriet's mother's on the way down. That had been the other thing that had got him going – at home Harriet was forever shushing him in case the boys heard, but that night she'd taken her mummy hat off for once, and they'd both let rip. They were only two miscarriages in at this point, and while they hadn't been consciously trying for a baby they hadn't been *not* trying either. At breakfast the next morning she'd looked like Anne of Green Gables again, in her dungaree shorts and her cute little neckerchief, but she didn't half have a spring in her step. When their eyes had met over the muesli, she'd made a face that said, 'Do you think I might be?' and he'd made a face back that said, 'I really think you might be…' and they'd smiled conspiratorially, as if it were that easy. As if…

'… So, I'm thinking at twenty quid a pop it's a bit steep,' Gary was still on about the ruddy sound bath, 'but they reckon it's "healing" so they're obviously not going to stint on the Radox…'

'*Radox, sound bath*,' said Mark, 'ha ha, I see what you did there.'

'Anyway,' Gary continued, 'it does what it says on the tin. They *literally* bathe you in sound. It's all very chilled; very fucking meditative. You sit cross-legged on the floor and this Buddhist geezer creates all these different vibrations with the gong. I know it sounds random, but you actually do feel it touching the different parts of you. Even your internal organs…'

''Specially if you've taken a shedload of E, I'm guessing…' put in Mark. 'Please don't tell me you gave the inspectors a sound bath?'

'Too right I did. But that wasn't the half of it…'

'Uh-oh.'

'Well, the kids have got to participate, haven't they? It's hands-on, is music. You can't just stand at the front *telling* them shit, like they get away with in maths and geography.'

'Right…'

'So, I've given out a few tambourines and at first the kids are looking at me like I'm having a laugh. You'd have to see these kids; I mean, they're well hard. Not the kind you want to mess with – but, you know, they're giving me the benefit of the doubt, which is more than the inspectors are . . . '

The black was the only ball remaining now, and Mark was itching to pot it, but Gaz was in full spate so Mark leaned on his cue and bided his time.

'I start out gentle like, tracing the mallet around the very edge of the gong and it's making this weird, warbly kind of sound – a bit *Twilight Zone*, and the kids are proper giggly at first, but into it, I can tell. Then I strike it very soft and slow in different places, letting the sound die away completely before I do it again and I'm not even kidding – it's magic. It really touches you. So now I'm milking it – you know me and audiences, I mean it's not the Haçienda or 'owt, well, truth told, in some ways it's *better*. It's raw, man. It's what music *is*, you know. And now everybody's feeling it. There's this really nice vibe in the room and one of these kids – Nathan – fucking hard nut – starts shaking his tambourine, really soft, like, but not random. He's responding to the gong, really sensitive, really authentic. And then some of the others start humming in harmony – I think they go to the same church or summat, and the gong's still doing its thing and I'm not kidding, I'd have given me right arm to have got *half* that fucking vibe when we was in the studio yesterday. And best of all, me lad-o, the inspector's crying like a fucking baby.'

'So, you're off the hook?' Mark said, cheerfully. 'That's amazing, mate.'

He was pleased for Gaz, but also for himself, because now, finally, he would have his moment.

Gary raised his pint glass in a toast to his lucky escape, and Mark raised his bottle in response, before draining it and preparing to clinch his victory. After the day he'd had he bloody well needed it. He narrowed his eyes, shuffled the end of his cue between his cupped fist, prowled the table for the best angle, but the truth was any angle would do. The shot was a sitter; so much so that it would almost be a humiliation to pot it straight. He'd been playing second fiddle to Gary all night. Why not grab the limelight? Against his better judgement, therefore, he perched his buttocks on the edge of the table, slipped the cue behind his back, and went for the trick shot he'd seen Alex 'Hurricane' Higgins pull off in one of the finals of yore. Except that when Higgins had done it, the black had cannoned decisively into the pocket, winning the guy a cool half million and sending the crowd into ecstasies, but somehow Mark mis-hit it, screwing the cue ball away so that it didn't even touch the black, just dribbled feebly down the table, kissing the cushion and coming to a standstill on the edge of the corner pocket.

9

Yvette

'Oh, Juris, it's you,' Yvette said, barely bothering to disguise the fact that she was less than thrilled to see him. She tossed her car keys on to the kitchen island and they skittered right across it and hit the floor on the other side. Juris walked around it, picked them up and returned them to her. He tilted his head on one side and looked at her kindly.

'I am leaving shortly but can I get you cup of tea before I go? Kettle has just boiled. You seem bit upset, am I right?'

'Er, you could say that, yes,' Yvette said. 'Where's Jade?'

'She's in shower. I'm dropping her at store on my way to airport.'

'Oh, where are you off to?' Yvette said, unable to keep the hopefulness out of her tone.

'Pick up special client,' said Juris. 'Nice little earner.' He rubbed his thumb and forefinger together and gave her his twinkliest smile, then went over to the cupboard and took out a mug, reached for the tea caddy from the shelf, flipped the fridge open with his foot and retrieved the milk.

He knew his way round the kitchen better than Gaz did, Yvette observed.

'Sugar?' He turned to her and she shook her head. 'Sweet enough already,' he beamed, handing her the drink. He reached into the inside pocket of his jacket and pulled out a packet of cigarettes.

'You want?'

Yvette was about to shake her head in distaste when it occurred to her that she did, in fact, very much want. She was still reeling from Mrs Stacey's bombshell and a cigarette was exactly what she needed.

Juris jerked his head towards the patio doors and she followed him meekly out into the garden. He lit her cigarette and then his own. Yvette took a drag and shuddered as the nicotine hit. He didn't say anything, just looked down at her benevolently and smiled and smoked, and by the time she was halfway through her fag, the desire to get it off her chest had got the better of her.

'They've sacked me,' she blurted, almost enjoying the histrionic sound of it. It seemed theoretical, as though it couldn't possibly be true. Things like this didn't happen to her.

'Fifteen years, not a single day's sick leave and I'm out on my ear at the end of term.'

Juris made a cartoon face of shock and indignation.

'This is bad!' he said. 'Bad decision. You are knowledge economy. That's all this country has now. No factories, no banks even, soon, maybe. Teachers are not luxuries, you are necessities.'

'Well, I'm not a teacher, am I?' Yvette muttered bitterly. She was already regretting taking Juris into her confidence and she was feeling light-headed from the cigarette. 'I'm a teaching assistant. They're cutting us so they can afford to *keep* the teachers. Never mind that the teachers can't bloody teach without us to pick up the slack.'

'You should do strike like Uber drivers,' Juris said and Yvette looked at him in surprise. He was the last person she would have had down as an advocate of workers' solidarity.

'I didn't know you went on strike,' she said.

'I didn't need,' he said, smugly, 'I have special arrangement. But others get better deal from going on strike.'

Yvette frowned. She wondered what might be the terms of Juris's 'special arrangement' but decided she was probably better off not knowing. In any case it was all very well his criticizing the school system, but he obviously didn't realize what a bind the Head Teacher was in. Between a rock and hard place, really, as she had been at pains to explain to Yvette and the other two TAs, Christine Wheatcroft and Tiana Higgins. It might have been easier if Yvette could have hated Mrs Stacey for what she had done, in the same way she despised her deputy, Deborah Wakefield, for trying to purge the school of all its Raymond Bennetts so as to appear 'successful' by the narrow definition of Ofsted. But Doreen Stacey was old-school – literally. She had come into the profession with the aim of educating children; raising them up – it wasn't her fault that in the thirty years that had elapsed since she'd qualified, schools, particularly inner-city schools in deprived areas, such as Dale Road, had become underfunded holding pens, where children like Raymond, if they were taught to read at all, were taught not with the aim of delighting, enlightening or empowering them, but with the goal of recognizing an adjectival clause when it came up in a SATs test. Nor was it Doreen's fault that her budget had been pared to the bone, so that she now had the dilemma of whether to cut the ancillary staff or the book budget.

The irony! Yvette had left for work that morning, braced for a bomb to go off in their lives, but she'd expected it to be Gaz who'd detonate it, not her. Somehow the prospect of throwing everything up in the air and starting again had seemed bearable, even invigorating, when initiated by Gaz. If Gaz had been let go, it would have forced his hand – given him the push he needed to get behind the relaunch of The KMA and milk the Nineties nostalgia boom for all it was worth. She had been prepared for an upheaval of that kind – a temporary hole in the bank account that could be back-filled from the proceeds of a new album and a reunion tour. But to have precipitated the crisis herself, for Gaz to have *pulled it out the bag* – as his joyous expletive-filled text of that morning had told her – only for the family to come unstuck for want of *her* paltry wage, was unthinkable. She couldn't believe their situation could be so precarious. They had come from nothing and earned enough through hard graft in her case and raw talent in his (what hadn't gone up his nose, anyway) to get within a hair's breadth of owning their place outright. Three bedrooms and a bathroom all but paid off – her mum and dad would have thought it a palace. But they'd got greedy, hadn't they? And a kitchen refit had become a remodelling which had become an extension, which had become a hefty additional financial commitment. For the sake of a granite work surface, some underfloor heating and an integral waste disposal unit, they'd put the whole lot at risk.

She heard the patio door rattle open and dropped her cigarette quickly, pulverizing it under the sole of her shoe.

'Mum? Oh my God, are you *smoking*?'

Her daughter stepped out gingerly on to the patio in her bare feet, her damp hair giving off a synthetic passionfruit whiff. Her Aldi uniform, a size too big at the best of times, looked, on her tiny damp frame, as though she had raided the dressing-up box.

'Ah no, not really, just scrounged the one,' Yvette said. 'See if I still liked the taste . . . ' Her apologetic laugh stuck in her throat and threatened to become a sob.

Jade frowned at her suspiciously.

'As if you didn't go mad when you caught me and Ruby smoking, Mum . . . *Mum?*'

Yvette turned away and flapped her hand but Jade moved around her and peered determinedly into her face.

'Mum you're crying!' wailed Jade accusingly.

'She has been let go by school.'

Yvette jerked her head up and stared accusingly at Juris. Jade didn't need to know this yet. Not before she started her shift and certainly not before she submitted her loan application to student finance.

'Mum . . . ?' Jade peered disbelievingly into her mother's face for corroboration, and Yvette didn't have the heart to deny it.

'It's all right, love, I've got till the end of term to find something. We'll be fine. Maybe I can take your job at Aldi when you go to uni . . . ?' she said half-joking, but seeing the way Jade glanced anxiously at Juris made her heart sink.

'*If* I go to uni.'

'Don't say that, please, Jade, you're going.'

'University degree is not so desirable commodity in work-force now,' said Juris lugubriously and Yvette felt rage swelling in her chest. The nerve of him. How dare he talk about a knowledge economy one minute and, for his own selfish reasons, try and talk Jade out of going to Oxford the next?

'I think you'll find, Juris, that an *Oxford* degree is a passport to pretty much any job you want in this country, even these days,' she said, wishing to God she had never accepted his mug of tea or his horrible cigarette. Juris fixed her with a look of insolent amusement. It was just as well Gaz wasn't here, Yvette thought or there'd have been a punch-up.

'Yes, well when you've both finished deciding my future for me ... ' said Jade, 'I could do with a lift to work.'

'I can take you,' said Yvette eagerly but Juris had already plucked his car keys from his pocket, tossed them in the air and caught them again. How did he manage to exude such authority, such *swagger*? Yvette wondered.

Jade looked briefly stricken, the choice seemed suddenly a symbolic one.

'Go on, you go,' Yvette said, to put her daughter out of her misery, 'and make sure you eat something proper in your break.'

She watched Juris shepherd Jade back through the kitchen, hovering over her as she put on her trainers and then helping her into her neoprene jacket with ostentatious courtesy. As they left the kitchen, he glanced back at Yvette and winked.

10

Harriet

Harriet raced down the platform just as the train door slid shut. She pounded on the electronic button with her closed fist and after an agonizing pause the door re-opened, admitting her to a narrow vestibule crammed with disapproving fellow passengers.

"S'cuse me, sorry, I need to get to the next... sorry, sorry, I've got a seat reserved in...'

Lips were stretched and elbows resentfully drawn in as she weaved her way through the crammed carriages, sighing with relief when the doors of First Class at last hissed shut behind her. She checked her phone for her seat reservation.

'Forty-one, forty-two...' she muttered under her breath, eyes flicking back and forth. Typical. You paid a fortune for the privilege of a guaranteed seat and a cup of anaemic tea and then some entitled idiot went and sat in it.

'Excuse me,' she said, dumping her laptop bag on the table, 'I think you must be in the wrong... *Gary*?'

'Oh, hiya, Harriet. You going up North as well?'

Gary took out one of his earphones and blinked up at her in apparent bemusement.

'I am, yes ... ' she said. She could feel herself blushing. She liked Gary very much, had spent hours in his company over the years, had been to gigs and out for meals, and even on a couple of holidays with him (and Yvette and Mark, of course) but she could nevertheless count on the fingers of one hand the number of times they had been alone together. Theirs was a relationship that relied on the social glue of their other halves to cohere, and right now at nine-twelve on a Thursday morning, the prospect of spending two and a half solid hours in Gary's company without so much as a glass of wine to oil the wheels of conversation was a daunting one.

'You're all right, that one's free,' he said nodding towards the seat opposite.

'No, it's reserved,' Harriet said to him. 'See?' She pointed to the ticket sticking out of the head rest. Why was it that Gary always seemed to bring out the latent headmistress in her?

'Well, they've missed it now, anyway,' he pointed out as the train started moving. Harriet scrutinized the ticket. He was right, it was reserved from Euston. Gary removed his feet from the seat and she sat down with a shrug, but it went against the grain. Harriet liked to comply. If you were allocated a seat, you should sit in that seat. Gary smiled conspiratorially.

'I'm really meant to be in there,' he said jerking his head back towards Standard Class.

Harriet's eyes widened in surprise.

'They'll chuck you out as soon as they come round,' she warned.

'It's all right, I'll get an upgrade,' he said, 'record company'll pay. They should've got me First Class anyway. Tight gits.'

'You can't upgrade on peak services,' Harriet said and then, catching Gary's eye, cracked a smile. He wasn't the least bit bothered, she realized. What, to her, would be a sweaty-palmed wait while she rehearsed what she was going to say to the guard, was for him just a punt. He would probably enjoy the testosterone surge he'd get from arguing the toss almost as much as the illicit thrill of getting away with it. She reached automatically for her laptop and then decided that would be rude. She'd make polite conversation for a bit and then plead a deadline once the train got through Milton Keynes . . .

'So, what takes you to Manchester?' she said, and then, wrinkling her brow, 'Isn't it term time?'

'It is, yeah,' Gary said, 'I got compassionate leave.'

'Oh, Gary! I'm sorry . . . Don't feel you have to talk about it if you don't want to, obviously . . . '

'No, you're all right, it *was* a bit of a scam if I'm honest. I mean, me mam's not well, that's true enough. And I am going to see her – not that she'll know me from Adam . . . '

Harriet gave a sigh of relief. She had assumed someone had died.

' . . . But, just between ourselves, I'm also going to see our old producer. See if I can get him on board with this new material we're doing.'

'That's a lot to fit in in a day.'

'Yeah, well . . . as I say, I'm just popping into the home, like.'

'Where your mother is?'

'Yeah.'

Harriet frowned.

'Only I got the impression . . . '

Gary looked at her inquiringly.

'No, I just thought . . . that night we were round at yours, you didn't seem all that happy with your new material and what with the Ofsted report going so well and Yvette's losing *her* job . . . I suppose I just assumed you'd be . . . '

'Knuckling under? Yeah, so did I, but you know what? I can't bloody do it. It's too soul-destroying. What happened was, after the Ofsted . . . I take it Mark told you the story about me wresting victory from the jaws of . . . yadda yadda?'

She nodded, although Mark's account had not been framed in quite those terms.

'Well, when the dust had settled, I just felt flat – no, worse than flat. I felt really depressed. The thought of sticking it out for another ten years . . . ' he shook his head, 'thing is, any twat can teach kids music.'

'Oh, Gary that's not . . . '

He held his hand up.

'Seriously. I've been selling them short. I only got my shit together for that one lesson and d'you know why?'

'Why?'

'Because I had an audience. Might have been a couple of stiffs in cheap suits, but I rose to the occasion, didn't I? We made some fucking decent sounds that day, if I say so myself . . . '

Harriet glanced around the carriage, but most of the other passengers seemed too busy with their spreadsheets to be offended by Gary's language.

' . . . That's what I got off on, you see, the buzz; the high. I only really get that vibe from performing. All the other stuff – hits and album sales – that's just icing on the cake. It's the love you get from the audience. I'm a love junkie, me.'

He looked up at her with a sort of beseeching candidness in his eyes and she saw that it was true. Cynical, wise-cracking Gaz was no different from anyone else; no different from her. He just wanted to be loved.

'Isn't teaching a sort of performance?' she suggested, hesitantly.

Gary made a scornful, plosive sound.

'Would you rather teach chromatic harmony to an audience of bored sixteen-year-olds,' he said, 'or hear twenty thousand fans sing along to a riff you wrote in ten minutes on the back of a fag packet?'

Harriet considered this proposition. She knew Gary had been someone back in the day. Mark was always trying to impress upon her the iconic significance of The KMA within the canon of UK rock music, but if she was honest, she'd never been able to tell them apart from any number of other jangly, druggy Nineties pop bands. Until now she had discounted Gary's fifteen minutes of fame as a brief and embarrassing episode, the equivalent of her own short-lived dance career, undertaken to placate her mother, who by that stage had decided she wasn't cut out for academia. The day she was invalided out of her elite ballet school with anorexia was the only time Harriet ever remembered seeing her mother shed a tear. Pop music, Harriet believed, like ballet dancing and starving yourself, were things that you were supposed to grow out of. Real life meant knuckling down and accepting your fate. It meant getting a proper job in law or medicine or, yes, teaching. Of course, there would always be the gifted few who had been blessed (or cursed) with a talent they couldn't ignore and thank goodness for them – otherwise there would be no art exhibitions to take the kids to, or plays like the one that had moved her so much she had had to shut herself in the toilet during the interval and sob. And yes, The Beatles were, without a doubt, geniuses (Paul and John anyway), but she was not one of those who believed that Johnny Rotten was as important as Mozart or that Stormzy was the Shakespeare of the modern era. And Gary, let's face it, wasn't Johnny Rotten or Stormzy, he was the one-time front man of a band now so niche that not only had Harriet not heard of them until she met Mark, but nor had anyone she worked with, except the IT guy, and that pretty much said it all.

And yet … bumping into Gary out of context, in this tawdry First Class carriage designed to look like a gentlemen's club with its antimacassars and its bullet-shaped reading lamps and its push-button, wheelchair-friendly toilet that sent a waft of methane down the carriage every time someone went in or out, he seemed – literally – like a breath of fresh air. In his PVC windcheater and lairy sweatshirt, he was the authentic antidote to all the headphone-wearing, jargon-spouting suits around them and she found herself reappraising him. She was curious to know more, now, about this midlife gamble he was intent on taking – whether he had a timeframe in mind or a financial plan in place; what Yvette thought of it – but the train guard was approaching and any minute now he would be banished to the overcrowded cattle trucks behind them.

'Tickets, please.'

He was an older bloke. World-weary. Looked like he'd been working this route forever; seen it all. Harriet didn't give much for Gary's chances. She leaned forward and proffered her phone to be scanned by the guard's machine, even though it wasn't her turn yet.

'I was wondering if we could wangle an upgrade for my friend here ... ' she said discreetly.

''Fraid not, Miss. This is a peak service.'

He turned to Gary.

'If you want to stay in here, you'll have to pay the full First Class ... ' His voice trailed off and he frowned, his look of perplexity changing slowly to one of recognition and then delight.

'Gary Kershaw!'

Gary shrugged with a 'fair cop' nonchalance.

The guard looked to Harriet for corroboration and she nodded.

'Bloody hell. I was at your first gig at the PSV club in Moss Side. Seen you at Elland Road, The MEN ... Massive fan, mate.'

He shook Gary's hand, seeming quite overwhelmed.

'Are you all still in touch, like, you and John and Macca?'

Gary waggled his head evasively.

'On and off, you know, it's been a long time.'

The guard's eyes glazed over in a brief nostalgic trance.

'Couldn't do it these days, I don't know about you,' he said with a rueful smile, 'not and hold down this job.'

Gary grinned knowingly and Harriet found herself wondering what, as a mere fan, the guard had been expected to do, and whether, in dismissing whole tranches of popular culture as shallow and hedonistic, she hadn't, perhaps missed a trick.

By now the catering assistant was waiting to come through with the breakfast trolley. Gaz went through the motions of getting out his wallet and asking what he owed, but the guard waved him away.

'Don't worry about it, mate,' he said, and moved off down the carriage, smiling and shaking his head.

Harriet ordered her usual fruit and muesli and Gary made the most of his unofficial upgrade with a fry up. Harriet took a dainty mouthful and watched Gaz squeeze the contents of a second sachet of brown sauce onto the side of his plate.

He looked up and caught her eye.

'What?' he said, loading his upturned fork with baked beans and shovelling them greedily into his mouth.

Harriet grinned and shook her head indulgently and Gaz smiled, so that orange goo bulged at the corner of his lips.

'Don't take the piss.'

'I'm not,' she said, then, meeting his eye, 'I'm *not*.'

There was a pause.

'Why didn't you tell the guard you were getting back together? You'd have made his day.'

Gaz pulled a face.

'Don't need the pressure,' he said, 'he'll find out, won't he?'

They talked non-stop after that. They talked about Yvette losing her job and Gary handing in his notice on a wing and a prayer. They talked about Mark behaving weirdly and the awkwardness between him and Ollie. They talked about Ruby and Jordan's last stab at IVF. They talked about Gary's hopes for his remixed songs and Harriet's enthusiasm for her latest project and when at last she got her laptop out, it wasn't to do her work, but to show Gaz her designs for The Button Factory. She had never really talked to him about what she did, assuming it to be too dry and mathematical to be of interest to him, but it turned out he had done technical drawing at school and was more knowledgeable than she expected. He recognized The Button Factory as an early rave venue of the Madchester music scene, then a derelict death-trap known simply as Dawson's. This was in the mid-Eighties, when The KMA had been nothing but a twinkle in his eye. First time he'd done coke, he told her fondly, had been that night at Dawson's... and then the police had arrived and what should have been a beautiful night had turned into a pitch battle.

'Funny to see an iconic building like that all decked out for yuppies,' Gary said as he watched the drawings collapse in and out of three dimensions, 'cool though. I wouldn't mind a gaff there myself.'

'Oh, it's not-for-profit,' Harriet corrected him, hastily, 'they're housing association, so I'm afraid you wouldn't qualify. Six units, with communal facilities. Quite high spec considering it's public housing, but I wanted it to be sustainable. Although...' she pulled a rueful face, 'they're only halfway through the conversion and it's over-budget, so I think I might have to draw in my horns.'

Gary gave her a knowing look and she felt herself blushing.

'I hope you don't think I pushed the envelope on your kitchen extension?'

''Course not, it's beautiful,' said Gary.

'Because I'd never forgive myself if I thought...'

'Don't be daft, we love it. *She* does, the missus, no danger.' He jerked his head as if Yvette were in the next room and somehow the reference chastened them both.

'Kitchens are my downfall,' Harriet said, with a rueful grin, 'well … you saw that on the Button Factory plans. But I just think it's the heart of the … what … ?'

'Aren't you meant to be getting off at Macclesfield?'

Harriet glanced out of the window.

'Shit! How did that happen?' She bundled her computer into her bag and snatched her coat from beside her. Gary rose out of his seat and they made to kiss one another on the cheek, but bungled it and caught each other's lips. She could still taste brown sauce as she got in the cab at Macclesfield station.

11

Gary

Manchester, so much to answer for. Gary could never walk down Piccadilly station approach without the lyric coming into his head, although he'd been gone so long that these days, he didn't feel like it was Manchester that had to answer, but him. A strange war waged in his breast, whenever he came back to his city. There was a sense of pride and belonging that brought a swagger to his step, but there was also, increasingly, a sense of estrangement. Malmaison, what the fuck was that? Who were all these cocky bastards in suits, and why were so many of them women? Fair play, he'd just got off a London train, which accounted for some of the flashiness but a lot of it was home-grown, he could tell.

Walking down the curving slope towards town put him in mind of those renaissance paintings of the damned descending into hell. You'd got all these go-getters talking into their head-sets, stepping over beggars in their haste to get to their meetings. You'd got the stench of disembowelled human – well, all right, chicken-and-bacon melt – wafting out of Subway. Then, as you entered the concrete wasteland of Piccadilly Gardens, you'd got spice addicts careering about with mad eyes, eliciting barely a tut from the battle-hardened matriarchs heading to the Debenhams sale. All the deadly sins were here, with the possible exception of wrath and lust, the two to which Gary was himself predisposed, and that was only because the pubs weren't opened yet.

It had never been a conventionally beautiful city, like Paris or Amsterdam, but it used to have heart, at least. Back in the day there'd been none of this high-rise nonsense. No Selfridges, or giant Ferris wheels or toytown trams tootling about. Back then, you'd got mucky Victorian buildings and filthy canals; you'd got railway arches and anarchist graffiti. You'd got buses lumbering round town in packs like big orange dinosaurs. You'd got proper shops, like Lewis's that didn't just sell cheap tat, and proper pubs like The Crown that served decent draft bitter, not these poncy craft beers with names dreamed up on flip charts by blokes like Mark.

The Crown. His first date with Yvette had been in The Crown. Well, less date, more ultimatum. She'd told him she was pregnant, he'd accused her of making it up, she'd cried and said why do you think I'm drinking Coke then, he'd said I don't fucking know and she'd said you're horrible I don't want your baby and stormed out. He'd gone after her, of course he had. He sometimes wondered what would have happened if he hadn't. It didn't bear thinking about. Yvette would probably have brought up Ruby on her own in a council flat. Or worse, got with some no mark and moved to Timperley. She wouldn't even have been *called* Ruby. She'd have been called Charlotte or Fallon, because those were the names on

Yvette's shortlist until Gary persuaded her to call the baby after his nan. And as for Jade – she wouldn't have been born at all. What a head-fuck that was.

They were the best of him, those girls, without a shadow of a doubt. The best of both of them. Let's face it, Jade wasn't Oxford material on the back of *his* brain cells. He'd have traded his whole career for them two, no contest. All the highs of the band, the Haçienda, the raves, telly, getting signed, America, The G-Mex – none of it meant anything next to Ruby and Jade. But if it had been a choice between all that and Yvette, *just* Yvette well… with the benefit of hindsight, yes, for sure. She'd turned out to be a little diamond. More grit, more honest-to-goodness character in her little finger than he'd got in his entire flabby, middle-aged bod. But back in the day, dickhead that he was, he'd thought he could do better.

He turned the corner into Tibb Street. A woman walked past him – loose-cut blazer, expensive haircut, classy-looking leather hold-all. She had a look of Harriet.

'What's a wrecked old cunt like you doing in a place like this?'

Gary slapped Declan on the back, almost making him choke on his coffee.

Declan swivelled round on his leather-upholstered stool and embraced Gary warmly.

'Good to see you, Gaz,' he said and his voice was a bit choked up. They held each other for a moment, then with a lot of buddy-slapping, parted again. Gary looked around the airy coffee shop, all industrial chic and dangling lightbulbs.

'Didn't this used to be The Grapes?'

'No, mate,' Declan said, 'The Grapes is another block along.'

'So, what are we doing in here, then … ?' Gary said, remembering too late that Declan had just got out of rehab.

'Ah, shit! Sorry. Sorry, mate. I tell you what, though, you're looking good,' Gary lied, appraising his friend properly for the first time. Declan's once magnificent face was wasted. His yellow-tinged skin hung off his cheek bones like two sagging hammocks and his eyes looked rheumy as a pensioner's, but he was alive, and after the amount he had drunk, snorted and injected over nearly four decades, that in itself was a miracle.

'I feel good,' said Declan, implausibly, 'I really do. I know I've been here before, but this time it's for keeps. I've got this counsellor, Cyndi … '

'Oh aye.'

'No, nothing like that. She's been a meth-head herself. They're all former addicts, the counsellors, and what I get now that I didn't get before is that it's *my* responsibility. I will always be an addict, but I was forever blaming someone else. Cyndi says I have to forgive myself. See myself as someone worthy of wellness and wholeness.'

'Yeah?'

'She says as long as I cultivate humility I should be all right.'

'Very wise,' said Gary, unable to keep a hint of sarcasm out of his voice.

'She is. She's *fucking* wise,' agreed Declan, 'she's turned my life around.'

'Enough to want to come back into the business?' Gary said, holding his breath, in case the answer was no.

'Well, as I say, it's not about what's out there, it's about what's in here,' Declan tapped the side of his forehead, 'so, yeah, she … we … *I* … think I could give it a go.'

Gary nodded slowly, then patted him on the shoulder.

'I'm made up for you, mate, I really am,' then, after a brief pause, '*so* ... what did you reckon to the new tracks?'

It was nearly four by the time Declan left Gary at the tram stop in Piccadilly Gardens. He felt like a kid again, climbing on board with his pre-purchased ticket. He watched the stops come and go on the indicator board; Dane Road, Sale, Brooklands ... You'd not think a man of fifty-two who'd been chauffeured back from Madison Square Garden in a stretch limo would get butterflies in his stomach on a tram ride to Altrincham, but he did. By the time he'd stopped off in a garage forecourt to buy his mam some flowers, and negotiated the confusing ramps and hydraulically assisted entry systems of The Limes Senior Care Home, he was an hour late.

'Your sister will have your guts for *gaart*ers,' said the care assistant, a kindly black woman with a gold tooth and a Jamaican lilt still detectable in her Manchester accent.

'Has she been here long?' Gary said, bracing himself for Janice's huffy tolerance.

'She always here same time,' said the woman, elliptically, 'like *clark*work.'

She flung open the door to his mother's room, with a flourish.

'*Sar*pri-i-ise!' she said, pulling the door to on her way out.

The room was hotter than the reptile house at Chester Zoo, but Janice had her coat on.

She got up and gave him a token squeeze, brushing her cheek somewhere in the vicinity of his.

'Sorry, our kid,' Gary said, with genuine remorse, 'my meeting ran over.'

'You don't have to be sorry on *my* account,' she said huffily.

He stepped around her and looked for the first time at his mother, who was sitting on a vinyl-covered chair so vast as to make it appear the room had been scaled up. In reality, it was his mam that had been scaled down. It was as much as he could do not to gasp. She seemed half the size, if that, of the woman he had visited, when ... ? Six months ago? Nine? No, it must have been more than a year because it would have to have been half-term.

Whoever had combed his mother's hair and clipped it to one side had stopped short of putting her teeth in for her and, gazing up at him with her blue eyes, she had the look of the little girl in the horror film who, when finally cornered, is revealed to be a cackling crone. He went to kiss her but she winced away from him, so he put out his hand and touched her cheek. It felt ... not even like paper ... more like ashes.

'It's me, Mam, *Gary*,' he said and now her face hardened into one of resentment.

'Fuck off!' she muttered.

Gary recoiled. His mam never used to swear. She'd say bloody or bugger, if she was really pushed, but the F word had always been taboo.

'Easy, Mam,' he said with a nervous laugh, 'I'll have to get the swear box out.'

'You can't,' she said sourly, indicating Janice, 'that bitch has got it.'

He looked at Janice, a stricken expression on his face and she returned his gaze with sardonically raised eyebrows as if to say, where've you been?

'I got you some flowers,' he said, starting again with determined cheerfulness. 'Have you got a vase somewhere?'

His mother stared at him.

'I haven't got a pot to piss in, never mind a vase.'

'All right, Mam,' he said, laughing.

Janice sighed and took the flowers from him. She plucked some flyblown roses – presumably ones she had grown herself – from a cut-glass vase, dropped them somewhat dramatically into the rubbish bin, swooshed the vase under the tap and refilled it, before dumping his flowers in it and putting it back on the bedside cabinet.

'Thanks,' he said.

There was a silence.

'How's Alan?' he asked.

'His sciatica's bad,' Janice said.

Gary wasn't sure what sciatica was or whether it was treatable. It seemed that further inquiry would only expose the depths of his familial neglect so he just looked regretful and kept quiet.

'Will you thank Yvette for my card,' Janice said, after a moment.

'Your card . . . ?'

'My birthday card.'

'Oh. Yeah, sure.'

'Girls all right, are they?' Janice asked briskly after another pause.

'They're great,' said Gary, with some relief. 'Ruby's buying her own place and Jade's going up to Oxford in October.'

He could feel himself colouring, not only at the pretentious phrase 'up to Oxford', which had just slipped out, but also at his own economy with the truth. 'That's if we can persuade her it's worth getting a student loan, anyway,' he added in the interests of full disclosure.

He saw a look cross Janice's face, as though a penny had dropped.

'Ah . . . ' she said.

'Ah . . . what?'

'No,' she shook her head mysteriously, 'it just makes more sense now.'

'What does?'

'This,' she jerked her head towards him, then towards the flowers.

'Now, hang on . . . '

'But if you think there's going to be anything left after we've paid for this little lot,' she indicated the room with a gyration of her forehead, 'dream on.'

Gary felt his throat tighten with anger. He dropped his voice to an urgent whisper.

'That is out of order, Janice. What kind of person do you think I . . . ? No, don't answer that. I can see how this must look,' he felt anger rise up in him, as shame and indignation fought each other in his breast, 'but I'm here to see me mam. I know I've not . . . I'm not . . . ' he took a deep breath, in an attempt to master his emotions, 'I know I've not been very . . . dutiful.'

'Ha!'

' . . . And I know you've borne the brunt of the care and I'm grateful, I really am . . . '

Janice looked at him sceptically.

' . . . But I've come now because . . . because . . . '

Instinctively he looked towards his mother, as of old, to defend him against the ire of his older sister. His mam looked back, and for a moment it was as if the fog had lifted. Her hands fluttered up from beside her like two butterflies and she reached out to him, her face full of pity and love. He shuffled towards her and knelt awkwardly beside her chair as if to be knighted. She took his hands in hers, looked into his eyes and started to sing in a quavering voice.

'*In Dublin's fair city, where the girls are so pretty, I first set my eyes on sweet Molly Malone ...*'

Gary was a kid again, lying under his candlewick bedspread, staring at her silhouette picked out against the triangle of light from the landing, storing up the love and reassurance of the moment against the song's ending, when she would slip away leaving him with his terrors.

'*As she wheeled her wheelbarrow through the streets broad and narrow, crying, "Cockles and mussels alive alive-oh."*'

Gary lifted his mam's hands to his lips and made to kiss them, but she pulled away abruptly and her eyes clouded over again.

'Go fuck yerself,' she muttered.

'Mam!' Gary chastised her gently and glancing towards Janice, prepared to share a look of sadness, of wry humour, of newfound respect for what his sister had, unbeknownst to him, been dealing with this whole time, but Janice's chair was empty.

Gary made straight for the bar on the train home. He was wrung-out like a wet rag. He could have done with some coke really – had, in fact, banked on scoring some off Declan, but on reflection, it was probably just as well. Dec had produced some stonking albums on snow, but once the meth had crept in, things had tanked. Now that Declan was clean, Gary could see this album being the best thing The KMA had ever done. He was buzzing to go back and write the last couple of tracks – he fancied cutting loose on one of the songs and just going for it, John Squire-style. He knew what he was going to call it as well – 'Song for Jean', after his mam.

He slugged back the first Scotch in one go and bought another. He felt the steward's eyes on him as he poured the contents of the tiny miniature into a plastic cup. You'd have thought he was Ozzy Osbourne on a bender. Gary gave the guy a sarky smile, cheersed him, took his drink over to the vestibule, and watched the dusk descend on Stockport. It hadn't changed much – still a shit hole, hat museum or no hat museum. The doors juddered closed and the train moved off. He glanced at his watch. They'd be at Macclesfield in twenty. He remembered Harriet, dashing off the train this morning with her Burberry mac flapping and her cheeks still pink from their fumbled farewell and grinned to himself. She was a mad 'un. It was funny – he'd felt closer to her today than he had in all the time they'd known each other. She was all right, was Harriet.

Odds on she'd got an earlier train, but there was no harm in having a look. He headed down the corridor in the direction of First Class.

12

Mark

'They're here...' Mark felt Harriet's hand touch his knee under the table, and he thrilled at the unexpected pleasure of it. He watched his wife waggle her fingers in greeting at the foursome approaching them across the restaurant, a hesitant smile on her face, apprehension in her eyes. He wanted to say, 'Don't worry, I've got this, relax.' Anything to spare her, the world's sweetest introvert, from the discomfort of an evening in the company of new, intimidating people. New, intimidating people, moreover, on whom they needed to make a good impression. Jack's prospective in-laws; Maisie's parents. But he could not spare her, nor, for that matter, Ollie, who, even as he and Harriet clambered eagerly to their feet, remained hunched over his phone oblivious to – or perhaps contemptuous of – the usual social niceties.

'Tony Gould, very pleased to meet you.' The man kissed Harriet, acknowledged Ollie with a streetwise chin jerk, then pumped Mark's hand as if trying to extract some saleable commodity from his very sweat glands. He was tall, with a mane of floppy white hair and a stubble-covered lantern jaw. He looked like a Viking in a designer suit. 'And this is my wife, Tanya.'

Mark kissed Tanya on both cheeks. He was relieved to see, close up, that she was a good ten years older than Harriet, despite having looked ten years younger from across the room. And where Tanya was dressed in a bling-y, figure-hugging dress that focused all eyes on her unfeasibly pert breasts, Harriet looked, not demure exactly, no – but classy and sexy in that very individual way only Harriet could. She was wearing a vintage tea dress, buttoned to the neck, dressed down with a denim jacket and for all her slightly brittle politesse, Mark could feel himself glowing with pride. Tony Gould's company might be big enough to buy up Mark's with its petty cash, but as far as trophy wives went, Mark was definitely winning.

'Hi, Maisie,' said Mark, 'and congratulations again on your degree.' He kissed her on both cheeks and clapped Jack on the back. 'To both of you . . . ' He heard the faintest click of the tongue from Harriet and remembered. '*All* of you!' he added, bowing deeply to Ollie in a way which he only realized as he was straightening up, may have come across as ironical.

'So, *you're* Jack's twin!' said Tanya. She pulled up a chair next to him. 'Were you at Sussex too?' She went on without waiting for an answer, 'You don't look a bit alike.'

'Ollie graduated from Portsmouth a couple of weeks ago,' Harriet put in eagerly and Mark cringed for them both.

'Oh, how fabulous,' Tanya said. 'Do you know, I'm not sure I've ever been to Portsmouth,' she turned to Ollie, 'is it nice?'

Harriet opened her mouth to answer on Ollie's behalf but Mark laid a restraining hand on her forearm. There was a long silence. Mark wasn't sure whether Ollie was himself squirming, or was deliberately prolonging the silence to make everyone else squirm.

'It's all right,' he mumbled at last, 'if you like boats.'

Another baffled silence. Tanya Gould made a *moue* of cartoon amusement to the rest of the company.

'And do you...' she asked, turning back to Ollie, 'like boats?'

'Not really,' Ollie replied. Tanya threw her head back and gave a throaty laugh.

'I like you,' she said, patting his arm, then to the rest of the company, 'I like him.'

Menus were brought and champagne ordered.

Tony Gould proposed a toast to the graduates and once they had eaten their *amuse-bouche*, and ordered their food, Maisie showed them a brochure for the flat in Deptford for which she and Jack had just secured a mortgage.

'It's just round the corner from the gym, Dad,' Jack told Mark, 'so next time we work out, I'll get the key off the estate agent and show you round.'

'Great, yeah!' said Mark, and then, with a glance at Harriet, lest his eagerness be deemed favouritism, 'I meant to say, though, Jack, is it worth you still being on my gym membership? I've heard Deloitte bust your ass the first couple of years.'

Jack shrugged nonchalantly, one eye on his prospective father-in-law.

'They're actually really into well-being. That's one of the main reasons I took the job.'

'Respect,' Tony Gould said, half rising out of his chair to fist bump Jack, '*Mens sana in corpore sano*, as we gym bunnies say.'

Mark glanced at Harriet, hoping to share a secret smirk at the man's pomposity but either she hadn't noticed or she was too polite to acknowledge it. He flicked through the property brochure.

'Looks nice, yeah,' he said. 'But, hey, Harriet's the architect here...'

'Yes, indeed,' said Tony Gould, leaning forward, 'let's get a *professional* opinion.'

He propped his chin on the back of his hand and gazed at her, admiringly.

'Oh gosh, well...' Harriet blushed and flicked backwards and forwards through the glossy folder, 'it looks... I mean... of course it looks *lovely*. Great location, nice finishes...'

She darted a guilty glance towards Ollie.

'The only problem with London is the lack of floorspace...'

'Harriet's just converted two thousand square metres of Cheshire warehouse into affordable housing,' bragged Mark.

'Well, I'm still in the process actually,' his wife put in, 'we've run into a few problems.'

Mark wished she would overcome this habit of hers of telling everyone the unvarnished truth about everything. The Goulds didn't need to know that The Button Factory had gone so far over budget that the housing association were threatening to pull out.

'It's a fantastic initiative,' Mark interjected on Harriet's behalf, 'regenerating the North, bringing high-quality, sustainable housing to an area of inner-city deprivation...'

'I don't know that you can call Macclesfield *deprived*, Mark,' Harriet murmured and he felt himself redden.

'Ah yes, Cheshire,' said Tony Gould, 'too expensive for me now, alas...'

'Really?' Mark perked up, supposing Tony to be referring to some holiday home he was having to let go.

'Yes, we've got a plant in Widnes, but the labour costs have gone through the roof, so it looks like we might have to relocate production to Cambodia. Sorry, I'm in pharmaceuticals, I don't know if Maisie told you?'

'Yes, yes,' said Mark vaguely, 'I think she did mention something.'

'And you're in... advertising... wasn't it? *Much* more glamorous.'

'PR actually...'

'I'm never quite sure where one stops and the other starts. I leave all that to my marketing director.'

'Well, it's all brand communication, but...'

'Ah, the wine list!' Tony interrupted him, receiving the oversized folder from the sommelier and opening it across his own place setting and his wife's.

'Shall we have red or white? What's everyone eating?'

'I'm having steak,' said Jack, 'so whatever red you'd recommend, Tony...' Mark couldn't help cringing a little, whether at Jack's obsequiousness, or the fact that he felt himself superseded in the pecking order, he wasn't sure.

'*Turbot* for you wasn't it, Harriet?' Mark said, a little more loudly than was necessary, 'and I'm having the guinea fowl, so a nice dry rosé might be...'

'We'll have a Châteauneuf-du-Pape and a Chablis.' Tony snapped the Carte des Vins shut and handed it back to the sommelier, before beaming around the table. His gaze fell on Ollie. Mark closed his eyes, in silent prayer.

'So, we know what *these* guys are up to,' Tony said, 'but

what have you got planned? Bit of globetrotting? An internship? Or is Dad luring you into the advertising business?'

'PR,' corrected Mark, quietly.

Ollie shrugged.

'Give the kid a break, Tony, he's only just finished,' said Tanya Gould, indulgently. 'Good grief, no wonder this generation are so stressed out. We never had this when we were starting out, did we?'

She looked at Harriet for confirmation, although Botox notwithstanding, it seemed unlikely that they had been in the same cohort.

'*Thank* you, Tanya,' Harriet said, 'that's what I'm always telling Mark. It's ridiculous. No sooner have they jumped through one hoop than we're putting the next in front of them. They need to find out who they are.'

'Oh, "who they are",' scoffed Mark. 'I'm fifty-three and I don't have the faintest idea who I am. Too busy earning a bloody living. How about you, Tony, do you know ... ' he sketched air quotes, 'who you are?'

'I do, actually,' Tony said, taking a mouthful of the Châteauneuf-du-Pape which the sommelier had offered him to taste. He rolled it noisily around his palate, then tossed his head back, swallowed, and gave the waiter a confirmatory nod.

'Tanya and I went on the most amazing retreat in Bali a couple of years ago.'

'It was the year Maisie left for Sussex,' Tanya said, making a sad face at Harriet. 'Bit of a watershed for us ... '

'Turned out to be life-changing,' Tony went on. 'I went out there a zombie. Totally burned out. Not fit for purpose in the boardroom *or* the bedroom ... '

'Dad!' Maisie protested, with an apologetic glance at Jack, but Tony Gould could have slapped his cock on the table and demanded a tape measure and Jack probably wouldn't have turned a hair, he was so in thrall to the guy. Only Ollie seemed unimpressed – in fact, it was hard to tell whether he was even listening, so insolently vacant was his expression.

'Sorry folks, but it's true,' Tony insisted, tearing a bread roll in half with macho abandon. 'I came back – we *both* came back – different people, didn't we, darling?'

He popped half of it in his mouth and chewed smugly.

Tanya smirked at her manicure.

'What sort of retreat was it?' Harriet asked, a little too eagerly for Mark's liking.

'Well, it was bespoke, according to your particular needs,' Tony said, 'but the elements were things like,' he counted them on his fingers, 'rebirthing, gestalt, coffee enemas, tantric yoga, mindfulness – they took us apart and put us back together again – *literally*.'

'And that was ... helpful?' Mark asked.

'*Christ*, yes,' said Tony. 'I was a mess, wasn't I, darling? Didn't know my arse from my elbow. Drinking too much, not sleeping. By the time I got back I felt ten years younger. I don't know how I'd have handled the takeover without the grounding that retreat gave me.'

'You got taken over?' Mark said, hopefully.

'No, *we* took over Phyto-Nature. Big multivitamin outfit. The board thought I was mad to go for it, but the synergies were obvious and it's paid off big time.'

Mark felt his spirits lower a little further.

'The secret is to trust in the universe,' said Tony. 'I came back from that retreat and I swear to – I was going to say God, but I should probably say Shiva – we had the best quarterly figures in the company's history. But I can honestly say, hand on heart, even if they'd been the worst; if it had all gone tits-up, I'd have been OK with that. Better than OK. In some respects, it would almost have been preferable, because I'd have been able to draw on my moksha.'

'Your *moksha*?' Harriet wrinkled her nose prettily.

The waiter had arrived with the starters.

'It's Sanskrit for your life force; your inner strength,' he said. 'Ah yes... who else was having the lobster tail... ?'

'Actually, I'd better just... will you excuse me?' Mark got to his feet abruptly. He was feeling... he didn't know what he was feeling... a mixture of fear and shame and panic.

'Mark, where are you going?' Harriet protested. 'The starters are...'

But Mark was already halfway to the rest rooms.

He barged through the door, unzipped himself and pointed his penis at the long slate trough into which he assumed he was meant to discharge it. He strained and strained but nothing came. He rolled his head back and stared at the ceiling. What was he even doing? Ducking out at precisely the wrong moment. Making a show of himself and Harriet. Kowtowing to a simpleton like Tony Gould. Had he run away? he wondered. Had the man's sheer alpha-maleness seen him off? Was it as primitive as that? Was this, oh God... was *this* how Ollie felt... ?

At last a trickle of urine came, the last few drops dribbling onto the fly of his Paul Smith trousers. He caught his own eye in the strip of mirror above the urinal but could not hold its gaze.

Was this just the male menopause, or could it be his conscience catching up with him? Surely not the latter. It wasn't like he'd done anything illegal, just refinanced the company to take out cash that was his anyway. And what if he *had* used the cash to buy shares in an ethical cosmetics company, the same cosmetics company for whose new vegan product range Mark's team was about to launch a campaign? There was nothing wrong with that ... not much, anyway. He rezipped his fly, and washed and dried his hands, thrusting his chin one last time towards the mirror, and running his hand around the five o'clock shadow, not yet visible, but palpably there.

'I said you wouldn't mind if we started,' said Harriet, mopping up the last of her lobster juices. Mark sat down to a daunting slab of terrine.

'I was thinking,' he said, 'about what Tony was saying.'

'About homeopathy, you mean?' Tony said.

'Ah, no ... ' Mark said, 'before that – the stuff about reinventing yourself, making a change ... ' He turned to Harriet. 'Don't you think it might do *us* good?'

'A retreat in Bali?' Harriet asked eagerly.

'No, not a retreat,' said Mark, 'a real change. Throw everything up in the air, see where it lands sort of thing.'

'I'm not sure I like the sound of that very much,' Harriet said, with a comedy grimace around the rest of the group.

'Oh, come on. We don't want to be stagnating, do we? Rattling around in our huge house, waiting for these jokers to bring us their washing ... ' He indicated Jack and Ollie.

'Our apartment's got a built-in washer-dryer, Dad,' offered Jack cheerfully.

'Yeah, I meant more ... figuratively speaking,' said Mark.

'We're free now, aren't we? For the first time in our lives. The boys are sorted . . . ' he looked resolutely away from Ollie, 'we can please ourselves.'

'What about work?' said Harriet.

'You can work anywhere,' said Mark airily, 'that's the beauty of a job like yours.'

'But *you* can't,' Harriet said with a bewildered smile, 'you've got employees, clients . . . '

'Oh, you'd be surprised,' Mark blustered, 'good management's all about making yourself dispensable, wouldn't you agree, Tony? No . . . things would tick along very nicely without me for a while, maybe even for . . . anyway, yes, in the first instance, a sabbatical seems like a very attractive proposition, I must say . . . recharge our batteries . . . find our *moksha* was it, Tony?'

Harriet frowned at him, half in puzzlement, half appeal. Why are you being weird in front of these people, her expression seemed to say. What is going on? And Mark didn't know. He only knew that it felt as though the walls were closing in on him and he needed to be somewhere else.

13

Yvette

Yvette scanned the kitchen, J-cloth in hand. It was spotless. There was nothing left to clean. She had been so efficient, she was no longer needed. Surplus to requirements in her own home, now, as well as at Dale Road Primary. She perched on a stool at the counter and started scrolling through Situations Vacant on her phone; care assistant, courier driver, trainee bookkeeper … how had it come to this? She'd had a job she was perfectly happy with. A job she was good at; a job she loved. Not the one she'd aimed for as a teenager, but all things considered, not a bad one.

At five, Yvette had wanted to be a princess; at seven, a fireman, at ten a pop singer – preferably Blondie. By the time she *met* a pop singer, she'd set her sights on teaching. A more mundane ambition, perhaps, but a lofty enough one, considering where she'd come from. It had all been going so well. She'd been revising for her mock A levels in her bedroom – Piccadilly Radio on quietly in the background – when a track had come on with an opening riff that had her tapping her pencil on her rough book. Before long, she was nodding along to its swirling melody and by the time the lead vocalist came in, with his hypnotic gravelly voice, her life had, unbeknownst to her, already been knocked fatally off course. At the time, it had just been a catchy song. An earworm, that had made her pay special attention when the DJ had faded it out, apologetically, in time for the pips, but she had made sure to catch the name of the band. The KMA.

Still, no regrets. She wouldn't be without Ruby, not for the world. Talking of Ruby, where the hell were they? She and Jordan should have been back half an hour ago, by rights. Did that mean good news or bad? More likely bad, on balance, Yvette thought, twisting her wedding ring round her finger, anxiously. If the scan had shown up something wrong, they'd have had to stay for a debriefing. If all was well, they'd have been sent on their . . .

That was them. She hopped off the stool to go and meet them, then thought better of it and sat back down. Act natural, don't add to the pressure. She plucked a leisurewear catalogue off the recycling pile and started leafing through it. She heard murmuring in the hall, a zipper unzipping, shoes being kicked off and then the pad of footsteps on the stairs. Oh God, they were going straight up to Ruby's room, that meant they couldn't face her . . . but no, wait, more muffled conversation, they were coming back down.

Her fingers fumbled on the pages of the catalogue.

'Oh, hi!' she said, as they came in to the room. 'I expect you could do with a cuppa. Did you manage to get a seat on the train?'

God, she was good. Give that woman an Oscar. They

probably thought she'd forgotten what they'd gone for. She looked up now and met Ruby's eye and her face must have given her away.

'It's all good, Mum!'

'The HCG's through the roof!' Jordan crowed.

'We saw the heartbeat.'

'It's worked. It's taken. We're going to have a baby!'

Yvette shrieked and flung her arms wide, gathering them both to her. Their scalps smelled sweet and salty, like family, like the baby would smell. Her grandchild. Who needed a job? She had a job.

'Oh, Ruby! Oh, Ruby!' she couldn't stop saying it. They did a dance.

'Sit down. Sit. You need to calm down. Breathe. Cup of tea. I'll put the kettle on.'

She steered Ruby towards the sofa, hugged Jordan again, smiled up at him. He looked shit-scared, like Gary had been, but up for it, like Gary hadn't been. She picked up the kettle with trembling hands.

'Where's Dad? Should I phone him?' Ruby asked.

'He's in Manchester again, but you can try him . . . '

The water gushed into the kettle, drowning out the first few sentences of Ruby's phone conversation.

'So, you are *pleased* then?' was the first thing Yvette overheard. She regretted not briefing Gaz first. He could be tactless sometimes, if his head wasn't in the right place – could blurt out any old thing.

She pressed the on switch and reached for the tea bags, listening intently. Why all the long silences? What the hell was Gaz saying? He never talked for this long.

'Yeah, yeah, just now,' Ruby said, already sounding, if not deflated, then less than ecstatic. What was he *thinking*, the big lummox? God, typical Gaz. Way to piss on their chips. Surely he could have let them have their moment, whatever it was he was so taken up with?

'Oh right, I didn't ... yeah, no, that sounds ... Yeah. June ... I know, I know ... Gemini, like you.'

Another long silence. Yvette gave up all pretence of making tea. She turned round, folded her arms, listened in. Ruby had the phone tucked into her chin. She was looking downwards. She was saying less and less.

'It's not because of us, is it?' she said at last. 'Because I'd rather not buy a place at all if it means ... '

She fell silent again. Yvette made eye contact with Jordan, who shrugged perplexedly.

'No ... no, 'course I'm not,' Ruby was saying, a break in her voice, 'no, yeah. I know you are. Well, no, not champagne, 'cos it wouldn't be good for the ... yeah, yeah, definitely – when you get in. I know you are. I know, Dad. No, 'course you haven't. I'm fine ... yeah, see you later.'

Ruby cancelled the call and handed her phone to Jordan as if in shock.

'What's up?' said Yvette warily. 'Was he not pleased?'

'Where's Chorlton?' Ruby asked in a small voice.

'South Manchester, why?' said Yvette.

''Cos Dad said he'd seen a dead nice house there that you might buy,' she blurted, and burst into tears.

'Now you listen to me,' Yvette said, putting down the kettle and going over to the sofa. She bent down and gripped her daughter firmly by the shoulders so their eyes met. 'I'm going nowhere till that baby's in primary school. I've not waited six years and seen you go through hell to send the kid an Amazon voucher on its birthday. I'm going to be a hands-on gran!'

She squished onto the end of the sofa and put her arm round her daughter and Ruby burrowed into her embrace like a baby animal seeking solace. They sat for a moment – mother and daughter, hair tangled together, chests rising and falling until their heartbeats slowed and synchronized. Yvette let out a deep silent sigh and Ruby lifted her head up.

'You're not going to knit stuff, though, are you?'

14

Harriet

'Let your body melt into the floor and your mind float free,' the yoga teacher intoned.

Harriet lay on her mat, tense as a sprung trap.

'As each new thought occurs to you, acknowledge it and let it drift away. Allow yourself to succumb to the deep peace of relaxation.'

She opened one eye and peeped sideways at Yvette, lying a few feet away on Harriet's second best yoga mat. For a novice, her friend seemed to have got the hang of things all too easily. Her knees were splayed, her chest rising and falling in an attitude of deep repose. Harriet closed her eye again and tried once more to empty her mind.

She had first gone to yoga to cure her stress-incontinence after having the twins; she'd barely been able to cough, in those first few months, without wetting her pants. But by the time her pelvic floor was back in shape she was hooked. Amid the hectic blur of young motherhood, her one-hour hatha yoga sessions were an oasis of calm. Gradually, as her abdomen grew flatter and her muscles stronger, the practice came to represent something more – an exercise of power over the parts of her body she could control, to make up for her powerlessness over the ones she couldn't – her reproductive organs. By the time three miscarriages had become four, yoga was a mental health must, the mindfulness a useful technique for hauling her thoughts out of the rat run of failure and back into equilibrium. Nowadays, with the prospect of a third child dwindling as she headed inexorably towards middle-age, she came mainly for this – Savasana – corpse pose. Ten minutes of self-induced nothingness. Ten minutes reprieve from being Harriet.

'Let relaxation embrace each of your limbs in turn. Let it soften your belly, your lower back, your thighs...'

Harriet thought of Mark's behaviour that morning in bed. The way he had tilted his phone screen away by degrees, as she had turned her gaze toward it with, she had thought, undetectable subtlety. Her buttocks clenched involuntarily and she shifted her weight a little on the yoga mat. She was used, if anything, to the traffic being the other way. Mark checking up on her; constantly taking her emotional temperature, saying things like 'penny for them', which immediately made 'them' murderous. She hadn't really appreciated, until Mark had started acting strangely, to what extent throughout their marriage her own neuroses had only found expression against the background of Mark's equanimity. She was the anxious, needy, fretful one; he the soother, the pacifier, the rock. Except just lately, somewhere within him, she thought she could sense the early rumblings of an earthquake.

She risked a deep inhalation, but on the exhale, feeling her rib cage start to shudder with distress, she stalled the breath and held herself taut again, counting the seconds in her head as a distraction.

'And when you're ready, bring your focus back to your body, wriggle your toes... wriggle your fingers... give yourself a full body stretch and in your own time, join me on your mat in Padasana.'

Harriet hauled herself together like a handful of cutlery, and turned to face the teacher, legs crossed, hands in prayer position. She kept her eyes lowered, but was still aware of Yvette glancing across, perhaps to imitate the pose, perhaps curious about her state of mind.

'... And bringing your hands to heart centre, honour yourself, your fellow human beings and finally, the universe.'

The yoga teacher beamed around the group, then, holding prayer hands up to her forehead, murmured:

'Namaste.'

'Namaste,' replied the class in a reverent whisper.

'Namaste,' muttered Harriet bitterly.

'That was great,' Yvette said afterwards, as they rolled up their mats and shuffled into their trainers at the side of the room. 'It's funny, I always thought yoga would be too hippy dippy for me, but I actually feel really...'

Her voice petered out as she caught sight of Harriet's face.

'Are you OK?' Yvette said softly, putting a hand on her arm.

A gaggle of women paused on their way out of the door.

'Feel free to join us for coffee, ladies,' called one.

'Will do,' said Yvette.

Déjà Brew had been a fixture in their neighbourhood for nearly two decades – an old-school coffee shop that had defied gentrification; there was no risk of bumping into the yoga posse here. With its chintzy lampshades, varnished pine tables and strip-lit refrigerator cabinet full of fruit-inspired salads and anaemic quiche it was a hipster-free haven; a place where mums set up camp for the day with their buggies and muslins and brittle chatter, where rain macs steamed on the backs of chairs and people in fleeces read yesterday's *Guardian* from cover to cover while insipid cappuccinos cooled at their elbows.

Harriet sat at their usual table and watched Yvette banter with the middle-aged woman at the counter before weaving her way between the tables, tray in hand. Harriet pulled the chair out as she approached and helped her unload the coffees and two plates, one bearing a croissant, the other a scone. Yvette emptied a sachet of sweetener into her cup and stirring it thoughtfully, looked up at her friend.

'Why didn't you say?' she said in a tone of kindly reproach.

'Say what?'

'That you were ... ' she shrugged, 'down. Sad. Whatever.'

'You've got enough on your plate. Besides, I didn't really know I was till we got to yoga.'

'It is allowed, you know.' Yvette gave her an admonishing smile and Harriet thought how attractive her friend still looked behind the careworn expression and the war paint. Yvette was beautiful in a way you might easily miss. Not only because age had softened her fine jawline and years of over-empathizing had left crow's feet around her eyes. Yvette's beauty was an ephemeral thing because she didn't believe in it herself, except when she was 'done up' as she called it, when, ironically, her natural radiance was hidden beneath a carapace of glamour.

Now, with sunlight turning her cheeks a luminous rose, her blonde hair corkscrewing over one eye, and a random bit of mascara gluing two lashes together, Harriet thought she had never looked lovelier.

'I know it's *allowed*,' Harriet said.

They both smiled.

'Is it Mark?'

'It's Mark.'

They blurted in unison and then laughed. Harriet took a breath and then launched in.

'I don't know, lately he's just... absent. Even when he's in the room, he's not in the room, if you know what I mean. He's distracted. Always checking his phone and Mark was never like that. He used to get on at *me* about it... Then he tries to make it up to me by being all dutiful. *Can I get you anything?* sort of thing, like he's the bloody butler. Yes, you can get me something, you can get me my husband back.'

'What is it do you think, Work? The boys?'

Harriet shrugged.

'I don't know. I feel like he's keeping secrets. If I didn't know him better I'd think he was having an affair,' she said, pulling a comical face.

Yvette burst out laughing, the force of her scorn blowing scone crumbs across the table, which she harvested again with the side of her hand, blushing slightly.

'I know, I know, he's not the type.' Harriet rolled her eyes. She broke off a bit of croissant and chewed it thoughtfully.

'He's so jittery, though. Ants in his pants. I don't think it's work. Well, only in the sense he seems to have lost interest in it. Ever since he's had a bee in his bonnet about this retreat

Maisie's parents went on in Bali – you know, I told you they had this amazing...?'

Yvette nodded and sipped her coffee.

'... Well, ever since then he seems to want to drag *me* off somewhere. A sabbatical, he called it. Like *I* can have a sabbatical. Like either of us can. Mark owns the company. You can't just duck out for a year, can you? Not without handing over the reins, anyway, and once he's done that...'

'Oh, it'll not be thought through,' said Yvette. 'Gaz is the same. Throw everything up in the air, never mind anyone else. It's a mid-life crisis, is what it is.'

'Just what I need!'

'Look out for the Harley-Davidson,' Yvette said.

They laughed.

'Or in Gary's case the portable electronic drum machine.'

They laughed again, then both sipped their coffees.

'Ollie's moved back home, hasn't he...?' broached Yvette.

'Yeah.'

'Could that be...?'

'Well...'

'Not that I'm saying they don't get on or any...'

'Honestly, Yvette, sometimes you could cut the atmosphere with a knife!' Harriet blurted. It felt like lancing a boil. And now that she'd started, she found she couldn't stop.

'... It's like, Mark walks into a room and Ollie walks out.'

Yvette made a pained expression.

'And if I go after him, Mark thinks I'm pandering to him and then *we* end up falling out. It's like Mark thinks everything Ollie does, he does to spite him... did I tell you he's shaved his head?'

'Mark?'

'No, Ollie.'

Yvette made a crying face.

'All his lovely hair ... ' she said.

'I know,' Harriet agreed, 'it's not an easy look to carry off ... '

'Still,' Yvette said, 'it could be worse. One of Ruby's mates has got those lobe-stretcher things ... I mean, I'm quite broad-minded, but when you can see the *room* through someone's earlobe ... '

'God!' Harriet shuddered.

'It's probably just a phase he's going through, anyway,' Harriet went on, 'but even if it's not, he is who he is. There's no point trying to change him. The trouble is, Mark always compares him to Jack.'

'Yeah, that can't be easy, for him,' Yvette sympathized, 'what with Jack walking straight into a flash job ... '

'And having a girlfriend ... '

'And buying a place ... '

Harriet stared pensively out over her coffee cup.

'It's not the norm, though,' Yvette reassured her, 'Jack's the exception. Not being funny, boomerang kids; that's all anybody talks about now.'

'Try telling that to Mark,' Harriet said. 'He won't have it. I've said to him, Mark, they *all* come home now. It's not like it was for us.'

Yvette nodded.

'It took Celia Kendrick's Milo nine months just to get a job in Tesco Metro,' Harriet went on. 'She's gone back to doing his washing like he's never been away and he doesn't pay a penny in rent.'

'Same as our Jade,' said Yvette grimly.

'Oh well, yes and no. Milo Kendrick's got some Mickey Mouse degree from Manchester Met, your Jade's just marking time before she goes up to Oxford.'

'*Is* she, though?' said Yvette.

'*Isn't* she?'

Now it was Yvette's turn to look troubled.

'I don't know, Harriet. I'm really worried about her. She says she doesn't want to get into debt, but I think that's Juris talking. He seems to have some kind of hold over her and I don't know if it's just security, 'cos he's her first proper boyfriend and she thinks you have to get with the first fella that asks, like I did with Gaz...'

'...Oh, I'm sure she'll come to her senses before...'

'...Or whether she thinks, what with me losing my job and Gary's situation being up in the air... I've told you his latest daft scheme, haven't I?'

'No?'

'He's only talking about moving back to Manchester.'

Dread clenched Harriet's stomach. She blinked stupidly at her friend.

'You're not *going*...?'

'Well, *I* don't want to, 'course I don't. *My* life's here. My mates. *You.* The girls – my grandchild'll be here, for goodness' sake. But you know what Gaz is like...'

Harriet thought back to their encounter on the train the previous week. She did know what Gaz was like, yes, and that too, if she was honest, was part of her dismay. After fifteen years of being friendly strangers, they had had a breakthrough on that journey and finally bonded. She'd seen him puff up with pride when the ticket inspector turned out to be a KMA fan and wither with shame when he'd talked about his mother. She'd seen him quietly intrigued by her plans for The Button Factory, and buzzing at the prospect of playing live again. With every mile the train had moved further north, Gaz had made a bit more sense to her. She had seen him for who he was – a big kid, and a haunted man; a contradictory bundle of sensitivity and machismo, regret and ambition, tenderness and pugnacity. A friend.

'Property's through the roof up north,' Harriet heard herself say sourly. Yvette looked taken aback. 'But of course, you'll get a lovely place with what you'll get for yours,' Harriet backtracked, quickly, full of contrition.

'Well, as I say, we're not going,' Yvette replied, with the over-emphasis of one who fears she might be, 'and even if we do, we'll not be trading up. Not with our Jade's uni fees to think of and Ruby's baby on the way...'

Harriet clenched her hand beneath the table. She looked down before meeting Yvette's eye warily.

'What?' Yvette said.

'No, only, with the baby... I'd try not to invest *too* much at this stage. Don't get me wrong, I'm sure it's all going to be fine, only with IVF, you can't really afford to...'

'Oh no, they've had the twelve-week scan!' Yvette interrupted her. 'It's taken, apparently. They seem to think she stands every chance of going to term.'

A shaft of sun bounced off the plate-glass window of the coffee shop, and for a moment Harriet thought she'd gone blind. She had hoped, should this day ever come, to feel vicarious pleasure at the success of a project that had become almost a proxy for her own frustrated attempts to reproduce, but instead she felt a visceral stab of pure jealousy.

'...Oh well that's wonderful, gosh!' she stammered. 'Well done, them. How fantast...'

She couldn't finish the sentence.

15

Gary

You couldn't tell she was pregnant to look at her, Gary thought. Ruby's face might have filled out a bit, but she was still slim as anything. Jordan was the one who looked different. The lad was strutting around the place like the cock o' the walk, chest puffed out, smug little grin on his chops. Yeah, all right, son, so you weren't firing blanks after all, Gary felt like saying, but he couldn't begrudge the lad his pride. He worked hard, he loved Ruby and they'd gone through the mill to get here. As far as son-in-law material went, Gary had no complaints. It was one less thing to worry about, especially now the two of them had their offer accepted on the new place.

He and Yvette had finally got down there to have a look at it the other night. It was a rabbit hutch on a windswept cul-de-sac in Woolwich, but you'd have thought it was Graceland, to see how thrilled they were with it. While Ruby and Yvette had measured up for blinds, Gary and Jordan sat on the bare floorboards, watching Arsenal thrash Liverpool on Jordan's iPad. At one point, Yvette had got down on her knees and put her ear to Ruby's belly, trying to hear the baby's heartbeat. He'd felt touched seeing that. Touched and a little bit irritated. She was over-investing, that was the thing. She'd already bought them a Moses basket, but in the space of an hour, Gary heard her promise them a changing table, a highchair and a baby monitor. If they'd stayed any longer she'd have been stumping up for a granny annexe. He'd had to remind her on the way home that they'd already coughed up nine grand they hadn't got, to pay Jade's uni fees and she'd said she was well aware thank you very much. They'd just about thawed out – he'd made a feeble joke, she'd laughed at it – when, turning into Brenner Street, they'd seen the FOR SALE sign outside their house.

The timing couldn't have been worse. Obviously, they'd known it was coming. It had been up on the estate agent's website for a bit, but there was something about seeing the board there, lit up in the glow of the street lamp. FOR SALE, nearly thirty years of their lives. Twenty-eight Christmases, one home birth, umpteen birthday parties, Christ knew how many Indian takeaways, a shedload of booze, the odd bad trip, a fair few rows and an adequate amount of sex – not as much as Gary would have liked; probably more than Yvette could have done with. It had been his second-best life – a life spent in exile in the soft South; a life spent on the run from his early promise, but it had *been* a life, and he would miss it. He'd put the handbrake on and looked across at Yvette, who was staring straight ahead with a face on her like a slapped arse.

'It's for the girls,' he'd said, his tone more defensive than he'd intended.

'Yeah, right,' she'd snapped back viciously, and she'd

slammed out of the car and gone up the garden path without a backward glance.

The next morning she'd been out for the count and if Gary hadn't got his shit together he'd have missed his train to Manchester. Normally she'd have been chivvying him along, making tea, finding his phone charger, but it was obvious she had the hump, because the alarm went off and she just rolled over and went back to sleep.

'I'm off now, babe,' he'd said, in a perky whisper that didn't quite hide his irritation, 'I'll see you tomorrow night.'

She made a noise, half mumble, half snore. He hovered by the bedroom door.

'Aren't you going to wish me luck ... ?'

Snort ... snuffle.

' ... Whatever.' He picked up his holdall with a shrug. 'I'll ring you.'

As the train snaked north out of Euston, the guard's voice came over the tannoy welcoming them on board, and Gary thought he recognized the flat vowels and dry humour of the KMA fan who'd given him a free upgrade last time. He considered chancing his arm in First Class again, but decided it wouldn't be the same. Harriet was already up there anyway – he'd be seeing her later by prior arrangement. The thought gave him a nice warm glow. It hadn't even been his idea – it was Yvette who'd suggested it.

'Poor woman's stuck up there half the week while this warehouse thing gets finished,' she'd told him, with a pleading look on her face, 'doesn't know a soul. Do you think you could see your way clear to have a drink with her?'

'Yeah, whatever, no problem,' he'd interrupted cheerily, to her evident surprise.

They'd arranged it for tonight, which at first glance wasn't ideal, given Gary was signing a recording contract that same day. Then again, this was a different kind of record deal. Back in 1989, The KMA had signed to Factory over a six-course dinner at The Midland Hotel, two courses of which had been snorted in the gentlemen's restroom. They'd gone on to do a set at the Haçienda and while the whole world *claimed* to have been at that now-legendary gig, Gary must have been the only one who unarguably was, yet who had no recollection of it whatsoever. If anyone had told him then that their comeback contract would be signed over a teetotal vegan lunch in the Gay Village he'd have laughed in their face. And if they'd said he'd be following that up just a few hours later with a civilized snifter in the company of an out-of-town architect friend he'd have pissed himself laughing. Yet here he was, on his way to just such a lunch followed by just such a sundowner and given that Declan had brokered the deal and its success depended on Dec's staying clean and sober for the duration, not just of the meal but of the entire project, it was probably no bad thing.

Gary sat himself down in Standard Class, plugged in his headphones and, selecting the lead track from the new album, pressed play. Soon his eyes were closed, his head was bobbing and a smile was spreading over his face. It was a banging tune – melodious with a driving rhythm and a backing track of looping electronica. It was reminiscent of their old stuff but no pastiche. Declan had worked wonders with the production, clever fucker that he was. Gary's reverie was interrupted by the ping of a text message from Yvette.

Sorry I was a bit narky. Fingers xd for you today. 🖤 🖤 😅

Gary felt a pang of guilt. It should have been him apologizing, really. Yvette had been spot on about his motivation for moving. He'd dressed it up in concern for his daughters. It was true Ruby had needed a deposit, and their Jade needed her fees paid, but if Gary looked into his conscience, *really* looked, he had to admit that, when push came to shove, he wasn't making this move for the girls, he was making it for himself. The KMA were on the brink of a comeback and you didn't get too many second chances at their age. A grandchild was a beautiful thing, but so was a limited-edition vinyl picture disc.

He was about to reply to Yvette's text when a voicemail notification popped up. He pressed play.

'*Oh, hi, Gary, it's me.*' Harriet's voice kept breaking up, '*Listen... 'omething's come... here and I'm not sure I... make it over to... 'anchester... ter all... so I was...*'

The train went into a tunnel and the message cut out altogether.

'Fuck!' Gary muttered. He jabbed the phone repeatedly with his thumb, his stomach falling away in panic. At last the train emerged into the light. One bar, two bars, three...

'*... To come over here instead. I could show you round the site and there's a nice pub by the canal where we could grab a bite to...*' the message cut out.

Gary threw his head toward the ceiling and smiled with relief, and some other emotion he wasn't yet ready to admit to.

Gary was in an upbeat mood as he got off the train at Macclesfield. By no means pissed, but not completely sober either. The band had signed on the dotted line in the vegan place and drunk a toast in Matcha tea, then, when Declan and his weird American girlfriend had fucked off, Gary, John and Macca had repaired to The Grapes for a celebratory pint. They'd had a whisky chaser as well, because it wasn't every day you got a second bite at the cherry, and then John had headed home to Chorlton in an Uber and Macca had gone to meet his missus in town to look for a wardrobe. Rock 'n' roll.

The guard at the exit barrier in Macclesfield had never heard of The Button Factory.

'Oh, you mean *Dawson's*,' he said, when Gary explained. 'Yeah, it's left at the lights, right at the end and then follow the lane as far as you can go. Can't miss it.'

It sounded like a doddle, but it turned out to be a twenty-minute uphill slog on a winding B-road, with commuter traffic and no pavement. By the time the sign for the site entrance came up, Gary's trainers were caked in mud and the drink was wearing off. A double iron gate ahead was padlocked. Having failed to get a signal on his phone or to discern any sign of life, he was beginning to wonder if Harriet had given up on him and gone home, when he heard a cry in the distance. He turned around to see a figure in a high-vis coat, overalls and a hard hat, jogging towards him, waving both hands in the air.

'Gary!' Their eyes met across the barrier and she half laughed, half panted with evident relief. Harriet had always had a bit of an androgynous thing going on, style-wise and Gary had always liked it; so that now, got up like a brickie, tendrils of hair escaping from under her hard hat, smear of lip gloss, she looked pretty much irresistible.

'Get you, Sir Alfred McAlpine!' he teased as she fumbled

with the padlock and swung the gate open. They went for the double peck, each guessing the wrong side, so that Gary ended up grazing the side of her lips with his mouth, just as he had on the train that time. Pulling away, he noticed dark circles under her eyes and a pinched, pale look to her complexion, and she noticed him notice and started fidgeting and apologizing and adjusting her hat which had got knocked out of true by their encounter.

'Blimey, it's like the *Marie Celeste* in here,' he said, following her onto the deserted site.

Pallets and skips were everywhere. Abandoned forklifts stood like dinosaurs, their necks rearing up in the pinkish light, but there wasn't a worker to be seen.

'I know you knock off early in the building trade but . . . ' he indicated, to right and left, the conspicuous lack of workforce.

'Yeah, no . . . We're . . . in a spot of bother, financially,' she admitted, biting her lip. 'Cashflow issues, it came to a head this afternoon . . . and, well, builders like to be paid, so . . . '

She turned her head away abruptly and darted into the Portakabin. Gary hovered awkwardly outside.

'Here you go,' she said a moment later, handing him a hard hat. A tissue stuck out of her pocket and her nose was conspicuously pink.

'Hey, I'm sorry, mate,' Gary said quietly. 'Listen . . . ' he waved his hand vaguely towards the warehouse, 'this must be the last thing you feel like. We don't have to if . . . '

'No, no, it's OK,' she said, with a heartbreaking brightness, 'you're here now. May as well have a look round. I'm sure it's just a hiccup. Well, it's *got* to be really!' She attempted a nonchalant laugh but her voice cracked and they trudged towards the still heavily scaffolded building.

'I like how you've kept it quite scuzzy,' Gary said gazing up at the imposing eastern façade. Other than new windows, some subtle repairs to the brickwork and a retro BUTTON FACTORY sign like the one Gary had seen on Harriet's computer, the outside of the warehouse still looked largely as he remembered it.

'Thanks ... I think ... ' she said, laughing.

'No, it's good. I didn't mean ... '

Things had become so tense between them, every remark so loaded, but it was nice; kind of like being a teenager again.

Harriet led him into a bright atrium from which a wide, open-tread staircase led up to first and second floor accommodation. The interior of the building was as smart as the exterior was scruffy. It had been stripped back to the bare bones, then re-imagined in a totally distinctive 'Harriet' kind of a way. All the services, plumbing, lift and stairs were located in the centre, and interior walls had only been erected where privacy and sound-proofing necessitated it, so that the living spaces flowed around the outer margin of the structure, giving each self-contained flat a high-ceilinged, light-drenched, industrial vibe. It was all state-of-the-art – exposed brickwork, wrought-iron spiral staircases, mezzanine sleeping decks, more Canary Wharf than Cannery Row. He recognized various signature 'Harriet' flourishes, from their own kitchen extension at Brenner Street – reclaimed oak floors, concealed lighting, granite work surfaces. By the time they had completed the tour, Gary could see how she might have let the budget get away from her.

'I'm gobsmacked,' Gary said, shaking his head in appreciation and it was true. 'Honestly, Harriet, you should get an award or something. It's just ... it's really fuckin' beautiful. I'm not even kidding.'

'Thank you,' Harriet's voice wavered, 'that means a lot. I just hope the people it's meant for get the benefit ... ' Her voice faltered again and Gary thought she was going to cry, but she took a deep breath and, rallying, reached for the handle of a heavy aluminium door. 'Come up and check out the roof space – I'm in two minds what to do with it.'

As they emerged onto a vast flat roof, surrounded by low parapet walls, Gary made a long low whistle. To the west was Jodrell Bank – space-age marvel of Gary's youth, to the east the Pennine Hills, bathed in late-afternoon sunlight.

'Not a bad view, is it?' Harriet said. 'What I'm thinking is, raised veggie plots this side – kiddies' play area over there, and I'm thinking we'll go Perspex with the barrier, rather than mesh so you still get the ... '

'You don't want to be wasting a space like this on kids,' Gary interrupted, scandalized. 'This is your party space, this is. You'd have your decks over there in the corner – great acoustics ... ' he spun round, mapping the imaginary scene with his open palm, 'stage there, and that wall there, you could paint white and project your vids onto it. I tell you what, if you're short of dosh, you've got a little goldmine up here.'

'Do you think ... ?' Harriet asked doubtfully.

'Defo. Rig up some of them old-school fairy lights, maybe even get a jacuzzi. They'd be over from Manchester faster than you can say Media City. Arty-farty film previews; up-and-coming bands, you name it ... '

'Well, I'm not sure the local council'd go for it; not on a permanent basis, unless the tenants were on board, but I suppose we might be able to get a short-term licence; plug the funding gap ... ' She looked at him hopefully and then gazed out across the hills. Gary watched her expression turn wistful, then pensive, then troubled, as if the sheer scope of the problem had defeated her again. She gave an involuntary shudder which seemed to jolt her back to the present moment.

'Goose walk over your grave?' He took a tentative step towards her, arms outstretched.

'Sorry?' she frowned and smiled; hovering on the edge of his embrace as though unsure whether she could trust it.

'It's an expression. Me mam used to say it.'

She stepped forward at the precise moment Gary dropped his arms to his sides and they were left looking at each other, too close for a normal friendly interaction, yet too embarrassed to acknowledge what had almost happened.

'What does it mean?' Harriet asked, taking a half-step backwards.

Gary shrugged.

'I dunno.'

Gary felt bad now. Like he'd killed the mood. Harriet seemed nervous and shy – a million miles from the glowing, confident businesswoman he had met on the train that time. He wished she would be that Harriet again; he wished he could make her see how good she was – put a smile on her face.

She shivered and looked at her watch.

'So, yeah, I booked us a table at the Lock-Keepers,' she said. 'That's where I stay when I'm up here. The food's nothing special but it's handy ... that's if you still ... ?'

Gary wrinkled his nose as if he'd had second thoughts and for a moment, she looked utterly crestfallen.

'Nah ...' he shook his head slowly, met her eye and smiled, 'I've got a better idea ...'

16

Mark

'Oh, hey, Mark... ?' Ambrose scooted his chair back as Mark passed the open door to his office, 'Planet Beauty?'

Mark kept his head down and strode on towards the refreshment station. He tipped some fresh beans into the grinder compartment of the coffee machine, remembering too late that he was supposed to be switching to decaf for his nerves.

Ambrose appeared in the doorway and Mark pressed grind.

'Oh, sorry, Ambrose, I didn't see you there,' he lied, when the grinder had whizzed its last.

'I don't want to hassle you Mark, it was just... I'm assuming you'll be leading the Planet Beauty presentation... you know the vegan thing? Only...'

'No, no, you're fine, bro. You should hold the ring on this one. You're much more up to speed than me on the sustainability story, and to be honest, I've got a lot of...'

'*Really?* Are you sure?' A grin spread slowly across Ambrose's face. 'Because Sadie seems to think this is them dipping a toe in the water – if they like us, she can totally see them coming across from...'

'No!' Mark said, punching Ambrose's shoulder a little harder than he'd intended, 'No-o-o-o!' He turned the punch into a playful two-fisted pummel. 'Sorry to disappoint you, pal, but it's not that big of a deal. Honestly. Sadie's getting ahead of herself there. This is just a one-off, a side bar sort of a thing, the vegan range. Very low key. Very, very small. They're just trialling it in a really low key way. I mean,' he tilted his head and looked rueful, 'they're with GO! for all their other stuff and with the best will in the world, we haven't got the reach to compete with GO! So...'

His hands trembled as he took the now-full coffee mug from beneath the dispenser. He could hear buzzing, like someone was using an electric shaver inside his head.

Ambrose made a cartoon shrug.

'*That's not what Sadie said,*' he sang the words, as if to neutralize any impression of contradiction. 'She said Feiner want to pivot the brand in a more ethical direction. She said because of the bad press they've been getting, with, you know, the whole animal testing and child labour thing, she thought they'd see more synergies with *our*...'

Mark thumped his coffee cup down on the work surface so hard that it sloshed onto his shirt cuff. Ambrose jumped.

'With the greatest respect, Ambrose, Sadie's not the boss. *I'm* the boss and if I say Feiner aren't coming over to us, they're not coming over to us, *capiche*?'

'Er, yeah, right. Got it,' said Ambrose. 'Thanks for the heads-up, Mark.'

As Ambrose's footsteps receded down the corridor Mark cringed.

Capiche. Jesus! He sounded like Tony Soprano. Was this what happened when you bent the rules? You did one tiny thing a little bit wrong... not even wrong, just made a completely innocent mistake on an obscure, technical level and suddenly you were descending, Macbeth-style, into moral depredation and psychological torment. Mark stared at the back of his hand which was smarting, the skin scarred pink and spotted with blobs of dark liquid. He caught his breath, then remembered slamming his coffee cup down on the work surface. Splashback, that's all it was. He closed his eyes in relief. Splashback. Jesus. It was like a metaphor for what was about to happen. What might happen. What *mustn't* happen when the auditors came in next week. Fucking sod's law they'd chosen this year to do a forensic audit. It was normally very light-touch – literally just a nod-through, nothing-to-see-here job. Still, it would be OK. He hadn't even signed the Planet Beauty contract until after the refinancing; the refinancing that had released the money for him to buy a *very* few Feiner shares for his own personal portfolio. And, it didn't matter either way, because Feiner would never have offered them Planet Beauty, given they were contracted to GO! for all their other brands, if it weren't technically an independent product, produced by a subsidiary of a subsidiary that you'd need to be Sherlock Holmes to trace back to Feiner itself.

Mark looked down at his coffee mug. How long had he been standing here? He stuck the tip of his finger experimentally into the murky liquid. It was tepid.

He was breezing out of the lobby, one arm thrust into the sleeve of his puffer jacket, when he passed Sadie coming in.

'Oh, hi, Mark,' she stopped and gave him a puzzled smile, 'where are you off to? I thought we had a...?'

He wrangled his other arm into its sleeve and zipped the jacket, as if to insulate himself against any attempt to deflect him from his purpose.

'Yes! Something's come up. I've got to … er … Can you hold the fort for a bit?'

'But Mark, we've got a team meeting … ? Will you be … ? *Mark* … ?'

He barged out through the revolving door and into the street, taking great restorative lungfuls of polluted London air. He'd just go for a walk round the block … have a think. Get a *decent* coffee; or maybe a kombucha, something to give him a bit of a lift. He took his phone out of his pocket and started composing a text to Sadie, then thought better of it, switched his phone off and started walking.

It was almost a surprise when he ended up outside his own front door. Five and a half miles in what had seemed like no time at all. In other circumstances, he'd have considered it a worthwhile achievement – might even have consulted his Fitbit to see how many calories he'd burned. But he'd barely been aware of putting one foot in front of the other, had only the vaguest, dreamlike impression of rushing traffic, sirens, the bleeping of pedestrian crossings, someone yelling, 'Wanker!' out of the open window of a white van. Then, finally, the faint blurred reflection of his own face in the stained-glass panel of his own front door. He had homed, instinctively, like a pigeon; found the only refuge he knew in a world that was orbiting away from him. He put his key in the lock and turned it, feeling relief well up in him like a sob.

And then he smelled bacon and heard the sound of the

TV and for a moment, he thought he was in the wrong house after all.

'Hello...?' came a suspicious-sounding voice from the living room.

Shit! Ollie. He'd forgotten, in his bubble of self-preservation, that his home was no longer the safe haven it once was. Just like his place of work, it had become a minefield – one false move could blow everything sky-high.

'Yeah, only me,' he called out, 'just... er... came back to get...'

He unzipped his jacket and made for the stairs, loosening his tie as he went. It felt like a noose. He needed a shower, he needed to cleanse himself.

The living-room door opened and the angry skinhead that was his son stuck his head into the hallway and glared at Mark.

'Hi,' Mark, said, trying not to visibly recoil from the alarming sight. There was something about the shape of Ollie's cranium, the combination of vulnerability and aggression that this new 'hairstyle' was the wrong word... *tonsure* evoked, that Mark would never get used to.

'What are you doing here?'

'I live here,' replied Mark, a little more doubtfully than he intended.

'No, I meant...'

'Actually, Ollie, I'm feeling a bit off-colour, so I might just...' he waved his hand vaguely towards the first-floor landing.

'Oh... right...' Ollie sounded chastened, but resentful, as though he suspected Mark of feigning illness.

'You're not having a heart attack, are you?' he added,

suspiciously, as though there might be no depths to which Mark might not sink in order to make him look bad.

'*No!*' snapped Mark, stung by the suggestion.

'All right, don't freak. I'm just ruling it out. A lot of men your age don't even realize they're having one until it's too late.'

'What do you mean *my* age? I'm fifty-four. I work out. I've got a resting pulse rate of sixty beats a ... '

'OK, OK. Jesus! You wouldn't be the first stressed executive to have a heart attack. It goes with the territory, doesn't it? All those expense-account lunches and impossible deadlines, not to mention selling your soul to the highest bidder!'

'Oh sorry! I didn't realize you were so contemptuous of the profession that puts a roof over your head, and paid your uni fees. Oh, and allows you to lie around for weeks on end watching daytime fucking TV without ever sullying your soul by applying for anything so ethically fucking compromising as an actual *job*.'

He regretted it as soon as he'd said it. He saw Ollie's face pucker in pain, then the shutters came down and his son's grimace became a sneer.

'Is that what you think you do, a *job*?'

'I think I do a job, yes. That is the usual definition, when you sell your expertise, your services, whatever, in exchange for money.'

'Your *expertise*?' Ollie's face was contorted with scorn. 'How much expertise does it take to manipulate stupid people into thinking they want shit they don't need that's going to get chucked into landfill in two minutes flat, just so you can drive a fucking top-of-the-range Lexus Hybrid and feel like the big dick in town?'

Mark closed his eyes. Best not to engage ... he was feeling slightly queasy. He grabbed hold of the bannister rail and hauled himself up three stairs at once. Behind him, Ollie made a contemptuous valedictory noise; a tut or a teeth-kiss. Whichever it was, Mark was back down those stairs in seconds flat, his face pushed up close to his son's.

'As a matter of fact,' he snarled, 'my company, yes *my* company that I set up from scratch with a fucking bank loan and the sweat of my brow happens to have won the best ethical campaign award every year but two since I set it up. It has a carbon negative website, a commitment to climate-responsible design and a socially inclusive recruitment policy.' At the word 'policy' a gobbet of shiny spittle flew across the very small gap between Mark's mouth and Ollie's face and lay glistening on his son's cheek. Neither of them acknowledged it.

'In addition, we have just persuaded a huge multinational cosmetics company to trial a range of eco-friendly products which, if successful, will provide the basis for an ethical reinvention of the brand which will stop the illegal hunting of sperm whales overnight. So, you can sit there in your fucking tracky bottoms, wanking over *Tellytubbies*, or whatever it is you do, but some people ... *some people* are out there trying to do their best in an imperfect fucking world and if you don't like it you can ... '

'Mark!'

At the sound of Harriet's voice, Mark came to, as if at the snap of a hypnotist's fingers. He wheeled guiltily around to see his wife collapsed slightly against the front door in shock. He hadn't even heard her come in. He opened his mouth to explain, closed it again and then, as if in slow motion, swivelled his gaze back to Ollie who was looking at him with an expression of utmost contempt.

'Ol, mate ... listen, I ... Christ, I don't know what came over me ... like I said, I'm not really on top of my ... I haven't been feeling all that ... ' He put a conciliatory hand on his son's arm, which Ollie removed as if it were leprous. Then, without even looking at him, his son went back in the living room and closed the door.

'What the *hell* was that?' Harriet said.

'I know it looked bad but ... '

'It didn't just *look* bad, Mark ... '

'But you didn't hear what *he* said! He said I was worthless and immoral and I was wrecking the planet ... all I was doing was pointing out that a bit of gratitude might not go amiss, given he was living under our ... '

'*Gratitude?*'

Harriet screwed her face up in disbelief.

'Yeah ... gratitude,' Mark repeated, uncertainly.

'He's our son, Mark. This is his *home.*'

Mark opened his mouth to speak but didn't trust himself. His body felt too compact a parcel to contain all the conflicting emotions inside him – fury and shame and hate and love and regret. It seemed there was nowhere he could be any longer where he didn't have to reckon with his own inadequacies – not home, not work. He clamped his hand across his mouth and stared at the floor until he felt composed enough to speak.

'You're right,' he began, raising his eyes, I'm sor ... '

But Harriet had gone.

17

Yvette

'I'm off now, babe,' Gary whispered hopefully. 'I'm a bit late, so... ' Yvette could hear the wheedle in his voice. Normally she'd have caved in and given him a lift to the station, but she was still sulking about the house sale so she rolled over and feigned sleep. She heard a sigh, then the aggrieved thud of Gary's feet on the stairs and finally the slam of the front door. As the house settled back into silence, a twinge of guilt assailed her. She had, after all, signed her name next to his on the estate agent's contract. It had been a mutual decision. But he didn't have to be so bloody happy about it.

She hauled herself up in bed now and looked about her, nostalgic in advance for the memory of this perfectly pleasant but otherwise undistinguished double bedroom which, until the FOR SALE sign had gone up, had always struck her as a foot too small in every dimension and in need of a makeover. Now it seemed the loveliest of rooms – light and airy, the view of the council flats tactfully screened by the branches of the laburnum tree. Apart from Gaz's dirty clothes flung in a heap in the corner, it wouldn't have looked amiss on *Location, Location, Location*. The stripped pine furniture wasn't what she'd choose now and the faux fur throw was, on reflection, a bit naff, but she prided herself that for once, the estate agent's hype was not misplaced. It *was* a deceptively large three-bedroom terrace, immaculately decorated throughout. Fuck Gary! Fuck him for making her move. Except he wasn't, not really. She was the one who'd egged him on to give up work and have another crack at music. But that was when the prospect of being a grandma had seemed a distant dream. Now that she had heard the baby's heartbeat she wondered that she had ever gone along with it. By the time her grandkid was born she'd be two hundred miles away. She groaned and rolled over, pulling the duvet over her head.

She dreamed that Ruby was in labour and the two of them were on the street, trying to flag down a taxi to take her to hospital. When a car finally pulled up beside them, the driver turned out to be Juris who rubbed his thumb and forefinger together, then, when she took a tenner out of her purse, drove off, laughing. In desperation, Yvette gave Ruby a piggy-back, but all kinds of obstacles got in their way – quicksand and barbed wire – and by the time she had staggered to their destination, Ruby had morphed into Gary and they weren't on the labour ward, but in the wings at the Manchester Arena.

By the time Yvette woke up again it felt late. She could hear the ear-splitting beep of a lorry's reversing siren in the street outside. The world was going about its business without her and her guilt at having done nothing was only matched by her guilt at having nothing to do. For the first few weeks post-redundancy, she had fretted no end about the kids she'd been keeping an eye on – Nicholas who seemed to be walking into a worrying amount of furniture since his mum's new boyfriend had moved in, Kady whose learning difficulties were just short of statement-worthy. But they were slipping away from her, these children. She wasn't sure if it was the antidepressants the doctor had put her on (the lowest dose, and just to tide her over) but already the faces were starting to blur into one another – the Ryans and the Raymonds, the Kylies and the Kayleighs. Just as well, really, they weren't her problem anymore, although sooner or later a handful of them would be everybody's problem. Just a couple in every year group; lads mostly – when all the TAs had gone and the Pupil Referral Units were closed down and there was nothing and no one to deflect them from all the trouble that was out there waiting to claim them.

Talking of trouble... she checked her phone, wondering if Gary had messaged her. Guilt had settled on her like a pall now. What if he hadn't made it on time? What if his ticket wasn't valid on the next train and he was late for the meeting with the record company and they decided the band was too flaky to sign after all? It would all be her fault for not giving him a lift. She reached for her phone and sent a quick text.

Sorry I was a bit narky. Fingers xd for you today. 🖤 🖤 😘

She had pressed send before she thought of Harriet. Would he remember that he was meant to be meeting her? She started to compose a follow-up text, but then thought better of it. He wasn't really one for social obligations, and as much as

Harriet might like to see a familiar face, they'd struggle to spend a whole evening together.

She hauled herself out of bed and tiptoed to the bathroom, mindful that Jade had been on nights all week, poor kid. Still, the end was in sight. Hopefully this spell at Aldi would be the last menial job Jade would have to do, now she was off to uni. Not just uni; *Oxford* uni. Michaelmas term, they called it – the name tickled Yvette. It reminded her of watching *Brideshead Revisited* with her mum back in the day. The dreaming spires, the punts, the stripy scarves ... It had stayed with her, that world. There had been a time before she'd got pregnant with Ruby when she'd hoped to go to university herself – not Oxford, she wouldn't have been so bold – but somewhere normal – Sheffield or Reading – where she could have wandered about in a university sweatshirt smoking Marlboro Lights with a clutch of library books under her arm. It might easily have happened, as well. The others had all gone – Caroline and Stephanie and Amanda. Stephanie was a lawyer for the United Nations now. Yvette had spotted her in the background on the news once. Then again, Stephanie hadn't been allowed out on a weeknight, so unlike Yvette, she'd not have been backstage at the Miles Platting Thunderdome on the fourth of September, 1986 which was when Yvette's university prospects had taken a nosedive.

Yvette stopped outside Jade's room. She could hear the murmur of her daughter's voice on the phone. She knocked tentatively and waited a moment. When all was quiet, she popped her head around the door.

'Shall I bring you some brekkie up?'

'No, you're all right,' Jade said, 'I'll come down.'

'Go on, let me spoil you. Egg, mushies and beans. How about that?'

'*Egg*, Mum?' Jade tilted her head in mock reproach.

'Oh, yeah. Egg's not vegan, is it? I suppose I could pop down the shops and get some of that Sosmix stuff . . . '

'Honestly, Mum, I'm not bothered.'

Yvette shrugged and was about to duck back out of the room when Jade seemed to take pity on her.

'We could go out for a coffee later if you want?'

'Oh well, yes . . . that'd be lovely. Let's do that then, or . . . ?'

'What?'

'No, I was just thinking. We could go into town and get your books off your reading list. Maybe have a posh afternoon tea somewhere . . . ?'

Jade looked doubtful.

'I don't think they'll have them in a random bookshop, Mum. People order them off Amazon now.'

'Oh no, yeah. 'Course they do. You're all right then, we'll just nip out for a latte later on . . . ' she started to pull the door to and then, remembering, popped her head back round, 'a *soy* latte.'

'I can't believe this place stays open,' her daughter said, shaking her head, as they took their seats in Déjà Brew.

'There's no need to look down your nose,' Yvette said, 'they were doing vegan food here before you were on solids.'

Jade bent down and sniffed the brown gloop in her bowl.

'It smells like . . . you know when you've left wet washing in the machine . . . ?'

Yvette gave her a withering smile.

'Sorry, Mum,' Jade said with a grin. The café door pinged behind them and Yvette watched her daughter's attention drift to the person who had just walked in. Jade frowned, then smiled, then half rose out of her seat.

'Ollie!' she called and waved.

Yvette swivelled round in her seat but could only see an emaciated, bald-headed youth in an oversized donkey jacket.

'That's not…' she started to say, then remembered that Harriet had lamented Ollie's newly shorn head when they had been sitting in these very seats.

'Hey, Ol! Looking fresh, mate,' Jade called, and Yvette was surprised at the familiarity of her tone. Ollie walked over and they embraced briefly, before he turned to Yvette.

'Hiya, Yvette.' He gave her an awkward hug, his body stiffening and arching away from hers, even as he imparted an emphatic triple shoulder pat.

'Come and join us!' Jade said, to Yvette's surprise.

Ollie glanced uncertainly at Yvette as if for validation and she nodded eagerly.

'OK then,' said Ollie, 'I'll just get a drink.'

He started to head back to the counter and then remembered his manners.

'Can I get you two anything?' he offered awkwardly.

'Nah, you're all right, Ol,' Jade told him and he sloped back to the counter.

Yvette leaned forward in her seat.

'I didn't know you two were mates,' she said in a conspiratorial whisper.

'We're not really *mates*. I just see him around now and again.'

'Around where?' Yvette frowned.

'I dunno. At the bus stop . . . he comes in the shop sometimes. Just . . . *around*. Why are parents so weird?'

'We just worry about you guys.'

Jade winced.

Ollie was paying for his coffee now and as he reached across the counter, Yvette noticed that the back of his hand was covered in black hieroglyphs. She leaned forward and murmured, 'What's wrong with Ollie's hand?'

Jade made a casual half turn.

'It's a sleeve, Mum.'

'A sl—? You mean it goes right up his . . . ? Oh my God, Harriet'll freak.'

'Harriet needs to get over herself,' said Jade wearily, 'it's not *Ollie* she should be worried about.'

'What do you mean?'

But by now, Ollie was in earshot. He manoeuvred a vacant chair across from a nearby table and sat down, staring for the longest time into his coffee, as if for conversational inspiration.

'So,' Yvette said brightly, 'what are you up to these days, Ollie?'

Ollie gave a little snort, which could as easily have been derisive as amused.

'Yeah, no . . . not much really. Just . . . ' He shrugged and his voice petered out. Yvette leaned forward and clasped his hand.

'Good for you,' she said, 'take your time. Paddle your own canoe. You don't have to be a straight in a suit like Mark and Jack, you know.'

Jade gave a silent-movie eye-roll.

'There's really interesting work available in the charity

sector, paid *and* unpaid, you know. Not that I'm suggesting you work for free, nothing like that, but volunteering can be a good route in or just a way to test the water, see what suits you, type of thing ... '

Yvette's voice trailed off and she felt for a moment the yawning gulf between her generation and theirs, as big – oh, easily as big – as the one that had separated her from her own parents. Only this generation gap felt all the more treacherous for being unanticipated. Had they honestly thought, with their raves and their pills and their glo-sticks, that the buck stopped with them? That their kids wouldn't find their loved-up self-indulgence as irrelevant, as medieval as their parents' idea of misbehaviour had seemed to them? Jerry Lee Lewis? Bill Haley's 'Rock Around the Clock'? *Tragic*. She had always thought of herself as a young hip and happening mum. She had Grime on her Spotify playlist and bought clothes from BooHoo.com. She was OK with piercings and not averse to tattoos, within reason – had even considered getting one herself – something small and tasteful and out of the way – but had never quite got round to it. Yet she had no more idea what these two did with their time, where they *really* bumped into each other, what secret virtual lives they led in chat rooms and on dating apps and for all she knew, porn sites, than her mum and dad had had a clue what went down at the Haçienda.

'I understand you're moving?' Ollie said stiffly, once a suitable hiatus had been left following the awkward careers advice.

Yvette sighed and attempted a smile.

'Looks like it, yeah ... back up North. Back to our roo ... ' her voice cracked and she looked down, clutching her coffee cup in both hands.

'Mum...' Jade placed a comforting hand on her mother's wrist and Yvette gave an exasperated laugh, but couldn't bring herself to look up.

'We'll be *fine*,' Jade soothed her, as if she had read Yvette's mind, 'Ruby will, Jordan will, the baby will, we *all* will...'

Yvette nodded. Her throat tightened and her eyes brimmed. They would; they *would* be fine without her – and that was the trouble. She shook her head, as if in self-disgust, smiled, fought back her tears and met Jade's eye.

'I know you will, babe, I know.'

18

Harriet

'This is it, number seventy-two,' Harriet said briskly, bending over to unlatch the lopsided wooden gate.

'Are you sure?' Mark looked dubious.

'What, you think a psychotherapist can't live in a terraced house?'

If Harriet sounded irritated, it was probably because she was doubtful herself. It was a neat enough little place, but the bird feeder and children's bikes in the front garden somehow undermined any air of professionalism. This was silly, Harriet knew. A brass plaque and an address off Harley Street were in themselves no guarantee of proficiency. Still – the domestic vibe made her twitchy. She'd been surprised that Mark had agreed to come at all – he'd always been suspicious of what he called 'psychobabble'. She didn't want to give him any excuse to wriggle out now. She met his eye, a challenge in hers, and he shrugged and rang the bell. It wasn't as though she'd pulled the therapist's name out of a hat, she thought, shifting uncomfortably from foot to foot. This woman had all the necessary credentials and had come highly recommended as a couples' counsellor by Harriet's friend Miriam, who was no slouch when it came to hiring professionals of all stripes. It was only as the light tread of Siobhan Carmichael (PhD, MBACP) could be heard approaching down the hallway, that Harriet remembered Miriam and her husband were now awaiting their decree nisi.

'Please . . . sit,' said Siobhan.

Her practice room, at least, looked the part; bright and book-lined, it had a businesslike desk and swivel chair and next to that, two low-slung seats arranged either side of a coffee table on which stood a jug of water, two glasses and, more ominously, a box of tissues. Mark stood back with ostentatious gallantry to allow Harriet access to the furthest chair and then perched anxiously on the other.

'So, I've read your assessments,' Siobhan said, with an encouraging smile, 'and it seems to me that you could certainly benefit from my psychotherapeutic approach. First of all, though, I wonder if you would like to tell me and each other what you believe has brought you here?'

Harriet shifted in her chair and plucked at one of her earrings. As far as *she* was concerned, Mark had brought them here. Mark's appalling treatment of Ollie, Mark's emotional repression, Mark's fucked-up, unacknowledged anger. She was just here to bear witness; to act as a catalyst to the raising of Mark's consciousness; not to scrutinize her own behaviour which had been, with the exception of one regrettable but never-to-be-repeated recent transgression, unimpeachable. No, this was on Mark.

'So . . . who'd like to be brave and kick off?'

Mark looked at Harriet, and she gave a sulky shrug.

'Oka-a-ay,' Mark began warily. He eased his Barbour jacket on to the back of his chair and sat for a moment, legs spread, elbows to thighs, fingers steepled in front of his pale blue V-neck in an attitude close to prayer.

'So . . . *I'm* here because my wife is the most important thing in my life . . .' Harriet rolled her eyes. 'My wife and my family. They are my rocks. Without them, I'm nothing . . . ' he took a deep, shuddery breath. 'I would also like to say, as mad as it sounds, that I'm *happy* to be here. I'm relieved. Because if *I'd* been Harriet, I'd have thrown me out on the spot. That's what I deserved. I'm ashamed of how I behaved and although I don't believe it was typical, there were . . . uh . . . extenuating circumstances . . . I think it's good to have this opportunity to clear things up.'

'It's not a bloody board meeting,' Harriet muttered under her breath.

'No, sorry, not . . . clear things up, obviously. That's glib. I mean . . . to examine what went wrong and why. To look at the wider context and . . . '

'Oh my God!' Harriet rolled her eyes. 'You see this is typical,' she turned to Siobhan, 'you'd think it was a public inquiry. *What went wrong and why?* He needs to take some responsibility! I came home to find him choking our son half to death while he yelled abuse in his face. *That's* what went wrong. And why? Well . . . how about because he hates him. There, I've said it.'

She turned defiantly back to Mark, who sank back into his chair, ashen-faced.

'It might actually help if you addressed Mark directly,' Siobhan ventured gently.

This, a rebuke, Harriet could tell. Take responsibility for your actions. Own the pain you are causing. So yes, she would. She *would* own the pain, because *Mark* needed to own the pain he'd caused Ollie. She swivelled round and glared at Mark.

'You attacked our son.'

Mark slumped in his chair and stared, hollow-eyed, into space for what felt like a full minute, then met her gaze.

'You're right,' he said, 'I was … physically and verbally abusive to our son,' he stopped and stared straight ahead for a moment, as though confronting for the first time the enormity of his crime, 'God, I'm so sorry, Harriet, I truly am.'

He was as well. Harriet could tell. She could feel her resolve crumbling at the sheer look of regret and self-loathing on his face. But she *needed* Mark to be the villain. If she couldn't put the blame on him, she might have to consider the role of her own recent conduct in creating the chasm between them.

'It's not *me* you should be apologizing to,' she said sulkily.

'No, I know. And I've tried to apologize to Oliver … to Ollie, I have, but he doesn't want to know.'

'No, well, are you surprised? I mean it was *naked*, your hatred of him. It was in his face. Literally.'

'I *don't* hate him,' Mark protested, 'if anything, it's him that hate's … '

'Oh no! Don't try and turn it round. You're the parent. You're supposed to love your child unconditionally.'

'*Do* we always love our children unconditionally?' interjected Siobhan.

'I do!' said Harriet.

'But if you didn't, how would you deal with that?'

'Well, I wouldn't strangle them for a start...'

Out of the corner of her eye Harriet saw Mark drop his head again in shame. She felt a twinge of pity.

'So, *Harriet*,' Siobhan swivelled her chair in Harriet's direction, 'before we take a deep dive into the family dynamics, can I just put the same question to you?'

'What question?'

'What do *you* think has brought you here?'

Harriet held her palms out and gawped.

'This!' she said, as if to indicate the rancour-filled air.

'*This*, being...?'

'This... spiel. This deluded, self-justifying *management-speak*...'

'Hmm. Before that, though... was there, perhaps, a more positive intention? A recognition that something between the two of you needed to be addressed...?'

Harriet frowned warily. What was she getting at? Had she somehow intuited Harriet's... not betrayal, no... that would be to elevate what had essentially been an accident, a drunken late-night fumble to the status of an infidelity...

'I don't know what you mean.'

Siobhan allowed the silence to lengthen. Harriet shifted in her chair, stared resolutely at her clasped hands, tried to suppress an unwelcome flashback – the click of a stylus on a revolving 45, the squeak of ancient couch springs, and the slap of flesh on flesh, drowned out by her own mounting yelps of excitement...

At last, when the ticking of the clock threatened to deafen them all, Siobhan glanced down at her notebook.

'Ollie's a twin,' she observed, 'that must have been chal-
lenging...'

'It was!' Mark blurted.

'Not really!' Harriet said simultaneously.

Siobhan tapped her pen against her pursed lips.

'What can sometimes happen in families,' she ventured, 'is
that twins become sort of proxies for any dysfunction that's
present in the...'

'*Dysfunction?*' said Harriet.

'Yes, I'm not saying that's the case with you, of course. I'm
just saying that's what *can* sometimes...'

'...There probably is a bit of that,' Mark glanced up, his
face creased and tired-looking. He could easily have been in
his sixties, to look at him, Harriet thought.

'Go on...' said Siobhan.

'Well, yeah, I think I see Jack as being more like me. Very
straightforward, what-you-see-is-what-you-get type of thing.
He just gets his head down, works hard...'

Harriet pulled a dubious face, but Siobhan was nodding
along sympathetically.

'...And Ollie?'

'Well, I've just never *got* Ollie in the same way. He's never
been a people person. Keeps himself to himself. I mean, he
just... There's a lot of guesswork involved, I'm not going
to lie.'

'He's more like me,' said Harriet, 'introverted and creative.'

'Ollie, *creat...?*' Mark started to say, then stopped himself.

'I think Ollie just *feels* it very much that, on paper, Jack
looks like the successful one,' Harriet said.

'On *paper?*' Mark blurted. 'Jack's got a first-class degree.

He's knuckled down and got himself a decent job within weeks of graduati…'

His voice trailed off and he looked guiltily from one woman to the other.

'Do *you* have a degree, Mark?' asked Siobhan.

'Ye-e-es…' Mark conceded warily.

'Of course he has,' muttered Harriet, 'and a "decent job". That's the blueprint. God help you if you don't conform.'

'And you run a PR business; interesting…' said Siobhan glancing at her notes again. 'Public Relations…' She left the words hanging in the air.

'Yes, because that's what I happen to be good at,' said Mark, 'but it's not like I want Ollie to be a clone. I know he's his own person.'

'You were going to offer him an internship!' Harriet glared at him.

'Yeah, only as a stop-gap in case he couldn't get anything el… OK, OK… I know.'

'What do you know, Mark?' Siobhan asked him gently.

'I know I don't get Ollie the way I get Jack,' Mark muttered. 'I don't get him but I do love him. We just don't have the same rapport. It's hard. He's always been sensitive… prickly. Life's been a battle for him, since the day he was… the day they were…'

He clamped a fist across his mouth. Harriet reached blindly for his other hand and clutched it in remorse. Siobhan stayed quiet and the silence stretched out, only punctuated by Mark's lachrymal gulps and sniffs.

'It was a difficult birth,' Harriet said quietly. 'I had Jack OK, but Ollie was breech. They were going to do an emergency

C-section and then it all got a bit … ' she tried for a laugh, 'iffy … '

'She nearly *died*!' Mark's voice was accusing, angry. 'He nearly … the birth nearly *killed* her!' Harriet shrugged. She couldn't remember, that was the trouble. She recalled having Jack. The pain, the lights, the tense atmosphere, the greasy, human smell, the relief. And then … nothing.

She let go of Mark's hand and flattening her palm across her mouth, turned her gaze through the French window to Siobhan's back yard. There wasn't much to see; buddleia and bindweed and a threadbare patch of lawn. She wondered if there was a Mr Siobhan and, if so, what he did for a living. Probably something worthy – a probation officer or a social worker. They didn't have time for gardening, that much was obvious. Something caught her eye over the fence – a line of washing in a neighbouring garden flapped like semaphore flags in the breeze – a man's football shirt, two towels, three tiny baby grows – one yellow, one pink, one pistachio. She felt a stab of grief.

'So … ' Siobhan said, after a tactful pause, 'we've talked about the flashpoint that brought you here, we've looked at some of the difficult feelings within your family. We've touched on Mark's work pressures, but we haven't really talked about the two of you. Your relationship … '

Harriet rolled her eyes.

'Before this recent flashpoint with Ollie, how would you have characterized your marriage?'

'Functioning,' said Harriet with a shrug.

'It was happy!' Mark protested, and Harriet looked up in surprise at the anguish in his tone.

'Happyish . . . ' he added, 'satisfying, anyway . . . '

Harriet looked down, smoothing the nap on her corduroy skirt.

'*I'm* not that satisfied,' she murmured.

Mark looked wounded and Siobhan eyed them both.

'She means sex,' muttered Mark.

'I don't, actually.'

'What *do* you mean, Harriet?' asked Siobhan. Harriet shifted in her seat and plucked at her earring.

'Intimacy, I suppose.'

'We're intimate!' Mark said.

'I'm not talking about kissing and touching. I'm talking about *communication*. Inhabiting the same space.'

'Well, that's been a tall order lately. You've been in Macclesfield. I've been working my butt off . . . '

'I don't mean *literally* the same space,' Harriet said. 'You can be intimate in a phone call, in a text; you can be intimate passing each other on the stairs . . . ' Mark looked baffled.

'I text you! I hold your hand!'

'That's not what I'm talking about, Mark. We're in different orbits. It feels like . . . I don't know . . . like we've been drifting apart for years without really noticing. I mean, yes, I've had a lot more responsibility at work, since the boys have been older and that's *good*, I've wanted to stretch myself professionally. But, well . . . a few things have happened lately that have made me . . . ' her voice faltered, 're-evaluate . . . '

The truth lay in wait, like a trap. She was aware of Siobhan's eyes on her, encouraging her; and Mark's, terrified, willing her to stop.

'What things?' Siobhan said.

'Our best friends are moving away.'

'That's ... difficult.'

A long pause.

' ... And, well ... their daughter, Ruby, who we're very close to – we're close to all of them, but Ruby in particular because we were both trying to get pregnant at the same time, she and I – anyway, yeah, she's done it ... through IVF, but even so. I mean, it's great and I couldn't be happier for her, don't get me wrong. It's just ... '

Mark looked across at her like a drowning man.

'Well, it's *hard*,' she went on, 'much harder than I expected. Because I always wanted a ... I'd like to have had a little girl ... ' her voice faltered. Mark leaned forward and stretched out his hand, but stopped short of actually touching her.

'Sweetheart, we're so lucky,' he cajoled, 'we've *got* our family. They've struggled just to get this far. And let's face it, for us, a late baby would have been, would be ... '

'It wasn't supposed to be a late baby ... '

'It was always going to be a long shot, love. We're a generation older than Ruby and Jordan ... '

'*I'm* not!' snapped Harriet, then, turning to Siobhan, 'Mark's older than me. I'm still in my early forties.'

'Oh, come on! You're forty-four. With the best will in the world, no one gets pregnant at forty-four. It's time to accept that it just wasn't meant to be ... Christ, I don't want to be a geriatric dad. It wouldn't be fair on the kid, it wouldn't be fair on Jack or Ollie ... it wouldn't be fair on anyone! As it is we've got a good chunk of life ahead of us. We've got security, money, we can please ourselves. Get out of our rut. Have an adventure.'

'What about work?'

'Fuck work! Life's short.'

'I've got The Button Factory to finish.'

'After that, then. You'll need a breather. We don't actually need to work at all . . . '

'Did it ever occur to you that I might enjoy my work?'

'Well, OK, I'll be your house husband.'

'You're being silly.'

'I'm being deadly serious. I want the next few years to be about us. I've decided, I'm going to sell my share of the business to Ambrose and Sadie. Take out a wodge of cash and call it a day while I'm still young enough to enjoy it.'

'Oh, yeah, I can just see that,' scoffed Harriet. 'Mr EVCOM Award, Mr Just Checking the Company's Ranking in the Top Independent UK PR Companies for the Seventeenth Time.'

She rolled her eyes at Siobhan.

'Honestly,' she went on, 'they'll have to prize the key to the executive washroom out of his cold dead . . . '

'I've already done it!' Mark interrupted a little wildly.

'What?'

Harriet swivelled towards him, a look of dismay on her face.

'I've resigned.'

19

Gary

'Just follow me and don't catch anyone's eye...' Mark pushed through the turnstile ahead of Gary.

'Blimey,' Gary muttered, 'I thought it was a gym, not MI5.'

It was bound to be like this after the snooker, he realized. Mark had made light of muffing the final shot, but it had to have hurt. Why *wouldn't* he get his own back, by making a meal of sneaking Gary into his snobby gym like it was Mar-a-fucking-Lago?

'By the way, if anyone asks, you're called Jack,' Mark said out of the side of his mouth.

'OK, Daddy,' Gary put on a silly posh voice, 'have you got my swimming trunks, Daddy?'

Mark threw him a pained smile and led the way to the changing room.

They stripped down to their gym gear and stowed their stuff in Mark's locker. Gary bent down to tie his laces and Mark eyed his trainers suspiciously.

'I'm not being funny,' he said, 'but aren't those the ones you had on in the car?'

'They're my trainers,' Gary said, 'if that's what you mean.'

'Only you're not really meant to wear outdoor ones inside … oh, never mind. Have you got a sweat towel?'

Gary leaned into the locker and took out the stripy beach towel Yvette had given him.

'I've got this,' he said.

Mark grimaced tolerantly.

'No worries, you can share mine.'

He shouldered his way out of the changing room, holding the door open for Gary in an exaggerated act of courtesy.

Mark might have had dedicated indoor trainers and a sweat towel and a stainless-steel hydrator bottle, but Gary was pleased to discover that his friend wasn't so much fitter than he was. They had been running on adjacent treadmills for nineteen minutes and twenty-three seconds. Every time Gary had increased his speed, Mark had increased his a little more. Now the sweat was flying and Gary's heart was thudding like he'd sniffed amyl nitrate. It was time to be the bigger man. He slowed the treadmill to walking pace, and with evident relief, Mark followed suit, mopping his face and neck before offering his soggy towel to Gary.

'You're all right, mate,' Gary said, bending over to wipe his sweaty brow on his T-shirt.

'Need a breather?' said Mark.

Gary gave him a look of utmost incredulity. They strolled over to the leg presses.

'You might want to go easy at first,' said Mark, adjusting his resistance weight to 100 kilos, 'you can knacker your back if you're not used to it.'

'You're all right,' said Gary again, and fixed his own weight at 110. They went hard for five minutes, their machines gradually falling in synch with each other in a way Gary found disturbingly intimate. He sped up ever so slightly, which Mark took to be a challenge and then they seesawed back and forth with a lot of grunting and sweating for another ten reps. By this time Gary's legs were jelly, but he was fucked if he was giving in. Luckily, Mark needed to take on fluids.

They sat beside each other, panting. Mark handed Gary the flask and he glugged gratefully.

'So ... ?' Gary gasped.

'What ... ?' Mark looked cagey.

' ... Elephant in the room?'

'Sorry?' Mark took another swig from his flask.

'Heard you'd been seeing a shrink ... '

Mark stared at him in dismay.

'Sorry. None of my business. Only ... you know what women are like.'

Gary mimed gossip with his hand.

'She's not a shrink. Me and Harriet have been having ... ' Mark turned his head discreetly, '*counselling*.'

'Oh shit. Sorry to hear that, pal. Didn't know you were in trouble.'

Gary had a brief flashback to Harriet's lace-clad arse, offered up to him for the taking on Declan's sofa. He had never meant for it to happen. Had genuinely thought to cheer the woman up by showing her Manchester, that was all. But that was what Manchester would do to you if you weren't careful. One minute you'd be having a cocktail in the Northern

Quarter, the next you'd be spinning the old Northern soul singles at Declan's place off your faces on sambuca ... Jesus! His best mate's missus. His missus's best mate. It didn't bear thinking about ...

'We're *not* in trouble,' hissed Mark, 'it's a positive thing. We're learning to be more fully ... ourselves.'

'O-*ka-a-ay*!'

'Look, if you're going to take the piss ... '

'No, honest, I'm not ... ' Gary held his hand up. 'It's a brave thing you're doing. Me and Yvette could probably do with some counselling if it comes to that.'

'Really?'

Gary considered for a moment. The prospect of finding out what Yvette was really thinking was not an entirely happy one. He knew she wasn't up for moving just as their Ruby was about to sprog, and he sort of knew he was taking the piss expecting her to. He shrugged.

'It'll keep,' he said.

They both started exercising again, slowly, halfheartedly.

'Anyway,' Mark confided, 'the upshot is ... I've packed in work.'

Gary stopped pumping and stared at him.

'You mean, for a breather, like ... ?'

'No, permanently. It was Harriet's idea, she thinks I'm a workaholic.'

'*Harriet* does?'

'Yeah.'

'So, you just ... *did* it?'

'I know. Pussy-whipped or what ... ?'

Mark's face was turning pink.

'...But, you know...' he gasped, 'it's not as if we need the money and like she says, we're not getting any younger...'

Gary was confused. This didn't seem to tally with Harriet's attitude at all, if he'd read her right.

'So, what, you're *retiring*?'

Mark shrugged.

'I guess so. Although I don't think I'll be getting an allotment any time soon. Harriet's got itchy feet. Says she wants a gap year!'

'*Harriet* does...?'

'Yeah, one minute she's got us driving across the States in a Pontiac, the next we're volunteering with Oxfam in Namibia. Go figure.'

Gary's alarm grew. Was Harriet baling because of him? If so, she'd got it all out of proportion. He'd wanted to show her a good time, cheer her up a bit, not trigger a marital crisis and a year of soul searching in the wilderness.

'What about this factory conversion she's doing?' he asked Mark, trying to sound casual.

'Yeah, that's on first fix now,' Mark said. 'It'll be finished any time.'

Gary recalled the cement mixers, the pallets, the heaps of sand. He widened his eyes doubtfully at his trainers.

'She's burned out with it. Really needs a break.'

'So, have a holiday. Don't fuck your life over!'

'No, the more I think about it, the more I know it was the right decision. I feel really... free. I mean, we're so lucky to have the option at our age; that's what Harriet's made me see. Life's not a rehearsal...'

He glanced across at Gary.

'Well, *yours* is, but you know what I . . . '

'Why don't you move up North?' blurted Gary, hardly knowing where the impulse had come from.

Mark looked puzzled.

'Seriously, there are some lovely properties in Cheshire. You'd get a palace for what your place in London's worth. Swimming pool, gym, the lot. Wouldn't half get Yvette off my back an' all.'

Mark pulled a face.

'Sounds a bit *Footballers' Wives*, no offence.'

'Oh, none taken mate,' said Gary wryly. 'Seriously, though – Manchester's got a lot to offer and if you don't like the 'burbs, you can be in the city centre. Why go to Namibia when you could have Ancoats? Honestly, it's like Shoreditch only without the wankers. So fucking hip it'll make your eyes water. Fine dining; night life. Viagra for the soul, mate.'

Mark wobbled his head as if pretending to consider.

'Yeah, well, could do, I s'pose . . . '

20

Mark

Mark had expected to own Gary in the gym. They might be more or less of an age, but Gary was way flabbier than him, not to mention chock full of cholesterol, if Yvette's cooking was anything to go by. Yet with seven press-ups to go, Mark was out.

'Oof!'

He collapsed face down, chest heaving from the exertion. Powering on to their agreed target, Gary switched tactfully from a motivational bellow to a loud, self-congratulatory whisper.

'Ninety-six, ninety-seven, ninety-eight, ninety-nine. One *hundred*!'

He collapsed onto the mat, exuding an unseemly triumphalism, to Mark's way of thinking.

'Sauna?' Gary said, raising his head.

Mark hauled himself up and considered. All that intimate gloom and hot eucalyptus-infused air. He wasn't sure he trusted himself to keep his shit together if he got in the sauna with

Gary now. It was as close as atheists came to confession. He glanced up at the clock.

'Pushed for time, mate,' he lied, 'just a quick shower for me.'

Gary barged back into the changing room like it was the saloon at the O.K. Corral and Mark followed behind. He opened the locker and they stripped off, Gary flaunting his cock and balls, like a prize heifer, Mark shielding his discreetly behind a fresh towel. Gary was still going on at top volume about how glad he was to be moving back up North because London was a shithole. Luckily there was only one other man in the changing room and he just carried on applying athlete's foot powder as if he hadn't heard.

'You ought to at least come up and have a butcher's,' Gary insisted as they walked towards the showers, 'it's not like it used to be. We've got electricity up there. Hot and cold running water; the lot . . . '

He glanced wryly over his shoulder for a reaction, and Mark obliged with a sardonic grin, but he could feel it fading even as he stepped into the shower cubicle.

The space wasn't especially small, and Mark had never suffered from claustrophobia, yet he had to steel himself, now, to shut the door. He shot the bolt and slid down the wall into a despairing crouch. It felt like his life, that was the trouble – the walls closing in, slowly, inexorably. Oh, he could hold them back for a bit – step away from work, whisk Harriet off to some paradise island somewhere, but who knew what would be waiting for them when they got back?

Ever since Ollie had moved back to Moorcroft Road, Mark had felt displaced; unwelcome. It wasn't anything very dramatic – a crumby plate left by the sink, the TV permanently on standby, a barely detectable scent of hostile male about the place. And the worst of it was, since the counselling session, Mark knew he had no right to feel this way. The fault was not with Ollie, the fault was with *him*. *All* the fault, for *everything* – the state of his home, the state of his business, the state of his marriage, the state of the world. He'd given it his best shot and he'd failed, just as his mother had predicted. He reached up and turned the tap on full, then, under cover of the noisy cascade, he sobbed.

'Well, that was a lot better than I thought,' Gary said, pushing back through the turnstile with a spring in his step. 'If we weren't moving up North I might have thought about joining. Mind you, there's a dead nice park near where we're buying in Chorlton, so I might just go jogging instead.'

Mark reached into his pocket for his key and the Lexus flashed its headlights at them.

'Decent little motor that,' Gary said. 'I s'pose you'll have to give it back now ... ?'

Mark felt his chest tighten.

'It's no great loss,' he said, as nonchalantly as he could, 'I always thought it was a bit "sales rep" anyway ... '

'It *is* a bit, now you mention it,' agreed Gary. 'You want something a bit more edgy at your time of life. Nice little vintage Alfa Romeo. Something like that.'

They got in and reached, simultaneously, for their phones.

Mark noticed Gary grin mysteriously and jab his keyboard three times with his thumb, before returning the phone to his pocket. Mark's phone was alive with notifications; several urgent emails from Ambrose, subject heading: AUDIT, a couple of scary-looking ones from the Financial Conduct Authority and a speculative promotional mailshot from a criminal defence solicitor.

His voicemail was full as well. His stomach clenched with nerves and he threw the handset, unchecked, back into the glove compartment.

They were halfway home and Mark had just pulled up at a red light when Gary muttered something about cigarettes and dived out of the passenger door into a nearby newsagent's. Mark gripped the wheel and glanced uneasily in the rear-view mirror. What was he supposed to do? Sit here blocking the left turning lane even after the lights went green, or drive round the corner and risk a ticket for waiting on a double red line? This was typical Gaz – Mr Spontaneity; Mr Cool – oblivious to the grief he caused everyone else.

Mark decided to stay put, much to the frustration of the driver behind him, who gesticulated frantically for a full sequence of the lights, before pulling around the Lexus with a squeal of brakes and a string of expletives.

'Sorry, mate,' Gary said casually, as he hopped back into the passenger seat, unwrapped his cigarettes and tossed the cellophane into the footwell. 'Bloke turned out to be a Man City fan,' Gary jerked his head towards the newsagent, 'reckoned he knew someone might be selling a season ticket.'

He engaged the in-car cigarette lighter which had never, until that moment, been deployed, and then started on about how Mark and Harriet could do a lot worse than Didsbury. Mark opened both front windows, pointedly, and then, his vision briefly obscured by the smoke haze, pulled out into the path of a passing cycle courier.

'Watch where you're fucking going!' the youth shouted, slapping his hand angrily on the roof, so that Mark swerved back towards the pavement again.

'I tell you what,' Gary said, shaking his head disapprovingly, 'you don't get road rage like that up Nor . . . '

'Can you shut the fuck up about Manchester for five minutes?' Mark bellowed, his jugular vein throbbing. 'I know you're the salt of the earth. I know you tell it like it is and your football teams win all the trophies and you can get fish and chips and a pint and still have change from a fiver, but watch my fucking lips. Wild horses wouldn't drag me up there!'

PART II

Up North

21

Yvette

'Ooh this is lovely,' Yvette threw her head back and stared up at the stars, 'so luxurious. I feel like . . . ' she felt the bubbles coursing around her neckline. 'Who do I feel like? Some glamorous Sixties pin-up . . . '

'Julie Christie?' Harriet suggested.

'Raquel Welch?' offered Gary, hopefully.

'No, I dunno . . . who lived in a commune?' She could feel her voice slurring slightly from the Martini.

'Charles Manson?' Mark dead-panned.

'N-o-o-o!' Yvette splashed her hand playfully on the surface of the hot tub.

'Mark!' Harriet scolded. 'That's horrible.'

'Yeah, well, I'm against all this decadence.' Mark indicated the jacuzzi. 'It's a crime against the environment. Not to mention a spawning-ground for bacteria.'

'Mate, I've never seen anyone get their kit off faster than you just did,' Gary pointed out, 'you can't really come over all Greta Thunberg when you're the first one in.'

Mark made a 'fair cop' face.

'Besides, it's solar-powered,' said Harriet. 'It'll only fire up if the solar panels have generated enough electricity over and above what's needed for the rest of the building.'

Hearing this, they all reclined a little more smugly into the foam.

'Is that how you see this, then, a *commune*?' Harriet nudged Yvette – she seemed quite taken with the idea.

'No-o-o! 'Course not. They were for hippies, weren't they?' Yvette replied. 'I just meant ... ' What had she meant?

'It's just great that at *our* age ... '

There was an ironic groan.

'No, not that we're *old*, but just ... when most people's lives are getting smaller – kids leaving home, work winding down ... '

'Speak for yourself!' said Gary. 'Mine's winding back up.'

'Yeah, no, whatever ... ' Yvette said impatiently. 'It's just great to be trying something different. I never went to uni, or anything, so I always felt like I missed out on that whole flat-sharing thing where you all muck in together ... '

' ... Eat spag bol and get gonorrhoea,' teased Mark.

'No! Don't be daft.' Yvette chastised him with a playful splash. She could feel herself turning pink and not just from the heat of the tub. 'I just always liked the idea of sharing your life with people, you know, cooking together and staying up late and having a laugh.'

'Oh, me too!' enthused Harriet. 'I am *so* up for that. We should try and set up some sort of rota, don't you think ... ? I mean, obviously we'll want to do our own thing some of the time, but what if, say, Mondays, Wednesdays and Fridays, we commit to eating together and take it in turns to cook?'

'Good luck with getting Gaz in a pinny,' said Yvette.

'Excuse me! The girls used to love my spaghetti al Pomodoro.'

'You must have made it all of twice,' scoffed Yvette. She turned to Harriet, 'Can of tomatoes tipped over a bowl of overcooked pasta. Eat your heart out, Jamie Oliver.'

'Sounds all right to me,' her friend enthused. 'You see, that's the beauty of a commu… of communal living. We can *learn* from each other – expand our repertoires…'

'Liking the sound of that!' Gaz wiggled his eyebrows and Harriet giggled.

'Well, if we're having a cooking rota we'd better have a cleaning one too,' Yvette said, 'for the common parts, anyway.'

'Oh, I'd thought we might get a cleaner,' Harriet demurred.

Yvette felt her smile slipping. It wasn't just the expense, it was the idea you'd *pay* someone to clean up after you. She knew she was the one with the problem. You didn't have to be from the Home Counties, these days, to afford a cash-in-hand cleaner. She just couldn't see herself sat round all day reading *Take a Break* while some poor Polish kid vacced round her feet.

'Anyway, we can talk about it,' Harriet said equably. 'We're friends, aren't we? And friends talk about stuff.'

Mark raised his glass.

'To friendship!' he said.

'To friendship,' they all murmured and to her surprise, Yvette found herself welling up.

'Aw!' Harriet said. 'Come here!'

She scooped Yvette towards her and planted a clumsy kiss on her forehead.

'What . . . ?' she asked, bewildered, as Yvette's tears brimmed over.

'No, it's just . . . this place . . . ' Yvette gasped, waving her hand to indicate their new living arrangements, 'it's so lovely. I keep having to pinch myself. You are clever, Harriet.'

And she meant it. She'd never thought to live somewhere as beautiful as this. So much space and elegance, everything top of the range. She wished her mum was still alive to see it, although, if she had been, Yvette knew she'd not have been able to resist bringing them down a peg or two. The glass-fronted cupboards would have been dust magnets, the bathroom tiles a bugger to clean, the open brick work 'not her idea of cosy'. And it wouldn't even have been bitterness or jealousy, Yvette knew; just an almost religious conviction that people like them should keep their heads down, not get airs and graces, above all, *not tempt fate*. Well, enough of that.

'It's me who should be pinching myself,' Harriet told her with a reassuring squeeze. 'You guys saved our bacon. If you hadn't come in with us . . . ' she shook her head, 'it just doesn't bear thinking about.'

'Same,' agreed Yvette. 'I was in pieces when the Chorlton house fell through.'

'When we got gazumped, you mean,' muttered Gaz.

There was a pause.

'I don't know how you swung it, Mark!' said Yvette. 'The financing and everything.'

'It's called "thinking outside the box",' Mark said.

'How d'you mean?'

'When you find a creative solution to a problem by coming at it from a totally new . . . '

'Oh, I get you! Yeah, *that's* what it feels like. This whole thing... like we got out of jail free!'

Mark did a double-take.

'*Jail?*' he said.

Yvette knew she wasn't making much sense but she didn't care.

'No, I mean, because we get a jacuzzi, but it's a *sustainable* jacuzzi. And we get all this lovely designer-y space, but we're *sharing* it, so it's cool. And we'll grow our own veggies and take turns to cook, and go for lovely long walks, but if we're not feeling it, we can just go, "Right, I'm off to bed with a Pot Noodle to watch *The Voice*."'

'Has anyone got the faintest idea what she's on about?' Gary appealed to the others.

'She's on about this, mate, *this*!' Mark waved his hand lavishly, to indicate the vista, the freedom, the possibility. Yvette nodded her head in urgent agreement and felt briefly dizzy. They'd got Mark all wrong, she thought, he had a very spiritual side.

'I mean, just *look* at those stars,' he murmured now, tilting his head back in wonder. 'I thought you were a songwriter, Gaz...'

'Yeah, I'm not fucking Don McLean...'

'Who's Don McLean?' asked Harriet.

'Oh my God,' Gary pretended to choke on his drink, 'what decade were you born in again? No don't tell me...'

Harriet smirked.

'I don't think it's an age thing,' Yvette said a little tetchily, '"Starry, Starry Night" is a classic.'

Mark started to croon the opening verse, slightly off-key,

then Gary joined in, his more melodious voice putting Mark's to shame. They finished, gazing sentimentally into each other's eyes, the women applauded and everyone laughed. There was a collective sigh and then they reached for their drinks, which were for the most part, empty.

'*He* lived in a commune, you know,' said Mark draining his glass.

'Who, Don McLean?' said Harriet.

'No, Vincent Van Gogh.'

'Oh ... '

'Probably why he ended up topping himself,' said Gary drolly.

'*No-o-o*,' Harriet corrected him. 'He was very troubled – a lot of geniuses are.'

'Not me!' Gaz said, with a cheeky grin.

'You think you're a ... ?' Harriet turned to him with an expression of scandalised disbelief, ' ... Oh my God, the vanity!'

Gaz narrowed his eyes at her jokily and Harriet responded with a sarcastic head wobble. They were chalk and cheese, her husband and her best friend, Yvette mused. For years she had watched them dance around each other socially, never quite managing to connect. Yet here they were bantering away like they'd gone to school together. They had ... what was the word? Rapport. She supposed she should feel pleased.

She was starting to dehydrate now, from the heat and alcohol. She had the telltale beginnings of a migraine, and her fingers looked like melting birthday candles.

'I think I might get out,' she said, 'I'm turning into a prune and I said I'd Skype our Ruby at nine.'

She stood up unsteadily, keenly aware that the leopard skin swimsuit which had been keeping everything lifted and separated when she'd first got in, was now waterlogged and drooping. So reluctant was she to draw attention to herself that she almost stumbled in her haste to get out of the tub and had to brace herself on Gaz's shoulder, before making her way across the terrace in as dignified a manner as her slight squiffiness would allow.

'Mind how you go,' Harriet called after her. She heard one of the men make some jokey remark and then the three of them laughed and for a minute Yvette was back in the school canteen, glancing over her shoulder as she went to the serving hatch to get a fresh jug of water for Caroline Braithwaite, Stephanie Henderson and Amanda Clarke – hoping they were saying what a good sport she was; fearing they were saying what a mug she was.

She was going to have to get over herself if this living together malarkey was to work, she decided. She needed to be her own person; do her own thing. Even if her own thing consisted of pooping the party in order to check in with her eldest daughter.

She went down the spiral staircase to her and Gary's room and heaved their bedroom door over the thick carpet they'd had laid on top of Harriet's tasteful polished concrete. Gaz had told her off for shoving the door too hard, scared it would break the hinges, but Yvette wasn't overly worried – it was their room and their door and they were their hinges to break, now that they were equal partners in The Button Factory, as she'd pointed out. And as impeccable as Harriet's taste was, Yvette had no desire to live in a show house. She could appreciate the functionality of the vast communal kitchen-diner and the quirkiness of the adjoining Scandi-style den with its eco-compliant wood burner and its sunken sofas; but if they were going to share so much of their living space with other people, she needed a bit of something that was hers. So, she'd ordered the carpet, and bought some lovely turquoise velour cushions at Harvey Nicks in Manchester, and she'd made a tasteful arrangement on their new bureau of Gaz's gold disc and some nice framed photos of the girls, and one of those frond-y, low maintenance ferns in a retro pot and whilst it might not live up to Harriet's standards of Zen minimalism, it felt homely to Yvette.

She padded through to the en-suite and turned on the shower. A noisy wall of water tumbled from the dustbin-lid-sized shower-rose, filling the room instantly with steam. She'd got so used to dithering on the candlewick bathmat at Brenner Street, waiting for the water to run hot, that it took her by surprise. Once inside, it was bliss. She closed her eyes and let the warmth cascade over her, plastering her hair to her head, pummelling her limbs, turning her whole constitution liquid. Every so often she would be assailed by some emotion; barely even a thought . . . gratitude that they had a home again . . . guilt that the four of them were living in a place that could have housed twelve . . . relief that it was less her fault than Harriet's . . . concern that they had made a rash move . . . reassurance that they had released a nice wodge of money to help out their skint, hardworking daughters – and finally panic when she realized she'd lost track of the time and one of those daughters might even now be Skyping her from the poky little second bedroom in Woolwich, which, despite being nearly five months into her pregnancy, she was still superstitiously calling 'the guest room'.

Yvette turned the shower off and hurried to the bedroom, her feet leaving great soggy prints in the carpet. By the time she'd grabbed her laptop, flumped down on the bed and opened it up, it was ten past nine. There were no missed call notifications though. Phew! She raked her hands through her hair, took a moment to compose herself, then called Ruby's number, anticipation and anxiety mounting in her belly.

'Mum?' Ruby's face appeared as if from outer space. She looked bemused. Had she forgotten? Jordan leaned across, and waved at Yvette. There followed a brief, silent-movie-style conflab between Ruby and Jordan before he made good his escape, leaving Ruby looking slightly miffed.

'We did say we'd Skype?' Yvette reminded her brightly.

'Yeah, no. We can. How are you?'

'We can do it another time if . . . '

'It's fine, Mum. How are things?'

Yvette nestled herself into the pillows, to demonstrate their luxuriousness.

'Yeah, lovely. Just got out of the jacuzzi. You'll have to come up . . . '

'No, we will, definitely. Only, you know how it is with Jordan's schedule . . . '

'Oh, yeah, I didn't mean straight away or anything. You'd love it up here. You can taste the fresh air compared to London, and the *views* . . . '

'You like it then . . . ?'

'Oh yeah, it's gorgeous.'

'And you're all getting on OK?'

"Course, yeah. No, it's really good. Really, really nice. But how are you? You're not overdoing it, are you? Don't be commuting in the rush hour when you could go in a bit later, will you?'

'It's fine, Mum, honestly, I'm being really sensible.'

'I know, I know you are … and … the baby? Have you felt it kick yet?'

It felt strange saying 'the baby', as though acknowledging its existence might jinx it somehow. Ruby would have had her third scan by now – they didn't take any chances with IVF pregnancies. She might even know the gender, but if she did, she wasn't letting on, and there was no way Yvette was asking. Not only because of the jinx thing, but also because if they wanted to tell her, they'd tell her. Tightness came to her throat and tears to her eyes. It was 1985 again and she was sat on her quilted nylon bedspread next to her mum. Behind their heads, Gary Kershaw, rock god and father of her unborn child loured down from a poster, a Fender Stratocaster thrust at a phallic forty-five degrees from his crotch.

'Well, you're not the first and I dare say you won't be the last,' her mum had muttered without meeting her eye, 'so we'll just have to make the best of it, won't we?' and she'd reached across and given Yvette's hand a brisk pat. That was about as affectionate as it got with Yvette's mum.

Yvette had vowed to do things differently and she had. They'd been close, her and Ruby. Too close, if anything; shared nail varnish, fags, secrets … a bit unhealthy, really. It wasn't until Yvette had had Jade over a decade later that she'd figured out a daughter doesn't really want a mate, she wants a mother. So, maybe Ruby's evasiveness now was just payback for all that intrusive parenting; maybe she was keeping Yvette at arm's length on purpose, and she'd find out whether she was getting a grandson or a granddaughter when they saw fit to tell her. Or maybe they just didn't know...

'Mum, where've you gone?'

'Oops, sorry,' Yvette blinked quickly to dispel the tears and turned the screen back to face her with a breathless smile, 'laptop slipped. Oh my God! I've just seen myself... State of my hair! I look like a Furby. Listen, I'd better go and blow-dry it... we've got people coming over tomorrow.'

'People...?' Ruby looked vaguely interested.

'Just this old friend of your dad's called Declan. You know – the producer for the band? He's going to see whether the downstairs might convert into a sort of live-in studio type thing for him and his girlfriend...'

'Sounds good...'

'Well, we'll see. I s'pose I might see a bit more of your dad if he was living above the shop.'

'I'd have thought you might want to see a bit less of him...'

'Ha ha.'

There was a longish pause.

'Well, look, I'll let you go,' Yvette said. 'You get yourself an early night. Give my love to Jordan and make sure you...'

''K, Mum. Skype again soon. Love you.'

Ruby's face froze briefly on the screen and then vanished.

22

Harriet

Harriet had laughed in Mark's face when he'd suggested they buy out the housing association and finish converting The Button Factory themselves.

'Hark at you Roman Abramovich,' she'd said, a little unkindly, in retrospect. 'There's no way we've got that kind of money.' But Mark had assured her they did. He said if they got their own builders in and changed it up a bit – fewer units, higher spec – the apartments would be catnip for all the media types that were moving up North in droves. They stood to make their money back and then some, he'd said. Harriet had wavered. On the one hand, she was sorely tempted by the opportunity to finish the job and salvage her professional reputation. On the other, she was troubled by the dubious ethics of turning what was meant to be a social housing project into a private money-spinner. Then she'd got the phone call from Yvette that had made her mind up once and for all. Not only had Yvette and Gaz been gazumped on their dream home, but Gaz had been abusive to the estate agent, and now no one'd show them anything that wasn't next to a chemical works or riddled with damp.

'I'm at my wit's end,' Yvette had wailed. 'Honest to God, Harriet, I'd rather sleep in a cardboard box than stay at Gaz's sister's place.'

'You might not need to . . . ' Harriet had said, half frowning, half smiling as her mind alighted on an idea so serendipitous, so obvious, so irresistible, as to seem written in the stars. 'I think I might have the solution.'

It had been a learning curve. Pitching in together; sharing a communal space – albeit a very *spacious* space. Harriet doubted any of them – even Yvette, who normally had empathy to burn – understood how uniquely hard it was for her; the architect. She'd had to let go of her original plan for the building and redesign it in collaboration with three people whose company she loved, but whose aesthetic preferences left a lot to be desired. There had been many days when she'd wondered whether she was doing the right thing. She missed London and she missed Ollie like mad. It killed her to think of him microwaving meals for one like a lonely pensioner while the four of them shared gourmet dinners and smoked weed.

Then there was the responsibility she felt for the cost overruns and unforeseen delays. The stud wall that had been wrongly demolished and hastily re-erected, the piece of Carrara marble trimmed five centimetres short, both of which the builders had charged for; neither of which she had queried. And finally, there was the secret shame of her . . . thing . . . with Gary in Manchester. The knowledge that, even as she repressed any latent desire to repeat it, their new communal lifestyle would bring the two of them into casual contact more times in one day than her and Mark's marriage had in a typical week, testing their will-power with every piece of cutlery passed, every door held open.

Yet for all these misgivings and mitigations, Harriet was already finding that her new life had brought with it a joyous sense of rightness, of *fit*. It was as though she had been dropped, with a satisfying clunk, into a slot precisely honed for her. It was a feeling she could only remember having had twice before – on sleeping with Mark for the first time and on learning she was pregnant. The truth was, she had fallen in love; with The Button Factory, with Macclesfield, with the *North*.

For Harriet, brought up in Surrey, the nearest thing to wilderness had been Box Hill, where Jane Austen's Emma had picnicked, and from the top of which, on a clear day, you could see Dorking. Compared to that, The Button Factory felt like Wuthering Heights, sitting among properly rolling hills with views of blasted trees and distant chimneys and a *viaduct*, for goodness' sake. Then there were the skies – huge and mercurial – watery blue one minute, pewter the next; now yawning wide with sunshine, now crouched upon by thick black clouds. And all this dark satanic stuff going on just two stops by train from the hip metropolis of Manchester, with its culture and its curry mile and its good-as-you swagger, where you could do Happy Hour in the Northern Quarter, snap up a vintage handbag in Affleck's Palace and eat the best tapas outside Barcelona, all for less than the price of a 'menu fixe' in Shoreditch.

So yes, there had been plenty of positive reasons to take

this mad leap into the unknown – reasons so compelling that they had drowned out the quiet voice of caution that normally whispered in Harriet's ear. But there had been some murkier motives too – easily the murkiest being her exasperation with Mark. Having him at home all day might have been bearable if retirement had improved his mood, but it only seemed to have made it worse. He'd been unrecognizable – listless one minute, manic the next. It was like having a restless poltergeist wandering the house, getting underfoot and causing ructions. Not that he wasn't doing his best. Since they'd done the couples counselling, he'd been making an effort with Ollie, treating him less like a pariah and more like a foreign exchange student whose strange habits and occasional gnomic utterances must be tolerated. Even when Ollie had appeared one evening with a large dragon tattooed on his neck, still suppurating beneath a layer of cling film, Mark had just peered at it curiously and then withdrawn with a curt nod of the head. Harriet had been so shocked she'd had to go out of the room and compose herself.

Yet even Mark's newfound tolerance smelled wrong to Harriet. It was as though he was acting a part. It had been the same when she'd raised the issue of his reckless unilateral decision to retire at fifty-four. He had smiled beatifically and trotted out the line that he was immensely proud of what he had achieved but PR was the sort of business in which you needed to be hungry to thrive. Sadie and Ambrose were hungry; he was satiated. He actually said the word *satiated*. Then he continued to waft around the house, trying, for all he was worth, to project the vibe of someone comfortable in his skin, whilst betraying all the telltale behaviours of someone coming apart at the seams. There was the compulsive phone checking and the conspicuous secrecy (he'd even started taking it to the loo with him). There were the night sweats and the anxious mumblings in his sleep. There was his annoying habit of replying to Harriet's cheery conversation-openers with non sequiturs that proved he wasn't listening. And there was the impotence. Harriet couldn't remember the last time she and Mark had had a satisfactory sexual encounter. For something like two years, Mark had been phoning it in; a bit of fake groaning, a thrust or three, and then he'd roll off her and reach for a tissue she suspected he didn't actually need. Desire – heart-stopping, throat-constricting, thigh-melting desire – had not featured in their love-making since... she didn't even want to think about when.

Yet here was Mark, four months on, stargazing from a hot tub, apparently a changed man. Relaxed, expansive; flirtatious even, assuming it was Mark's and not Gary's foot that Harriet could feel stroking her inner thigh as the four of them bantered about Don McLean. And it had to be Mark's, surely? Gary wouldn't risk it. Not after what had gone down between him and Harriet in Manchester.

They had done the cocktail thing and the shopping thing and the tapas thing, both aware, on some level, that they were getting on unprecedentedly, *unfeasibly* well. But it had all felt very matey and light-hearted; not really flirty at all. There had been some banter and some awful jokes and Gaz had threatened to take Harriet dancing, but she'd refused on the basis she had two left feet and he'd said the penalty for being a stick-in-the-mud was to come back to Declan's and listen to some top tunes (Declan being in Austin at his girlfriend's graduation) and she'd agreed to this. Gary had played her some music, which hadn't done much for her until they'd started on the second bottle of wine and then, just when she was getting into it, he'd handed her a joint and told her to go easy and the next thing she'd known, they were all over each other on Declan's 1930s sofa. She'd woken the next morning with a raging hangover, a pattern of concentric circles on her cheek and a sinking feeling in her stomach.

She'd felt terrible the next morning. Gary had tried to be gallant – offering her toast, apologizing for the fact that Declan only had instant coffee – as if she would even *taste* the coffee. Neither of them could meet the other's eye. All Harriet could think of was how often, over the years, she'd reassured Yvette that Gaz was a changed man and wouldn't dream of cheating on her, even if he *could* still pull, which frankly, Harriet doubted. In fact, when she thought about it, she'd said so many rude things about Gaz in the past – calling him at various times (and with affectionate contempt) a professional Northerner, a throwback and a narcissist – that she had inadvertently created the perfect smokescreen for an affair.

'I think I might get out,' Yvette said now, standing up so abruptly that she caused a small tsunami in the hot tub. The foot that had been caressing Harriet's inner thigh was swiftly withdrawn. Yvette waded across the middle of the jacuzzi and clambered over the side, giving Gaz's shoulder a proprietorial squeeze as she went. Harriet, Mark and Gaz turned as one and watched her progress tipsily across the roof terrace towards the triangle of light cast by the open door.

'Mind how you go,' Harriet called after her solicitously.

'It's a jungle out there,' Gary said drolly. Harriet gave him a sarky smile and they laughed. She thought perhaps she should follow Yvette indoors, rather than stay out here with the men, but she'd missed her cue now and it would feel contrived, as though there were some impropriety in being left on her own with them which, in view of her and Gaz's recent track record, there absolutely was. It was for this reason, she told herself, that she *must* stay, not only to allay suspicion, but to prove to herself and to Gaz, that from now on their relationship would be strictly platonic.

She rolled over onto her belly and lowered her head onto her folded arms so that all she could hear was the throb and churn of the water.

She had not been lying there very long, when the mystery foot returned, its arch now pushing up experimentally against her pudenda. She moaned into the crook of her elbow and pushed back against it. It was OK to do this, because it was Mark's foot. It had to be. In fact, as long as it *was* Mark's foot, it was better than OK – it meant he'd got his mojo back, which was miraculous. She lifted her face from the pool edge and glanced over her shoulder but the two men were deep in conversation, discussing Arsenal's new signing as casually as if they were propping up the bar at the local. And they said men couldn't multi-task. She lowered her head again and parted her legs a little, unable quite to believe that she was going to let it happen. His foot was circling rhythmically now, and Harriet stilled the guilty voice inside her head and focussed instead on the ache of pleasure that was building between her legs. She pushed back hard against it and was rewarded with a reciprocal increase in the frequency and intensity of the kneading. At last, when it seemed she might have to cry out, she bit down instead on the soft flesh of her upper arm and, with a discreet tensing of the hips, she came.

She lay there for several moments, breathing in the faint chlorinated tang of her flesh and watching the coloured lights of the jacuzzi glow through the churning foam.

'He just goes to pieces in front of goal,' she could hear Mark saying, 'he's lost it. The fans know it, he knows it. It's only Arteta that can't see it.'

'Well, now you're up here, maybe you want to start following a decent team like … oh hello, Harriet,' Gary smirked at her, 'we thought you'd nodded off.'

Later, in bed, arching over her with a raging hard-on, Mark didn't mention the game of footsie and Harriet was too astonished by his rampant libido to inquire.

It had to have been him, she reasoned, as he scrunched his eyes shut, clenched his jaw and pushed deep inside her. Gary might be a cool customer, but even he wasn't cool enough to bring off his best friend's missus right under said best friend's nose. Yet as she closed her eyes and focussed intently on the bud unfurling now between her legs, it was the doubt she clung onto, the doubt that brought her, rushing headlong to ecstasy.

23

Gary

'Declan, my man!' Gaz walked out onto the newly laid gravel in front of The Button Factory and greeted his friend with a handshake-cum-hug.

'So, this is you now, is it?' Declan pulled back and squinted at the north façade. 'Come a long way from the Rawcroft Estate, haven't you?'

There was admiration in Declan's tone, but also, unless Gary was imagining it, a hint of mockery.

'I'm a lot nearer to it now than I've been for the last thirty years, mate – physically and, you know, *spiritually*. It feels great to be back up North, I'm telling you. Good for the creative juices.'

'I don't know that you can call Macclesfield "up North",' said Declan. Gary gave a wry grin.

'It'll do me. Now, do you want to do the tour first, or have a coffee or what?'

'Well, I wouldn't mind a quick butcher's at the space first, 'cos I'm buzzing to know if I've got a new studio. It's a long way to come just for a social call.'

'Fair dos.' Gary shrugged amicably and led the way. It was hard to get used to the new, focussed Declan. Granted, he was a better prospect by far for the band and the album launch and ... just about everything, really ... than the old drug-addled Declan; only, Gary had kind of preferred him when he was off his face.

As far as drugs went, The KMA had fallen into two camps. Macca and Declan – the shy creatives – liked downers; weed, ketamine, Rohypnol and, latterly, smack, which as everybody knows, will knock you off the top of the charts faster than Kylie in a one-piece. It was these two who, with their trippy lyrics and innovative production techniques, gave the band its intellectual and emotional weight. Gary and John, on the other hand, front man and drummer respectively, had been the gobby exhibitionists. They'd brought the energy, the vibe and, yes, the groupies. Naturally, they'd been all about uppers – poppers, molly and eventually, crack, which for a while had been the ultimate upper before it became the ultimate downer. But the writing had been on the wall for the band by then anyway. Too much money, not nearly enough discipline and 'artistic differences' by the shedload. Declan was a lost cause so the record company had foisted a new producer on them who'd got no fucking idea what The KMA were really about. No wonder the album had tanked.

This time it would be different. They were older and wiser. Their creative talent had had two full decades to mature. Plus, they were desperate. No one was going to piss it up the wall this time round, that was for sure – not now they knew what *real* work looked like. Gary unlocked the up-and-over door that gave onto the ground floor of the factory and led Declan inside.

'Hang on, let me...' He fished around for the switch and flooded the room with light.

'Wow!'

'Yeah, I don't think space'll be a problem,' Gary said, his voice echoing around the room, 'and it'll not be hard to sound-proof, 'cos them walls are thick as. It's more *light* really, and how you divide it up into living and working. If you're still after moving in here with... what's'er face.'

'Meadow.'

'That's the one.'

Declan paced the floor purposefully, as though already making calculations in his head.

He narrowed his eyes and sucked his teeth and tapped things into his phone.

'And your place is...?'

Gary jerked his head upwards.

'One floor up, but as I say, Harriet's done this type of thing before – theatres and that, so she's savvy on the sound-proofing. The ground-floor windows got bricked-up back in the day, but Harriet says they'll not be difficult to reinstate. Full disclosure, though, you're facing onto the car park, so you've not got the views we get upstairs, but I don't reckon anybody'd mind if you share the roof terrace – I'll take you up there in a bit. It's un-fucking-real. You'll need to see it anyway if we're going to have the album launch there. Harriet says we'd have to get a health and safety certificate but she reckons it's just a formality and...'

'Harriet says this, Harriet says that.' Declan stopped tapping notes into his phone and regarded Gary with a wry grin. 'You've got it bad, haven't you?'

Gary gave him a sarcastic smile.

'No, just, she's the architect. I mean, *I* could have a go at sorting your windows and your sound-proofing if you'd rather – fix you up in a nice little flat with your jail-bait girlfrie…'

Declan bundled Gary's back to the wall and squared his elbow across Gary's chest.

'She's twenty-fucking-three, you cheeky cunt, and she saved my fucking life…'

They froze for a second, eyes locked, both riled and ready to fight. Then they caught themselves and backed off, authentic anger taking second place to necessary camaraderie.

'Just 'cos your missus doesn't go down on you any more…' Declan gave Gary's chest a playful poke.

'Fucking does.'

'Fucking doesn't.'

They pushed each other jokingly back and forth, until the anger had dissipated. Then they smoothed down their clothing with wry humour and finished with an uneasy fist-bump.

'So, you likey?' Gary said after a pause.

Declan cast a last appraising glance around the space.

'Me likey.'

'No, he's just a really lovely, really gentle guy, is Declan,' Gary told the other three housemates as they sat around the wood-burner later that evening, sipping Pinot Noir and discussing their potential new business partner.

'He had a tough few years after the band split, mind,' Yvette pointed out.

'Yeah, but he's right as rain now,' said Gary. 'His girlfriend's done wonders for him. She's a wellness specialist, apparently.'

'A *wellness* specialist?' Harriet raised an amused eyebrow.

'Yeah. Dietary advice, therapy, that sort of stuff ... right up your street, I'd have thought, H. Oh, *and* she teaches yoga. She could do private classes for us. Be good, wouldn't it?'

'*You*, doing yoga?' Yvette scoffed at Gary. 'I can just see that.'

'That's the one where you bend over and wave your arse in the air, isn't it?' Gary said. 'I reckon even I can manage that. And I tell you what ... ' he smirked at Yvette, 'when *I* do it, there won't be a solar eclipse!'

Harriet gasped and put a sympathetic hand on her friend's arm.

'Hey, I was just kidding,' Gary said, registering the look of dismay on Harriet's face before the expression of hurt on his wife's, 'you've got a lovely arse.'

'I dunno,' Mark stroked his chin, seemingly oblivious to all the vibes that were flying around, 'it sounds like it could be a good fit – this recording studio idea, but don't you think we should get some sort of feasibility study, before we commit to a new business on the premises? *Two* new businesses, potentially.'

'Oh, there's plenty of time for that,' replied Gary, 'they'll not be moving in till August ... '

'*Moving in?*' Mark looked dismayed.

For a man who'd been toking on Gary's joint like it was a life support machine, he could have been a bit more chilled, Gary reckoned.

'That was the plan, wasn't it?' Gary replied. 'There's plenty of space down there and I thought we wanted to put it to good use. Make a bit of ... ' He rubbed his thumb and forefinger together.

'*Was* that the plan?' Mark looked at Harriet and she glanced uneasily at Gary and then back at her husband.

'*I* thought so,' she said.

Gary smirked into his wine glass.

'I wouldn't worry, darling,' Harriet told Mark, 'it's not like it's even the same space really. With the sound insulation and the separate entrance and everything... I mean, if you compare it to the housing density in London – your old terrace, for example,' she waved her hand towards Yvette, 'Declan and Meadow will be the equivalent of three doors down.'

'Yeah, think of the nutters *we* had three doors down...' Gary rolled his eyes.

'The Fergusons!'

'I never had a problem with the Fergusons,' said Yvette, huffily. 'Not after their Tommy left, anyway.'

'Got put away, you mean...'

Yvette glared at him.

'*Anyway*,' said Harriet, still trying to be upbeat, bless her, 'this is a very different scenario, because you can vouch for Declan, can't you? And it means having the ground floor occupied, which is better from the point of view of security and also... let's not beat around the bush, *financially*.'

She lifted her wine glass towards Mark's and Yvette's as if to cheers them and they both leaned forward, a bit halfheartedly to Gary's way of thinking, and clinked glasses.

'Now then,' he said, to change the subject and jolly everyone along, 'who's for a listen of *The Other Cheek*?'

'Who are they?' Mark frowned.

'Who are they?' Gary repeated, scornfully. 'You're a joker.

He's a joker. It's what we're calling the new album. Named after the title track. Trying it for size, anyway. What do you reckon?'

Harriet frowned.

'*The Other Cheek*? I don't get it. Is it biblical or something?'

Gary stared at her in amusement.

'It's a play on words.'

'Sorry... I don't...' Harriet shook her head. She was blushing, bless her.

'The KMA. Kiss my *Arse*. Turn the other *cheek*. Geddit?'

'So KMA stands for kiss my...? *Oh*, I never knew.'

Gary's face broke into a disbelieving grin. He nudged Yvette.

'She thought they were just random initials!'

Yvette stretched her mouth into a smile.

'Fancy me not knowing that...' Harriet said. She nudged Mark, 'Did *you* know?'

'Yeah... no, I... think I did. Anyway, yeah. *The Other Cheek*. Great title. Let's give it a listen.'

An anticipatory silence fell. Gary pointed his phone at the entertainment hub and pressed play. There was a hiss of static, then Macca's unamplified voice – '*A-one, a-two, a-one, two, three, four*' – followed by John's driving snare, a burst of electronica, Macca's funky little keyboard riff and finally Gary on guitar and lead vocal – the gravel of middle-age giving a bite to the natural sweetness of his pipes that surprised even him with its beauty.

'*I seen your face in the mirror, girl*
And there's sadness in your eyes
I seen your face everywhere I go
And it's telling me a big surprise.

It's telling me you got my number, girl,
It's telling me you want me gone,
It's telling me you got no hook
for me to hang my hat upon.
It's telling me you found my diaries
It's telling me you seen my juice
It's telling me you know when I'm out all night,
That I'm bringing you a cheat's excuse.
It's telling me you want this over with,
It's saying you're not mine to keep,
Well, I'm down on my knees,
And I'm beggin' you, girl, you gotta . . .
Turn the other cheek.
Turn the other cheek, girl,
You gotta turn the other cheek.
Roll over lay down and let me in,
You gotta turn the other cheek.'

A reprise of the chorus and then they cut loose, first Gaz on his Fender, then Macca on keyboards, before the whole thing degenerated into a delicious orgy of psychedelic improvisation and faded out, leaving all three members of his audience looking gratifyingly awestruck.

'Fucking fantastic, mate!' said Mark after a reverent silence. 'Great lyrics too. Very cool. That little sample in the chorus, *roll over lay down . . .* ?'

'Yeah, that's not a sample, a sample's when you . . . '

'Even so . . . nice touch. Nice little nod to The Stones there.'

'Status Quo,' Gary corrected him, 'it's ironic.'

'The Quo, that's right.'

Gary looked at Harriet and pulled a 'shoot me now'

face. It was, he realized, a kind of test. Would she blank him, out of loyalty to her hopelessly un-hip, irony-free-zone of a husband, or come on board? Harriet met his eye and gave a little smirk.

24

Mark

'Mark, is that you?' Harriet's voice was groggy with sleep. The bedside light snapped on and Mark froze, the neck of his new running top stretched over his nose like a bandit's mask.

'Sorry!' he whispered. 'Go back to sleep. I didn't mean to ...'

Harriet raised herself up on one elbow and squinted at him.

'What time is it? Why are you getting dressed ... ?'

'I'm just going for a run.'

'It's the middle of the night.'

'It's not, actually. You go back to sleep. I'll pick up some milk on my way back. We're nearly out.'

This to make his behaviour appear rational, to make it seem as though he was participating in the life of the house; a normal human being.

Harriet looked at him as if he'd gone mad.

'It's pitch black. You'll have an accident.'

'No, it's fine, I've got a head-torch. Honestly, pretend this never happened.'

He pulled the duvet up to Harriet's neck and planted a little kiss on her forehead. 'You go back to sleep.'

He switched the bedside light off and crept along the corridor to the kitchen.

He still didn't trust himself with the lights. He didn't know which switch was which and the last thing he wanted was to flood the vast, curtain-less room with light, to be *seen*. So, he stumbled around in the dark, filling his water bottle, shuffling into his running shoes and wincing at the deafening sound of Velcro on Velcro. He tiptoed down the stairs and pulled the front door to quietly behind him. The cold enveloped him at once, bone-chilling and hostile. He peered into the darkness until he could just make out the gate in the distance, then tiptoed towards it down the gravel drive. He was about halfway there when he realized he'd forgotten his headphones. The thought of retracing his steps to retrieve them was daunting. Then again, so was the thought of running with no soundtrack other than his own deranged thoughts. He turned his Spotify playlist on at low volume and tried securing the phone to his ear with the elastic band of his head-torch, but he had only jogged a few paces, before it fell out, face down on the gravel. He switched it off and zipped it into his pocket.

OK, so this was it. This was him. Coming to terms, working it all through, getting into a whole new ... he paused at the gate and looked up and down the lane, alarmed by a pale beam of light that flashed briefly over the hedgerows, until he realized it was shining from his own forehead. He set off in what he hoped was the direction of the hills. God it was tough. He was out of condition. He'd been meaning to join a gym since they'd moved, but as with everything else he'd intended doing

– signing up for evening classes, buying himself a mountain bike, ordering the books on his retirement reading list – it had somehow got deferred. It had all felt too provisional; a holiday from real life, not the thing itself.

How could this have happened? They had bought a button factory. It was absurd; Dickensian. Even more absurd was the fact they'd opted to share it, when they could have taken a floor each. This was down to Harriet. The extra cost of making two self-contained apartments, whilst considerable, could easily have been accommodated from Mark's . . . income stream . . . without the others even needing to know. But his wife had been so wedded to the kibbutz-like vibe of her original plan and so appalled at the waste of resources a more radical redesign would have entailed, that he hadn't really dared pursue it. Instead, he had gone along with her hippy-dippy 'best-of-both-worlds' philosophy and thus found himself living in what was, to all intents and purposes, a commune. He could just imagine the look of scorn on his mother's face had she lived to see it.

'Trust you to be fifty years behind the times,' she'd have said, 'it'll end in tears, you mark my words.'

He noticed a stile by the lane, and a footpath leading up towards the ridge. This looked about right. He clambered over it. The path was steep and hard to pick out in the darkness and in order to make his head-torch illuminate it, he had to tilt his chin down at an unnatural angle that constrained his breathing. Glancing up, he noticed the first blue gash of dawn above the limestone escarpment. What better metaphor for his new life? He would fix his gaze on that and run by instinct, he decided. Now he found his rhythm, and despite the odd stumble, began to feel . . . what was that feeling . . . peace? No, surely not. Peace was a state of grace forever denied him, since he'd committed a... not a crime, exactly, but a morally ambiguous act. No, what he was feeling was more like resignation; or resolution. Something beginning with 'res', anyway. A sense, if not of having left the past behind, then of seeing it for what it was... putting it at arm's length. All the bad stuff – the discord with Ollie, the years of frustration at not being able to give Harriet the baby she wanted, the guilt and shame (and relief) when he'd taken matters into his own hands, the grubbiness of his recent financial arrangements. It was all behind him now. The trail was cold. A brighter future lay ahead, if only he could feel deserving of it. Good things lay in store, shiny, optimistic things. That's what this revelatory crack of light on the hilltop seemed to be telling him, as it winched open the night sky by degrees.

Halfway up, Mark stopped to catch his breath, and turning to take in the view, was surprised at how high he had already climbed. The Button Factory was a matchbox far below him, the canal a line of black marker pen, leading his eye towards the red-brick huddle of Macclesfield. Beyond Macclesfield, some larger town with a viaduct and chimneys – Stockport, he supposed. And beyond *that*, squatting on the far horizon, Manchester, a city about which he had heard great things, but which he had yet to explore. London was nowhere. Not even a pinprick in the distance. London did not exist.

He pressed on now, grinding up the gears as the path grew steeper still, forcing himself to dig a little deeper, endure a little more until the sweat was flying off his forehead and his legs were trunks of jelly. He breasted the top of the ridge as if it were the finishing line at sports day, then bent over, panting and clutching his thighs, until his heart stopped leaping in his chest. Straightening up, he saw that light was everywhere and day had come. He could hear the occasional swish of a commuting car in the lane below, the distant hee-haw of the first intercity train. It was a new dawn, a new day and, yes, he was feeling good.

He took out his phone. Seven forty-five. The guys would be getting up soon. He remembered that the purchase of milk had been part of his cover story. Macclesfield must be – what? – a twenty-minute yomp away at most.

By the time he'd found his way there, via track and lane and towpath and tunnel, the day was in full swing. Weaving along the high street in his sweaty jogging gear and his head-torch, he felt conspicuous as a badger that had lost its bearings. Kids in school uniform nudged each other as he passed, mums with buggies exchanged indulgent glances, cars honked him as he jaywalked where no pavement was. He passed a Peacocks, an Iceland and a Poundstretcher and, unsure if any of them sold milk, and unwilling to subject himself to further ridicule by asking, was about to slink home again, when a man leaned out of a doorway and thrust a leaflet into his hand. Mark stopped and stared at it, uncomprehendingly.

'It's a reading group,' the man explained. Only then did Mark notice, in the shop window beside him, three ziggurats of books, each one topped by a bestseller.

'Men only, but not in a weird way,' the man added, with a wry grin. He was a ruddy-faced chap with a hipster beard, a pot belly and a brushed cotton shirt with frayed cuffs and if they'd met in London ... well, there were no circumstances under which they *would* have met in London ... but Mark had already made the fatal mistake of meeting his eye.

'Third Thursday in the month. Here in the shop. Led by yours truly. And men only, not because we're discriminatory at all, just because I did some research and found out that ninety per cent of local book groups are run by and for ... anyway, I can see you're busy ... '

Mark realized that he had been shifting from foot to foot, fairly leaking impatience and anxiety. This was London behaviour.

'No, go on, then,' he invited the man, with a huge effort of will, 'what are you reading?'

He made a little bargain with himself. If it was something he'd heard of, something he might conceivably want to read, not self-help, not crime, not environmental bollocks, he'd give it a go.

'*Fear and Loathing in Las Vegas*. Hunter S ... '

'No way!' said Mark. 'That's on my list.'

Forty minutes later, he emerged onto the street again with a hessian bag full of paperbacks, seven stamps on his loyalty card and a new friend.

He was feeling so elated, he just strolled into a newsagent's, bold as you please and asked the girl behind the counter if they sold milk.

She barely looked up from her mobile, but nodded towards a glass-fronted, larder-style fridge. Mark grabbed a four-pinter without even checking the sell-by date. He was scanning the papers on the way back to the counter, thinking he'd take Harriet a *Guardian* and earn himself some Brownie points when his eye fell on the headline of *The Financial Times*.

FCA RECOMMENDS TOUGH NEW PENALTIES
FOR INSIDER DEALING

'Hey, mister? What the … ? Come back … you haven't paid for … '

25

Yvette

Getting off the train at Oxford station, Yvette couldn't see a single 'dreaming spire'. Not that she expected the whole city to look like it did in the brochure, but as she and Harriet trudged down a dreary arterial road towards the city centre, past kebab shops and backpackers' hostels, she couldn't help feeling disappointed. Harriet had assured her the city centre was only a ten-minute walk away, but in her brand-new heels that rubbed like hell, it seemed a lot further to Yvette. She had been excited about this day trip and chosen her outfit with care, but the moment she'd walked into The Button Factory kitchen at six that morning, in her best smart-casual trouser-suit, to find Harriet munching muesli in skinny jeans, a parka and a cashmere scarf, she'd realized she'd got it wrong. That first misapprehension had set the pattern for the day.

Once they crossed the river, though, the city started to look grander and Yvette perked up a bit. The roads were wider, the buildings older, the trees more mature. With one eye on Google Maps, Harriet navigated them past the Ashmolean Museum, then along an upmarket shopping street, where her guide was momentarily distracted by a shearling coat in the window of Toast, before leading Yvette down a quaint pedestrianised passage, lined with second-hand bookshops. They emerged at the other end into the world of Inspector Morse. Here at last were the dreaming spires; the domes and the clocktowers, the bridges and the lawns. They strolled down a wide avenue, past ancient buildings with gothic windows and gargoyles, all in slightly different shades of mellow golden stone.

Harriet pointed out a cute little church across the way, claiming to date from 1422 and Yvette thought that if her own local church had looked like this one, instead of like a young offenders institution with a phone mast, she might not have lost her faith aged fifteen. Then again, if she'd grown up round here, she'd have been a different person entirely, the kind of person Jade might yet become. The kind of person she could see all around her now, cycling lazily past in vintage cardigans, scrolling on their phones in oversized check shirts; hurrying to lectures with their Fjallraven backpacks. They didn't look so privileged or remarkable that they couldn't have passed for ordinary mortals in Whalley Range or Streatham, but flocking here, in their natural habitat, it was easy to see they were a breed apart.

'Oh, this is lovely!' said Yvette. 'Hang on, Harriet, let me just get a picture for Gaz.'

She scrabbled in her bag for her phone and when she looked up again, Harriet was striking a pose on the balustrade.

'Well, I meant the view, actually, but yeah, go on then ... ' She adjusted her camera setting, pushed her face close to Harriet's, and, holding the phone at arm's length, took a selfie with a bit of building in the background.

'There you go, Gaz,' she said, 'see what you're missing!'

'Hey, you haven't sent it, have you?' Harriet grabbed the phone out of Yvette's hands and squinted at the picture. 'Oh my God! I look like Quasimodo.'

'I shouldn't worry,' Yvette said. 'He won't even look at it, his head's that far up his arse with the album release.'

'Well, I hope he knows what he's missing,' said Harriet, piously. 'It's not every day your daughter gets into the best university in the country.'

'Oh, he's *dead* proud of her,' Yvette said, 'it's not that. It's just bad timing. We were all set to bring her stuff down for the start of term, but then the record company organized a press junket on the same . . . ' her voice trailed off. 'Is that bad . . . ? It's bad, isn't it? We should've brought her. *I* should anyway. What kind of mum doesn't jump at the chance to take her kid to Oxford uni?'

'The kind who's got an even bigger kid at home?'

Yvette wasn't sure whether to be grateful to her friend for letting her off the hook, or miffed at her for shifting the blame onto Gary. As his wife, she'd always taken that to be her prerogative. Just lately, though, Harriet seemed to think Gaz was fair game. She was forever rolling her eyes and mugging behind his back like they were in an episode of *Friends*. The other night, Harriet had got them all playing Scrabble in the snug – *Gaz* playing Scrabble – you had to pinch yourself. He'd turned out to have quite a knack for it too, but when he'd gone out with 'JISM' on a triple word score, Harriet had got all giggly and dragged the dictionary out and then what had started as drunken banter had turned quite testy, like it was about something else altogether. Yvette hadn't known where to put herself.

Even Mark had been squirming a bit by the end, and he was on a different planet lately.

Yvette was worried about Mark. He was blatantly in the throes of a mid-life crisis. Everything was an act with him at the moment, this whole new persona he'd adopted since they'd moved – the dodgy facial hair; the men-only book group – it just wasn't him. There was something eating him up inside, she could tell. She'd been trying to pluck up the courage to ask him about it, but she'd held back because ... well, because that was his wife's prerogative.

The truth was, six weeks in, Yvette was finding it all a bit much. Communal living had been fun at first – eating together, kicking back with a bottle of wine in the den – it had all felt like an extra-long holiday. But a holiday was only a holiday if it was a holiday *from* something and this wasn't. She wouldn't have minded if she felt like she had an equal stake in the place. She'd never noticed Harriet's controlling streak before they lived together – why would she? But Harriet swanned around The Button Factory like the big I Am. Oh, she was careful to stick to the rules they'd drawn up, democratically, in a spirit of self-mocking co-operation that first week. Stick to your shelf in the fridge, if you finish something off, put it on the shopping list, if one couple cook, the other washes up. Except, in practice, when it was Gary and Yvette's turn to wash up, Gary would more often than not get an 'urgent' phone call, wandering off with the tea towel over his shoulder, so that Harriet ended up deputizing for him. Yvette would then have to bite her tongue as Harriet leaned across her to re-rinse items that didn't meet her exacting hygiene standards, a power play of which Yvette was already beginning to tire.

When the house purchase in Chorlton had fallen through and it had looked like Yvette and Gary were going to be homeless, The Button Factory had seemed like the answer to their prayers. It was so spacious and elegant, like something off *Grand Designs* and Yvette hadn't really thought much beyond how they'd all look on Instagram, cheers-ing in the hot tub. But since they'd moved in, she found she missed their own space. She and Gaz had their en-suite bedroom and it was all very chi-chi, but it felt more like a hotel than a home. She longed for their little house in London – the cosy front room where they used to hole up and play records; the scrubby little patch of garden where they'd kicked a ball around with the girls; the narrow staircase, where she'd known, sneaking home after a tipsy night out, which stairs creaked and which didn't. The smell of the place when you opened the front door – that intimate scent of meals and shampoo and old carpet and family. She ached for that smell.

'So, if you guys didn't bring Jade's stuff down, who did?' Harriet asked her now. Yvette looked shifty.

'Juris,' she said. 'Don't tell Gaz, whatever you do, he thinks it was Ruby and Jordan, but they couldn't get the leave in the end.'

'I thought she'd dumped Juris.'

'Oh yeah, she has. She just let him do it for old time's sake, she told me.'

'Right,' Harriet nodded, not sounding entirely convinced. 'Oh well,' she added, 'I doubt Juris'll be much of a match for the sort of men she'll be dating now.'

'I'm hoping men won't be top of her list,' Yvette said grimly. 'She's here to get her degree.'

'Oh yeah, no, I know,' replied Harriet, 'I'm not talking about marrying her off or anything, only, if she's going to have meaningless rebound sex, it might as well be with a viscount…' She wiggled her eyebrows and Yvette laughed in surprise. Harriet used to be such a prude.

'Oh look, here we are…' Harriet consulted her phone and stopped in front of a daunting building, which looked, to Yvette, more like a medieval castle than a college.

'We just need to find the visitor's entrance…'

She marched ahead a little way and then ushered Yvette towards a forbidding-looking double door of heavily carved oak, one half of which was open a doubtful crack, as if to discourage time-wasters. A discreet sign beside it read:

MAGDALEN COLLEGE
*Visitors please report to
the Porter's Lodge*

'Oh no, Harriet…' Yvette hurried after her and laid a restraining hand on her arm, 'she's not at *Mag*dalen College she's at…'

'*Maudlin?*' Harriet turned back to her with an indulgent smile. Yvette winced as the penny dropped. Magdalen, pronounced Maudlin… Dur!

She followed her friend meekly through the gate.

Once signed in, they passed through sunny quadrangles where students sat around on the grass chatting, or texting; in some cases, even reading. Again, they were not quite the Sloane Rangers or Hooray Henrys Yvette had been expecting. There was the odd preppy jumper, the occasional Alice band, but as with the cyclists earlier, they looked surprisingly normal. None of them looked like Jade, though. Yvette couldn't see anyone else in an Adidas top, a high pony and drawn-on eyebrows. No doubt by Christmas her daughter would have knuckled under and adopted the dress code that would smooth her passage here – the dungarees and no-make-up make-up, the cute little plaits. The uniform that was supposed to signify bohemian independence but which, to Yvette, just conveyed another kind of conformity.

Jade was waiting for them on the landing. When she saw her mother, her expression changed in an instant from eager fresher to homesick five-year-old. Yvette held out her arms and her daughter came to her. They embraced for a long moment.

'Let me look at you.' Yvette put Jade at arm's length again and interrogated her face. 'You're very pale.'

'I'm fine, Mum.'

'Are you eating properly?'

'Mum!' Jade rolled her eyes and jerked her head towards Harriet, waiting patiently behind them.

'She can't help it, sweetie,' said Harriet kissing Jade on both cheeks, 'she's a mum. Worrying's in the job description. Great digs you've got here!'

Harriet indicated the grandeur of the stairwell with its carved wood bannister and stained-glass window.

'I know, it's well posh, isn't it? Wait till you see my room.' Jade held the door open for them.

'Isn't this nice?' Yvette enthused, although in truth, the sight of it made her want to cry – there was something unbearably touching about this centuries-old scholar's cell, with its sloping ceiling and mullioned windows, temporarily prettified with a purple duvet cover and a Banksy poster over the bed.

'Oh, it's to die for!' Harriet said, putting a hand to her breast. 'Ollie's halls in Portsmouth were nothing like this. I mean, don't get me wrong, they were perfectly nice, but this is just ... *gorgeous*!'

'Yeah, it'd be a bit wasted on Ollie, though, wouldn't it?' Jade said with a knowing grin and both women looked at her in surprise.

Yvette sat down on the side of the bed, eased her shoe off and gave her ankle a surreptitious rub.

'So,' she said, 'tell us all about it. Met any nice people?'

'One or two.'

'Anyone you can get on with?'

Jade shrugged non-committally.

'What about the course?'

'It's all just reading at the moment.'

'How about the food?' said Yvette, in slight desperation. 'What are the meals like?'

'They're OK,' Jade said.

'Do you all eat together in the dining room?' asked Harriet. 'It must be amazing – all that history ... '

Jade looked shifty.

'I've not really got into the swing yet, but yeah, I will do.'

'Not got into the swing of *eating*?' Yvette frowned. 'I thought you said they offered a vegan menu. You do know we're paying for it, whether you use it or not?'

'Yes, Mum, and I am going to use it, it's just, they don't serve supper till ... '

'*Supper?*'

'Dinner, tea, whatever! And if I'm out and about its just as easy to get a vegan burger at Leon's.'

Harriet looked a bit pained at the snarky tone their conversation was taking.

'I don't suppose you could point me in the direction of the loo, could you?' she murmured to Jade.

'Oh, yeah, sure,' said Jade, 'it's just down the end of the corridor. I'll show you ...'

Yvette closed her eyes. She could have kicked herself. As if the money mattered. She'd got one precious day to spend with her daughter and already they were squabbling. It just all felt so awkward in front of Harriet. Yvette regretted inviting her now, but when Gary had pulled out at the eleventh hour and Harriet had stepped up, it had seemed like a fun idea. A girly day out; shopping, a pub lunch, perhaps a ride in a punt. But that was before she'd seen the lost look on Jade's face. It had never occurred to her that her stoical daughter, who had stacked shelves for twelve months, who had played second fiddle to her big sister's fertility dramas, who had just quietly got on with being a bit of a genius, might find Oxford University a challenge. It was obvious, now that a heart-to-heart was called for but equally obvious that it wouldn't be happening today.

She glanced around the room, now, wondering how long the two of them would be gone, wondering how bad it would be to have a snoop. Cocking an ear towards the door, she slid the bedside drawer open. It was empty except for a phone charger and a half-used packet of contraceptive pills. She felt a brief pang, but told herself they didn't necessarily mean anything. Young women had sex lives. Christ, she'd not exactly been Sandra Dee herself. There was no other evidence; no mementos or love letters. *Love letters* – as if anyone wrote love letters anymore, least of all Juris. She glanced towards Jade's laptop, standing open on the desk in screen-saver mode. He might send emails, though . . .

She leaned forward and, with a glance towards the open door, touched the mouse. A worried-looking woman loomed onto the screen and she leaped back guiltily, before realizing it was her own face, captured on the webcam. She approached again and scrutinized the FaceTime call-log down the left-hand side of the screen. Eight calls over five hours – all to one account. Bound to be Juris. A rock settled in the pit of her stomach. She could hear footsteps and chatter in the corridor now. In a panic, she snapped the laptop shut, and sat back down on the bed, gathering her foot into her hand, pretended to examine the blister on her heel.

'Even the plumbing's medieval,' Harriet said, breezing back into the room, 'very quaint though. Gargoyles on the cistern, if you can believe . . . oh dear, is it still sore? Here, let me see if I've got a plaster . . . '

Harriet scrabbled in her bag.

'Thanks.'

'Do you still want to go to the pub for lunch?' she asked doubtfully. 'It's a bit of a walk.'

'I'll be fine,' said Yvette, with a martyred smile.

She wasn't fine. It turned out to be a mile-long hike down the riverbank. After stopping to remove the offending shoe, Yvette had given up trying to join in Harriet and Jade's chitchat and had hobbled in their wake, returning the bemused glances of passing joggers and cyclists with dirty looks. By the time she limped up the steps into The Cherwell Arms, she felt like a medieval peasant, shivering with cold, the soles of her feet black. Harriet was talking to the maître d'.

'... Well, we were *hoping* for a table by the window...' she wheedled.

Jade turned to Yvette.

'Isn't this lovel...?' she started to say, indicating the elegant riverside dining room, with its white table cloths and smart clientele, 'Mum, are you OK?'

'I'm fine!' lied Yvette, glassy-eyed. 'I might just pop to the loo and freshen up, though. Tell Harriet I'll be back in a minute.'

She hurried across the polished floorboards towards a door with a brass-rimmed porthole and a sign saying TOILETTES.

There were two other women in the ladies – both Harriet-types, in expensively understated clothes, one re-applying lipstick in the mirror, the other dispensing hand cream into her palm. They were comparing notes on their Fresher children – Matthew (PPE; All Souls) and Alice (English; Balliol). Neither seemed to notice Yvette squeeze past them into a vacant cubicle. She locked the door and sank down onto the seat with a silent sob of relief. She gathered a wodge of toilet paper into her hand and spat on it quietly, before rubbing it back and forth over first one, then the other grimy foot, but the dirt seemed only to become more ingrained, less distinguishable from her DNA.

26

Harriet

'Shouldn't you be going?' Harriet cast a pointed glance at the kitchen clock.

'God forbid Jack and Maisie have to wait *two minutes* at Macclesfield station,' Mark said, with a sardonic eye-roll at Yvette, who was slicing bread at the kitchen counter. Seeing the look on Harriet's face, however, he slurped the last of his coffee and grabbed his car keys.

'Yep. Outta here.'

'He's a good dad,' Yvette said, with a sentimental head tilt.

'Oh, he loves it!' Harriet snorted. 'He can't wait to see Jack.'

'What time do Ollie and Jade get in?' Yvette asked delicately. 'I could go for them, save Mark running a taxi service all day.'

'Oh, he doesn't mind,' Harriet replied, although the thought of Mark picking up Ollie on his own made her stomach clench with nerves. Even with all the progress father and son had made recently – and notwithstanding Mark's generosity in letting Ollie live in Moorcroft Road, rent free – there was still the likelihood of prickliness between them, which was bad enough at the best of times, but the last thing she needed on this, her big night.

'We can see, anyway,' she added, 'plenty of time yet . . . '

'I'm doing scrambled eggs,' Yvette said, 'want some?'

'Oh, no thanks, I'm way too nervous.'

'You are going to eat something, though, before tonight? 'Cos it won't get going till much later than you think.'

'Yeah, no, I will. I'll have something later,' said Harriet vaguely – although she knew she probably wouldn't. She'd gone up a dress size since they'd moved here as it was – one too many of Yvette's hearty shepherd's pies. Tonight, of all nights, she wanted to look hot.

'Can I get your opinion on my outfit, actually? After you've had your brunch, I mean. I don't know whether to go with the leggings and T-shirt or the dungarees and cami. I'm just worried dungarees might look a bit tragic on someone my age . . . '

Yvette gave Harriet a quizzical look.

'Not on *you*, obviously,' Harriet corrected herself quickly. 'You can *totally* carry them off . . . '

'Honestly, Harriet, I can't stress enough . . . I know it's being filmed and everything, but no one's going to *care* what anyone's wearing and if they do, it'll have been a flop. Everyone's here for the vibe. It should feel really loved-up.'

'I meant to say, actually, do you think we need to search people for drugs as they come in? Because it'll be my head on the block if there's a raid or something . . . '

'A *raid*?' Yvette smiled.

'You used to get raided, didn't you, back in the Nineties?'

'Yeah, but that was when thousands of people went to deathtrap warehouses and got off their faces. I don't think the local constabulary are going to be bothered about a little roof party in a private property, miles from anywhere.'

Harriet felt herself going pink.

'Look, Harriet,' said Yvette, patiently, 'I know you've done loads to help organize this, the minibuses and the portaloos and the accommodation and everything...'

'... I'm taking over, aren't I?' said Harriet glumly.

'No, it's not that. I mean...' Yvette smiled, 'you *are*, but... I get that. I do. It was your baby, this building, and it's a bit of a gamble having the album launch here...'

'A *gamble*?'

Yvette winced.

'Not a gamble. A brave move...'

'I don't think it's a gamble. I've thought of pretty much ev...'

'... I know you have and that's great. It is. Gary appreciates it. I appreciate it. It's the perfect venue and you've left nothing to chance, only...'

Harriet searched her friend's eyes and Yvette cast her face upwards as if trying to translate a difficult abstract concept to a foreigner just learning the language.

'... You *have* to leave something to chance. It's *got* to be a bit spontaneous, otherwise you'll kill the vibe. And I know we're kind of faking it for the cameras, which isn't what happened back in the day, but once you're in the groove... you've just got to let go, do you get what I mean? You've just got to *go* with it?'

'No, I do. I get it.' Harriet paused, pursed her lips, then murmured half to herself, 'Think I'm going to stick with the leggings.'

Harriet left Yvette to her breakfast and went to the bedroom, to give her outfits one last try. She pulled on the leggings and posed in front of the full-length mirror, sticking her bum out at different angles. It wasn't for anyone in particular, she told herself, just for her own satisfaction. OK, that wasn't quite true. Tonight, of all nights, when Gary was going to be the big draw, when everyone at the gig would be basking in his celebrity, she craved some signal from him, some secret acknowledgement of her specialness. Just a glance, a secret smile to acknowledge they had history. *History* being the operative word.

There would be no more shenanigans – of that Harriet was certain. But surely no harm could come from fantasizing? She couldn't seem to stop herself, anyway. There was the one where she and Gary bumped into each other in the corridor after the set – she'd be buzzing, he'd be gagging for it. He'd bundle her into the bathroom, peel off her sweaty T-shirt and . . .

Or the other one. Trippier; more romantic. They'd meet by chance on the roof, after all the plebs had gone to the Premier Inn (which she'd had the foresight to block-book). As dawn broke over the Pennines, he'd thank her for everything she'd done to make his comeback gig the best day of his life, one thing would lead to another and before they knew it . . .

That's all they were, though, fantasies. And purely sexual ones at that. She didn't flatter herself that Gary was in love with her. *Christ* knew, she wasn't with him. She'd never have suggested they all move in together otherwise. She valued her friendship with Yvette too much for that – she still woke up in a cold sweat when she thought of the careless way she and Gary had betrayed the sweetest woman in the world. Just the memory of it, hazy is it was, made Harriet cringe with shame.

No harm, though, surely, in utilizing Gary's proximity, *leveraging* it, to use one of Mark's favourite words, in order to pep things up in the marital bedroom? Mark didn't need to know what was going on inside her head.

She was gazing at herself in the bathroom mirror, trying to work out whether her frown lines went away when she wasn't smiling, when she heard the toot of a horn in the car park below. She threw on some jeans and yesterday's T-shirt and hurried downstairs to greet Jack and Maisie.

'This place is *so* amazing!' Maisie said. She stood on tiptoe and puckered her lips somewhere in the vicinity of Harriet's cheek.

'Hey, Mum, how are you?' said Jack, giving her an easy hug before making to pick up their bags.

'It's OK, I'll bring those,' said Mark, 'you guys go ahead and do the tour and don't forget to tell your mother she's a genius.'

As they made their way up the stairs, the throb of Gary's bassline started to shake the foundations of the building, quickly followed by the thwack of John's drums.

'Is that them?' Maisie turned to Jack, wide-eyed.

''Fraid so,' said Harriet, her face beaming with reflected glory, 'that's in a fully sound-proofed studio as well, so you can imagine how loud it's going to be tonight.'

She was proud of how nonchalantly she said this – she might as well have had I'M WITH THE BAND printed on her T-shirt. Jack and Maisie both looked suitably impressed. Yet as she led the way through the lobby, the level of reverb was alarming. She could feel it jarring her whole skeleton as she walked up the stairs, sense the molecules in her body rearranging themselves in time with it. It was one thing knowing that there was going to be a gig on their roof terrace tonight, it was another to feel this pent-up energy pulse through the building deep into the substrate of the Pennines. She remembered the sour face on the jobsworth at the town hall who had granted her a temporary entertainment licence – how casually she had signed a form agreeing to keep the sound levels below thirty-four decibels adjusted, whatever that meant.

27

Gary

The band was huddled behind a stack of Marshall speakers, waiting to go on. Gary's heart was beating out of his chest but he felt invincible. He felt like Diego Maradona and Cristiano Ronaldo rolled into one; he felt like Bob Dylan at Budokan, Mick Jagger at Altamont, Ian Brown at Spike Island; he felt like a master of war, Jumpin' Jack Flash. He was the resurrection and the fucking life. This was what it had all been in aid of, what he'd chucked in teaching for, what he'd put Yvette through the mill for.

A bit of neck hair had got caught in his guitar strap but he didn't dare release it in case he nudged the Fender out of tune. He made a low gargling noise in the back of his throat and patted his pocket for his lucky pick.

The dance music stopped abruptly, the lights dimmed, the crowd hummed with anticipation.

'Ladeez an' gennelmen ...' the disembodied voice of their guesting DJ was laden with ironic showbiz-ery, 'I give you, the one-ah, the only, K ... M ... '

The rest was noise.

Gary had been a caged beast all day. They'd had a rehearsal late morning and it had gone fine, but there came a point when the songs weren't getting any tighter and the band members were rubbing each other up the wrong way. That was when you had to call time on it for a bit. Go and have a kip or a wander, or in Gary's case, a fag. He went to the kitchen and found Yvette, yakking on her mobile. Seeing him, she half turned away and lowered her voice. If he hadn't known better, he'd have thought she had a fancy man, but she was sound as a pound, his missus. Not like him. He winced inwardly at the memory of his most recent indiscretion. He'd honestly not had that in his mind when he's suggested he and Harriet go back to Declan's.

Who knew a side-effect of his rediscovered rock stardom would be a wandering cock? It wasn't like he hadn't had the opportunity when he'd been at Beresford Academy. There'd been no shortage of doe-eyed student teachers in the staffroom offering him green tea with benefits, but he hadn't had the heart back then; or maybe the balls. Yet now that he really needed to keep it in his trousers for the sake of … everything really; his career, his marriage, the roof over his fucking head, he'd managed to give Harriet the idea he was up for a fling. His lip curled in self-disgust, he was going to be a grandad, for God's sake.

'That was our Ruby,' said Yvette.

Gary looked up.

'They'll not be coming after all. She's really sorry. She says she'll give you a ring later.'

'Is the baby all right?'

'It's fine,' Yvette said. 'It's just a bit on the small side and the doctor said she should avoid strenuous activity.'

''*Course* she should. Jesus.'

'She thought you might be disappointed.'

'Well, I am, obviously. But it's a no-brainer. They can't come if it's not good for the b...' He couldn't bring himself to say the word.

Their eyes met, both clearly envisaging a worst-case scenario that had haunted them since Ruby first announced her pregnancy. Gary felt irritated with Yvette for not being up front about the phone call. She did this. Tried to protect him from stuff, like he was a little kid or something. As if the *gig* mattered, compared to...

'Jade'll be here in an hour, anyway,' she said, cheerfully. 'She's coming with *Ollie* if you can believe it...'

'Uh-oh. Found herself a posh lad at Oxford, has she? Oh well, anyone's got to be better than Juris...'

'No,' Yvette said, with an exasperated laugh, '*Ollie*. Ollie Pendleton.'

She jerked her head to indicate Harriet and Mark's quarters in the house. Then, seeing the look of perplexity on Gary's face, 'I know. They're mates, apparently. It's quite nice, though, don't you think?'

Gary shrugged. He wasn't sure which of their two lads Ollie was – the Mark wannabe with the flash job or the delinquent with the personality disorder; neither was son-in-law material in his book. He knew better than to say that to Yvette, though.

He patted his shirt pocket.

'Do you know where I've left my fags?'

'You're supposed to be giving up.'

'Oh yeah, 'course,' he said, 'on the day I front my first gig in eighteen years.'

She sighed.

'They're in your denim jacket on the back of the bedroom door.'

'*A-one, two, three, four,*' John counted them in and in no time the building was pounding, the lights were pulsing and The KMA were chugging and funking their way through 'Ravin' Mavis', their most reliable floor-filler. The crowd went berserk, arms waving, heads bobbing, faces turned heavenwards like the acolytes they were. They played the seven-inch version and then segued straight into 'Turn on a Sixpence', which took the crowd to a whole new level of demented flailing, accompanied by the blowing of whistles and, in the case of a few die-hard middle-aged fans, the ill-advised stripping off of T-shirts. Gary finished with an ironic, punk-style scissor kick and the place erupted.

He grabbed a towel from behind the speaker, wiped his face and chest, poured a stream of water into his mouth from a plastic bottle, then went to the front of the stage, shielding his eyes from the lights and took a look.

'Hiya,' he said, with a smirk. The audience went mad. Credit to them, they'd really hit the brief. It could have been 1989 out there. He could see Aztec-patterned sports shirts and Fila tracksuits; he could see smiley tees and bucket hats. He could see bowl cuts and feather cuts and mullets – and that was just the women. If they'd called up the baggy army and said, 'Your country needs you,' they'd not have got a better turnout. Funny thing was, a lot of them looked like kids – which was to say, under thirty, which was to say, people who hadn't even been born when The KMA's first album came out, so either Declan's girlfriend had invited all her hipster mates or the PR had got a load of Instagram influencers to turn up. Either way the video was going to look the part. Gary had been worried the whole thing might come across a bit panto – bunch of old twats trying to turn the clock back with a rooftop rave, but there was nothing said 'relevance' like a twenty-two-year-old in a D-cup.

'Right then,' he said, readjusting his guitar and an excited murmur went round the audience. He'd taped the setlist to the front of the stage, but he wouldn't be needing it. It was second nature, this, like riding a bike. He turned and nodded at the lads. John raised his sticks above his head, and they were off again, freestyling to 'Copper Night Rate'. Gary went over and duetted with Macca, bent double over the keyboard like a mad professor, then they both turned to the crowd, who cheered their approval. Next, Gary backed up, using his guitar like a paddle, and paid homage to John, sat drumming away with a look on his face like he was receiving holy communion and a blow job at the same time. Another cheer of affection. Finally, Gary made his way back to the front of the stage and milked all the love that was out there just for him. He felt like he'd died and gone to heaven. They played three or four crowd-pleasers and finished the first half with 'Coming Up', their biggest hit. The crowd trailed down the fire escape towards the portaloos and the merch stands, the lads in the band high-fived each other and filed off stage.

It was a walk in the park, as far as Gary was concerned.

First half: warm the crowd up with the old stuff; second half, blow their tiny minds with the sheer brilliance of the new stuff. *The Other Cheek*; both sides, played in album order, no dumbing down. Naturally, Declan had disagreed, disagreement being in his job description. *He'd* been for smuggling the new material in among the old hits so as not to freak out the fan base. Gary thought this approach was for wusses, and said so, with perhaps more finger-jabbing than had been strictly helpful to his case. At their age, he'd told Declan, they couldn't afford to fuck about. They were after a second career, not a comeback album that got them on Graham Norton and then sank without trace. He'd got his way in the end, set-wise, but as they trooped downstairs for a well-earned breather, Gary's adrenaline levels were as high, but no higher, than the stakes.

Yvette had been right about the fags. They were in the pocket of his denim jacket, two floors up, on the back of the bedroom door. Finding his lighter was another matter. Gary ransacked the bedroom drawer, checked his dressing-gown pocket, even got down on his hands and knees and peered under the bed. He suspected Yvette had hidden it on purpose – well, the joke would be on her when he had a stroke from the stress of looking for it and she had to push him round in a fucking wheelchair. Surely to God he deserved five minutes to calm his nerves? Five minutes on his tod, on the roof, to get his head straight for tonight. He was stomping back down to the kitchen to light his fag off the gas ring when he remembered that he'd seen a box of matches next to a scented candle in the communal toilet. He barged in, then stopped short. Harriet was in front of the mirror, her mouth frozen in that involuntary 'O' that women made when they were putting on lipstick. An 'O' that, in this case, brought shameful memories instantly to mind. Their eyes had scarcely met in the mirror, before he was backing out again, apologizing.

'It's OK, Gaz, I'm done, you can come in ... '

'No, you're all right, I'm not even ... I was looking for a light, actually.'

Jesus! As excuses went it sounded flimsy as fuck.

'Oh, a *light*, of course. Why didn't you say ... ?' She pursed her lips and looked up at him all sexy and sceptical. Christ, she smelled good – no one had the right to smell that classy and that sexy at the same time. He gestured towards the window ledge, where there was indeed a box of matches next to the scented candle, but instead of reaching it for him, she shrank backwards, inviting him to lean across her and fetch it himself. His arm brushed her breast, and by the time he'd taken hold of the matchbox, her hand was on his belt.

It might have been complacency, or it might have been that they'd overdone the stimulants, but the second half didn't get off to the greatest start. The lights went down and instead of the reverent hush that had greeted them in the first half, there was chatting and laughter at the back. Then, just as John was counting them in on 'If It Be Your Won't', someone dropped a glass and Gary lost it and had to start again. They got into a bit of a groove after that and the crowd got dancing but not really with the same commitment they'd shown in the first half and Gary could see Declan out of the corner of his eyes, giving him 'I told you so' looks from the mixing desk.

But then then they did 'Turn the Other Cheek' and the

crowd went off. It was like magic, like alchemy. Something about that song, its catchiness, its gorgeous chiming melody hooked the past up to the present in a way that everyone suddenly seemed to get. It was 1989 and it was 2018. The young were old and the old were young. It was as if the last thirty years hadn't happened. Like there'd been no shoddy compromises and no disillusionment, no chucking people on the dole, or cutting coke with rat poison, no knocking down The Haçienda to build luxury flats; no 'Things Can Only Get Better' when you know things will only get worse. No city bankers, no bloody learning outcomes. He looked out into the mosh pit and his eyes fell on his missus, dancing like no one was watching, eyes closed, arms ravelling over her head like she was chucking stars up in the sky and she could have been sixteen again, she looked that carefree and fresh and fucking beautiful. She was a diamond, that woman; a keeper. He knew it now like he'd never known it and he wished, Christ, he *wished* he'd not let her down.

28

Mark

Mark had never really got it; the fuss about rave music, house, techno, whatever you wanted to call it. He'd always been more of a Blur man; Oasis at a pinch. Britpop, anyway. Until Gary's comeback gig, that is, when suddenly it had all made perfect sense.

The drugs had helped. Not that he was a complete novice in that department – he'd tried weed and coke, of course he had – he'd even tried magic mushrooms at boarding school, to no great effect. But hand on heart, he'd never found a stimulant that was more to his taste than a pint of craft ale or the scent of Harriet's hair on a summer's day. Until now. How in the name of God had he never tried Ecstasy before? Well, he knew how, actually. He was the wrong demographic. Too young for the second summer of love, too old for the third (had there *been* a third?); too middle class; too straight; he hesitated to say too *male*, because it was Gary that had slipped him an E when he'd been hanging with the band, about an hour before they were due on stage and blokes didn't really get more macho than Gary.

'See how you go with that,' he'd said with a wink, and Mark had looked down at the parma violet in his hand.

'Are you taking the piss?'

But he'd downed it anyway, with a vodka cocktail, for good measure. For a while, Mark was convinced Gary *had* been taking the piss – the pill didn't seem to be having any effect and it wouldn't have been the first time Gary had set him up. But by the time he'd had a bit of a mingle on the roof terrace, and then a bit of a dance, the band were due on stage and something magical had started to happen.

They'd been right at the front – him, Jack, Maisie and Harriet; a family again – which was heartwarming enough before you factored in any chemical high. He'd spotted Ollie lurking somewhere with Jade, too, which was an added bonus. He couldn't figure out what was going on there but whatever it was, it had to be a step in the right direction for his sociopath son. Theirs seemed an unlikely friendship; then again, he didn't really know Jade. If he was honest, he hadn't paid her much attention, preferring the easy charm of her older sister, who he'd spent more time with, thanks to Ruby and Harriet's little fertility club. At one time he'd almost had a word about it. It never seemed quite right, to him, for Harriet to be hand in glove with someone ten years her junior, especially when Yvette was left out of the loop. There had been a time when he forever seemed to be interrupting cosy little conflabs about conception-friendly diets or positive envisioning. You'd have thought *they* were the sisters, not Ruby and Jade. Then again, as Harriet never tired of reminding him, she was closer in age to Ruby than she was to him – by a year, he pointed out, a year! At any rate, the upshot had been that since the kids had grown up, Jade had seemed a bit remote, a vague presence in the background with whom he'd had few dealings, except for the one time he'd asked her, via Yvette, to fill out a client survey about a new diffusion trainer range because she fell into the right demographic. It was only when he'd heard that she'd got into Oxford, that it occurred to him there must have been more to her than met the eye.

As a matter of fact, what with Ollie's tattoos and Jade's chavvy style, the two of them fitted in better here than Mark did. Despite kindly fashion advice from Yvette, he wasn't really loving the baggy vibe. His somewhat portly good looks required well-cut clothing to show them to their best advantage. In loose-cut jeans and a smiley T-shirt he looked a foot shorter and a stone heavier and the bucket hat had been the final indignity.

Having two left feet didn't help, but something was starting to happen now. Slowly, unaccountably, he was coming to feel less alienated; more comfortable in his skin. He was starting to feel the love. Everything was going to be OK, he told himself, repeating it like a mantra until he started to believe it. Everything was going to be OK because no one here was judging him; everything was going to be OK because his family was reunited, in relative harmony, against all the odds; everything was going to be OK because this was it now; no more babies – *ever*; everything was going to be OK because he was as crazy about his wife as he had been on the day he'd met her; everything was going to be OK because he'd escaped the shallow world of PR, without the sky falling in. And as the now-familiar intro of The KMA's 'Coming Up' filled his ears and he started to nod along to its shuffling, optimistic beat, a big involuntary smile broke over his face. Life wasn't, after all, the hard-knock grind his mother had gleefully warned him about, but a mind-altering space-voyage of love.

Moving as one with the crowd, his face gurning with happiness under the strobe lights, Mark felt his heart open up like a flower. He held the backs of his hands up in front of his eyes and it seemed to him his veins reconfigured themselves into strings of Christmas lights, carrying a pulse of sheer joy around his body. Everything was going to be OK.

Driving to Chapters in Macclesfield, twenty-four hours later for the inaugural meeting of the men's reading group, Mark was feeling less than OK. His euphoria had long since evaporated and he'd had some twat in a Range Rover up his arse most of the way. It hadn't been there and then it had, looming in his rear-view mirror, drawing dangerously close, then dropping back again. For a while he thought it was just a macho driver impatient to overtake, but even when he moved onto a straight section of road with plenty of room, it continued to tail him.

Or did it? He'd been feeling peculiar all day. Not just peculiar; wrung-out, melancholy and a little bit paranoid. It was to be expected. You couldn't have an up without a down and everyone in The Button Factory had looked a bit green around the gills that morning; everyone except Harriet, anyway. It must have been getting light by the time she'd finally made it to bed, but she'd been up by eleven, bright-eyed and bushy tailed, brewing coffee and asking anyone who came in the kitchen if they wanted a bacon butty, a phrase which tripped uneasily from her Home Counties lips. Mark had groaned in response, and then sprinted to the sink, where he'd braced himself for several seconds against the desire to vomit.

'Ollie not up yet?' he'd asked, eventually, after downing a couple of glasses of water and perching gingerly at the breakfast bar.

'He left a while ago,' said Harriet. Mark looked up guiltily, but there was no edge to her tone, no implied 'where the hell were you when he needed a lift to the station?'

Instead, she rubbed his back soothingly and smiled at him as though, for once, he had done something right.

'That's a pity,' Mark said, and to his surprise, he found he meant it.

Mark pulled up outside Chapters bookshop and the Range Rover accelerated past, nipping through an amber traffic signal before he could check the number plate. He could see a dim light coming from inside the shop, which suggested he had got the right night. Damn. He peered at himself in the vanity mirror. He looked like death.

'You should go!' Harriet had urged him. 'It's a great way to meet like-minded people.'

'Like-minded *men*,' he'd corrected her gloomily.

'Even better,' she'd beamed.

He'd smiled wanly and she'd taken his cheeks in her hands and kissed him on the nose. She was a changed woman, his wife, since they'd moved up here and as much as this warmed Mark's heart, it was also freaking him out a little bit. This new, sexed-up, confident persona of hers seemed to have brought out his ambivalence. All his uncomplicated alpha-maleness had deserted him. The man who had given more PowerPoint presentations than you could shake a stick at, who was hailed for his after-dinner speeches and his camaraderie, now felt intimidated at the thought of a men's book group in a provincial book shop. It had come to this.

He glanced once again towards the shop's dimly lit frontage.

'Fuck it,' he muttered and had started the engine to make good his escape when the door pinged open and the bookshop owner appeared on the pavement, resplendent in a Ramones T-shirt and a pair of ill-fitting Levi's, cranking his hand to indicate that Mark should lower the window.

'I thought it was you! Great you could make it. Don't worry, you're fine to leave your car here after five thirty.'

Mark smiled grimly, unplugged his seatbelt and got out. He followed his new friend into the shop and through to the children's section at the back, where three fellow bibliophiles were reclining awkwardly on a cluster of brightly coloured beanbags.

'Good OK, well,' their host said, 'it looks like it'll just be the five of us, so we might as well get cracking. Shall we start by introducing ourselves? You all know me, of course. Steve. Steve Norris – aspiring novelist and proud Maxonian ... ' he turned to Mark, 'that's a native of Macclesfield, by the way. And everyone, this is our latest recruit, Mark. Mark's just moved here from ... ?'

'London,' muttered Mark, as if it weren't written all over him. 'Great to meet you all.'

There was an awkward pause.

'Colin Grimshaw,' said a portly chap in an Icelandic sweater, 'IT consultant of this parish.'

'John Mottershead,' declared a dour bloke in a fleece, folding his arms across his chest as if reluctant to divulge more.

'... And Piers. Piers Cooper.' A snaggle-toothed fellow in suit trousers and a UCLA hoodie leaned forward and shook Mark's hand. 'Solicitor, two doors up. For all your conveyancing needs...'

'Ah,' said Mark, 'too late for me, alas, I've done all the moving I plan to.'

'So, you're a convert, are you?' asked Piers.

'A convert?'

'You like it up here? You're here to stay?'

'Oh... yes. Very much. The whole lifestyle change is proving very, er, beneficial.'

'And whereabouts are you? In the town, or...?'

'Ah, no. A little way out... I don't know if you know it? The Button Factory.'

There was a palpable cooling of the atmosphere. The other men exchanged glances.

'What...?' Mark smiled warily.

'Waco, you mean?' John said. He nudged Colin and smirked.

'Now then, chaps,' Steve, the bookshop owner, frowned.

'That's what they're calling it,' John shrugged, 'you know, after the ranch in Texas where that cult leader slept with all the women and then shot the place up.'

'Oh, well, you've got the wrong end of the stick there,' Mark said with a nervous laugh. 'We're not a cult, I can assure you. Far from it! We're just a bunch of like-minded people who decided to throw in our lot together and rescue a local heritage building from the bulldozer.'

'So, it's *not* a commune?' Steve looked slightly disappointed.

'Er, well, it depends what you mean by... we do have some communal *facilities*. We wanted to make the most of the building's unusual layout, and focus on self-sufficiency – grow our own veggies and so forth, so... ' He looked around the group with a winning smile.

'*I* heard you've got a jacuzzi,' said John.

'Ah, well, yes, but... it's solar heated!'

'And a music venue in the basement.'

'It's a recording studio and we did obtain all the necessary permissions. It's fully sound-proofed... '

'So, how d'you explain that bloody cacophony last night?' interrupted Piers, his demeanour now distinctly chilly, 'because I live at least a mile away and I didn't get a wink of sleep.'

'Oh,' muttered Mark, 'sorry to hear that. I suppose it might have been a bit louder than we intended. It won't be happening again, I can... '

'An-y-way... ' Steve interrupted, 'it's twenty past, guys. Shall we get on with our discussion? *Fear and Loathing in Las Vegas*. A drug-fuelled, counter-culture road trip to the dark heart of the American Dream... anyone?'

Mark could hear his housemates cavorting as he parked the car. He glanced up and saw that the fairy lights on the roof terrace were on. Steam was billowing from the hot tub and he could hear the throb of dance music and the occasional shriek of mirth. No wonder the locals thought it was orgy central. The trouble was, now that the Ecstasy had worn off, Mark couldn't help feeling a certain sympathy with Piers, or whatever his name was. It was fair enough to have a licensed one-off event, but it was a bit much to have this sort of thing going on every night. The trouble was, some of Gary's mates didn't seem to have got the memo. Two days on, they were still hanging round like a bad smell; who knew where they were sleeping? He'd have to have a word. It wasn't on. Harriet had her reputation to think of; although you wouldn't know it to see her behaviour. Mark knew she'd had a sheltered upbringing and he was all for her playing catch-up, if it made her happy. But there was such a thing as discretion. If they wanted to be accepted in the town, they needed to play by its rules. Luckily, as far as salvaging reputations went, Mark was a pro. He'd reach out to the local community. Get Gary to make a charity donation from the proceeds of the gig; get Radio Macclesfield round for an exclusive KMA interview ... maybe even a live set. They were bloody lucky, if they only but knew it, to have a PR professional in their midst.

Mark went up to the kitchen. The lights were blazing and an open bottle of tequila stood on the work surface next to a melting tray of ice, several halved limes and a packet of king-size Rizlas. He poured himself a large slug, knocked it back in one and thumped his fist on his chest. He was going to go up there and read the bloody riot act. Someone had to ... He was halfway out of the room when his eye fell on a bundle of envelopes propped against the microwave. A Post-it note in Ollie's hand read:

Dad

Mark approached it apprehensively, plucked off the elastic band and flicked through junk mail, postcards, utility bills until he reached two weightier envelopes near the bottom. Both were addressed to him. One – cream, watermarked – bore the logo of the accountants who had been tasked with auditing Mark's old firm; the other – manila, flimsy, the addressee's name visible through a cellophane window, carried the imprimatur of the Serious Fraud Office.

29

Yvette

Yvette woke to a blur of white sky pressing against the Velux. For a second, she thought she must have died and gone to purgatory. But it couldn't be purgatory because Gary was lying next to her, the duvet rising and falling in time with his snores and there was no way the Almighty would have let him off the hook, not after last night. He'd have been heading straight for the other place. Besides, as Yvette knew only too well there *was* no God but Gary, no greater calling than The KMA. And it only took the briefest of flashbacks to last night's festivities for Yvette to recognize that what she was experiencing wasn't a spiritual reckoning, it wasn't even the perimenopause; it was the bitch of a comedown. They didn't call it Suicide Tuesday for nothing.

She swung her legs over the side of the bed, prompting a lightshow in her head and an overwhelming urge to vomit, but by the time she had reached the bathroom, there were other priorities.

She sat on the toilet, dry-retching, even as she peed. Looking up, she caught sight of herself in the mirror tiles she'd disliked from the moment she'd set eyes on them.

'What?' she asked her reflection.

State of you! it replied.

Fair point. Piggy eyes, flabby chin; it could have been her mother sitting there.

Yvette looked huffily away. She noticed a rogue flake of dried grout on a nearby tile, and set about scraping it off with her thumbnail.

What are you even doing? her reflection demanded to know.

'Multi-tasking?' she replied, hopefully.

That's not a task.

'Oh, shut up!'

Bitch had a point. When it came to displacement activities, Yvette was a past master. Since they'd moved here, she had colour-coded her wardrobe, de-pilled her woollen jumpers, sorted Gary's sock drawer and taken umpteen bags of jumble to the charity shop. But when had she last performed a task worthy of the name? She was done being a mother, done being a teaching assistant; she was too far away, alas, to take on a meaningful role as a grandmother. Even her wifely obligations had dwindled to a routine fortnightly fuck. Now that the practicalities of the move had been completed and Gary's ego cossetted through the album launch, what was she even for?

She decided she was going into town to get herself a job. Heading for the kitchen to rehydrate and get a caffeine hit first, the buzz of conversation stopped her in her tracks. She could hear laughter, shouting, shushing and the clinking of glasses. These were not early risers with regrets, like her, but twenty-four-hour party people who'd not yet gone to bed.

She could hear Declan's girlfriend's Texan bray and the needy guffaws of various hangers-on who ought to have known better. It didn't do any of them any credit. She despised them all but not as much as she despised herself for hanging back, scared to go into her own kitchen and put the kettle on.

She scuttled back to the bedroom. How had she allowed this to happen? What had made her think it was a good idea to give up their little house for this great big hangar of a building, where nothing was hers and she couldn't even make herself a coffee without having to barge her way through a bunch of freeloaders.

She clattered open the blind and barged around the bedroom, half hoping Gary might stir and ask her what was up, but the best she got was a leg flung over the side of the duvet, a euphonious fart and then a lip-smacking retreat into the pillow.

Feeling more and more defiant, Yvette wriggled into her smart-casual linen mix pants and a nice stripy blouse, which she buttoned just far enough for decorum's sake but no further. She spent ten minutes on her make-up and another five trying to tame her hair before giving herself a last appraising glance in the mirror. 'Mutton dressed as lamb,' she could hear her mother saying in her head.

She was poised to refasten a button or two when something stopped her. She tilted her chin this way and that, gave her reflection a defiant smile and murmured, 'Fuck it!' before snatching her car keys off the chest of drawers and fairly flouncing out of the room.

It was muggy outside and the sky was still a glaring white. Rain would be a relief. Yvette got into the little five-year-old

Ford KA she'd bought when the move had cost less than they'd feared, and reversed out from between Declan's Audi Quattro and a souped-up Ford Capri, whose owner was no doubt even now scoffing the last of her cornflakes.

The plastic-smelling tomb of the car made her retch again and as she turned into the lane she opened both windows and put her foot down, taking great gulps of hawthorn-scented air. Taking a bend at speed, she had to swerve to avoid a couple of kids, strolling side by side along the verge, deep in conversation. She was about to accelerate away, when she realized she'd nearly mown down Jade and Ollie.

'Jesus, Mum!' Jade jogged up to the car and poked her head through the passenger window.

'Sorry! I was just trying to clear my ... oh, never mind. Get in.'

She flipped the front seat and the two of them clambered into the rear. They drove for a few seconds in silence.

'Fancy just going off like that?!' Yvette said.

'You were asleep.'

'You could have woken me. I'd have done you some breakfast. Did you not think to say goodbye, even?'

'Mum, you didn't go to bed till stupid o'clock. 'Course we're not going to wake you, state you were in last night.'

Yvette pursed her lips.

'Plus, it's term-time,' Jade reminded her, 'I'd have thought you'd *want* me back in Oxford. I only came because you said Dad'd be gutted if I didn't.'

'Well, he would've been,' Yvette insisted, convincing neither of them.

There was silence, then a nervous cough from Ollie.

'I'm really glad *I* came, Yvette,' he said leaning forward. 'Thanks for inviting me. I'm going to download the new album when it comes out.'

Yvette caught his eye in the mirror and smiled. Who'd have thought, Ollie Pendleton – wannabe goth; sociopath; evil twin – pouring oil on troubled waters?

Yvette was signalling left for the station pay and display when Jade put a hand on her shoulder.

'You're all right, Mum, just drop us here.'

'Oh! I thought we might manage a quick coffee.'

Jade pulled an apologetic face.

'I've got a tutorial at four and if I miss my connection I'm screwed.'

Yvette shrugged and as her passengers clambered out, the truth of it hit her – both daughters were lost to her now, Ruby to motherhood, Jade to academia; be careful what you wish for. She plastered a brave smile on her face and was preparing to wave them off when Jade flung the passenger door open again, and, leaning across, bestowed a tender kiss on her mother's cheek.

'See you soon, Mum, yeah?'

Yvette's eyes misted over and she nodded her head briefly, setting her jaw against tears.

One hour or two? Yvette dithered in front of the ticket machine in the short stay car park. Probably two, given the task she had set herself. She fed in a fistful of change and took her ticket back to the car. Fat drops of rain were falling now and she didn't want to be doing the rounds looking like a drowned rat. She made a dash for Starbucks. It was empty except for a table of school-run mums and a bloke with a laptop. Yvette thought fondly of Déjà Brew, where she and Harriet used to go after yoga; its quirky retro scuzziness. Here, the barista was too busy polishing the coffee nozzles to bother serving her, despite there being no one else waiting. She might as well have been invisible for all the notice the yummy mummies took when she peered into their buggies and clucked in grandmotherly fashion at their not-very-prepossessing infants. So much for the warm and hospitable North. It was all just hype. Gary had sold her this move as a return to their roots; to authenticity and belonging. But it could have been Croydon for all the sense of belonging she felt. The high streets, the people, the atmosphere – all were interchangeable. Everywhere was the same when it came down to it. All that mattered was how you felt inside, and Yvette felt redundant; under-used, unseen.

She took a sip of coffee, scrolled on her phone, wrote Jade a text; then deleted it. If only she had sought out her daughter last night, sat her down, *talked* to her, but she'd been too busy trying to recapture her own youth; off her face from eight o'clock, boogying in a mini skirt after she'd sworn blind to Harriet that looking sexy wasn't the point. The shame of it. Not content with squandering her first chance to get close to Jade on the daytrip to Oxford, she'd just thrown away a second. What if it was her last? What if her daughter dropped out of uni and ran away to Latvia because her mother had been too up herself to listen? Then again, Jade had seemed happy at the weekend – more settled somehow. What kind of mother couldn't read her own daughter? True enough, Jade had always been more self-contained than Ruby, but the thought that she had more to say to Ollie Pendleton, tattooed misfit and parental scourge, than she did to her own mother, didn't say much for Yvette's parenting, did it?

Then again… she remembered meeting Ollie's eye in the rear-view mirror on the way here; the empathy in his brief, shy glance; the tact. What a contrast to the cross little boy and scowling teenager he had been. Yvette had always suspected there was another side to him and here had been the proof. Maybe in some small way, her intervention long ago had helped bring that about.

Rain lashed the window now and a polystyrene food carton flipped its way along the pavement in a sudden gust of wind. How jammy was Gary that it had held off last night? There'd been no plan B. Just a blithe KMA-style confidence that a make-or-break rooftop gig in the North-West of England in October would be blessed with dry weather, which of course it had been.

Yvette took her phone out of her pocket and flicked through her photo stream while she waited for her coffee to cool. She'd taken more pictures than she remembered, some blurry, others surprisingly good. Scrolling back and forth, she couldn't help smiling. It had been quite a night. If it hadn't quite managed to replicate the carefree spirit of their youth, it had at least been a shot in the arm for their middle-aged selves. The atmosphere had been one of almost manic urgency, an awareness that time was speeding up, that there were no second chances; that moments like this must be seized. She flicked back and forth. Loved-up faces loomed at the camera – Mark, bless him – he'd not thank her for that one; Harriet, pupils the size of saucers, looking unfeasibly youthful and annoyingly pretty. A gang of hardcore fans from the old days, one of whom Yvette had dated, still fancied himself just as much now, she could tell, despite a tragic comb-over. Back and forth her finger whizzed, zooming in here and there to check if that was so and so from wherever. The outfits were something else.

She was deleting some of the howlers, when her eye fell on a snap she didn't recall having taken. It was Jack, with his arm round Declan's girlfriend Meadow, their faces lowered intimately, some sort of clandestine chat going on. Yvette's mind went into overdrive trying to decode the meaning of the picture and its implications. Did they somehow know each other? A Texan hippy and a squeaky-clean buttoned-down City boy. It didn't seem likely. Was he coming onto her, then? This, too, seemed far-fetched. Meadow had a certain flaky appeal, but there was no way she was Jack's type. Yvette enlarged the image between her index fingers ... in, out, in, out she zoomed, before her digits froze an inch apart on the screen – was she imagining it, or was some transaction going on? Something passing from Jack's hand to Meadow's? Or even ... the other way round?

'Shit!' she said not realizing how loudly, until all four yummy mummies swivelled round simultaneously to fix her with disapproving stares. She was about to mumble an apology when something in her rebelled. They were grammar school types, these women – Amandas and Carolines all; much younger than her but still, by dint of their Bugaboo strollers and their whitened teeth and their leather jackets, somehow her self-appointed superiors. So, she stared them down, until, with much eye-rolling and muttering, they returned to their conversation. Yvette sat, straight-backed and finished her coffee, forcing herself to take leisurely sips; not to be seen to hurry, even though no one was looking any more. Then she got up and left, scraping her chair legs deliberately on the laminate floor, and leaving the door ajar behind her.

There were only a handful of adverts in the newsagent's window. A couple of house shares, a man with a van, a reliable teenage babysitter with references, and a woman called Trixie offering French lessons; maybe not a woman, come to think. Nothing for her, though. Perhaps she'd been naïve to think there would be. She should probably have looked online, but she was a great believer in the human touch and she'd promised herself she'd not go home without a job. She decided to wander up to the local primary school and butter up the secretary. They might have something. She'd be a dinner lady if it came to it, she wasn't proud.

Funny how things happened sometimes. If she had arrived five minutes earlier, it would have been Carol Tannock on reception, and Yvette would have had her negative impression of the townsfolk confirmed by the school secretary's off-hand attitude. As it was, Carol had nipped out for a fag, leaving the Deputy Head to cover for her.

'I'd give my eye teeth for someone with your experience, but I've just let two TAs go myself,' the woman told her, screwing up her pretty face in regret. She looked about twenty-five. They had a nice bonding chat about shrinking budgets, rising class sizes, social deprivation and pie-in-the-sky targets.

'Now if you had a teaching qualification...' Sadia said (they were on first-name terms by then).

'Ah, no ... I never got round to it,' Yvette pulled a regretful face. 'In another life maybe...'

'You know there's an FE college up the road that offers a fast-track BA in primary?'

'Not fast-track enough, I'm afraid. I've only got another ten years in me, if that. Besides, I don't know that I've got what it takes, you know ... ' she tapped her temple, 'up here.'

'Yvette,' Sadia put a hand on her sleeve, 'don't put yourself down like that. I've only just met you, but even I can see you could teach primary standing on your head.'

Yvette felt touched by the young woman's words. Why had no one ever said this to her before? Her teachers? Her mother? Her husband? All she'd ever heard was what she couldn't do and why. She couldn't be in sixth form with a bump because it would reflect badly on the school, she couldn't go to college because who'd look after the kid? If only one of them had told her 'you can' she might have been in Sadia's job by now; she might have been her boss.

Yvette got back to the car park to find a traffic warden printing off a ticket.

'Oh no you don't!' she yanked the door of the KA open within an inch of his face and reversed out of the space with a squeal of brakes before he could stick it on her windscreen. It was a hollow victory, she knew, the paperwork already being set in train, but she was feeling a bit *Thelma and Louise*. She headed out of town in the direction of ... home ... was hardly the word ... The Button Factory – her fingers clenched on the steering wheel and her jaw set in fury; fury with the jobsworth in the car park, fury with her mother for writing her off as a Jezebel aged sixteen; fury with her husband for prioritizing his personal fulfilment over hers. Fury, most of all, with her own docile compliance. She thought of the sweet young woman she'd just met in the school – younger than her own daughter, yet more astute than any careers advisor.

A sign on the other side of the carriageway caught her eye.

MACCLESFIELD FE COLLEGE
1/2 MILE

Yvette swerved into the right-hand lane, slammed her foot on the brake and barely noticing the outraged horn blasts of the drivers that she scattered in her wake, made a U-turn.

30

Harriet

Harriet sat at her desk in the broom cupboard that doubled as her office and tried to focus on the email. She was feeling, to use Gary's vernacular, rough as a badger's arse. It wasn't just a hangover. This wrung-out, woozy feeling had to be down to the drugs. Clearly you couldn't have Ecstasy without agony. She thought she'd got away with it; buzzing with adrenaline, still, the morning after the night before; making brekkie for everyone; lapping up the compliments and not wanting it to end. But she hadn't been to bed at that point. Once she did, it was like she'd been coshed. She must have slept the clock round and this morning, oh boy! Yvette had warned her coming down was no picnic, and she'd expected to feel a bit blue, not overcome by this horrid crampy nausea with an undertow of existential dread. She felt as though she wanted to cry and have sex and run a marathon and curl up in ball and protect every vulnerable creature in the world, all at the same time. And be sick. God, she felt sick. All of which grimness made it very difficult to focus on her work, which was probably why, at first sight, she'd mistaken the email for a charity mailshot and transferred it to junk. She'd paused for a second, some instinct telling her that wasn't right. She'd retrieved it and skim-read it with a growing sense of excitement.

From: Derbyshire Wildlife Trust

Dear Ms Constantine,

It was with great interest ... your conversion of Dawson's Button Factory ... state-of-the-art public housing ... (yes, well, draw a veil over that) ... exciting National Lottery-funded project ... convert a former water mill into a heritage museum and wetlands centre ... Peak District National Park ... invitation to bid in the first instance. Attaching a PDF of the brief and available any time to discuss, should you require ...

There was a tentative knock at the door.

'Come in,' Harriet said distractedly.

Mark poked his head into the room. He looked different. Younger but also older. At first Harriet couldn't work out why, then she realized he had shaved his beard off.

'Sorry. You're busy. Sorry.'

He started to withdraw.

'Mark, don't be silly. Come in, what do you ... ?'

'No, it's fine,' came his voice from the corridor, 'I won't distract you.'

'Oh, for goodness' sake!'

He stepped halfway in and hovered evasively. He was wearing a suit, and ... she sniffed the air ... aftershave.

'How's it working out, your ... ' He waved his hand to indicate the space.

'It's fine. A bit on the small side, I suppose, but that's my own fault ... Mark ... ?'

'Anyway, don't let me ... ' he interrupted her, gesturing towards the computer screen. 'You crack on ... '

'I've been offered a job,' she said, enthusiasm momentarily overcoming her irritation with him, 'invited to *bid* for one, I should say. Might not come off, but it's great that they asked me.'

'Fantastic!' said Mark. 'Go for it.'

What was the matter with him? He wasn't interested. He wasn't even listening; he had ants in his pants. He looked *terrible*.

'So, well, I'm just er ... popping down to London.'

'*London?*'

'Just to say hi to Ollie ... '

'You've only just seen Ollie.'

' ... And to sort out some outstanding ... work stuff.'

He frisked himself, for keys and wallet. Anything it seemed, to avoid meeting her eye.

'You said that was all done and dusted ... '

'No, it is. It is. This is more ... *social*, really. Ambrose wants to pick my brains ... he wants to know how best to organize the er ... finances.'

'Oh God. Poor you! Can't you just tell Ambrose to man up?'

'No, yeah, I will. I just ... '

'So, you'll be back for dinner? Because it's our turn to cook.'

Mark's eyes widened in dismay.

'Oh well, I hope so, yes. It depends. There's a chance I might be detained. I mean, I might ... stay over. If it gets too late, I mean. Probably won't, though. Anyway, I'll let you know. Love you, bye ... '

'Mark?'

But he had gone. Not a kiss, not so much as a shoulder squeeze. She'd have got more intimacy from a colleague. She bit her lip, wondering if it was her fault. Could Mark have rumbled her and Gary? No. He was away with the fairies, head somewhere else entirely. She started writing a holding email to the people at Derbyshire Wildlife Trust, but had only got halfway through when her conscience pricked her. She ought to at least give him a lift to the station – they hadn't really spoken since the gig. She hadn't asked him about his book group ... She pushed her chair back from the desk and, hearing his car start up in the courtyard, flung open a window and called his name, but the rattle of tyres on gravel drowned her out.

Harriet stood there for a minute, watching the car wind down the lane until it was out of sight. She paused briefly to admire the courtyard she had designed. The cedarwood ranch-style gate; the recycling shack, roofed with local slate. Yes, she was a good architect, she *deserved* to be in the running for the Derbyshire job ... She was about to duck back in again and get on with her email, when she saw a figure emerge furtively from the studio below her and hurry around the side of the building. Meadow. Where the hell was she off to in a dressing gown and Ugg boots? She was a funny one, that girl; moody and unknowable. Harriet didn't get her at all. She'd supposed it was because of the age gap, but some intuition told her now that it might be something else. She'd looked like she was up to no good. Harriet frowned. Where would be her best vantage point...? She bounded two at a time up the stairs to the bathroom where she had given Gary a blow job on the day of the gig. Balancing on the lid of the loo, she peeped out of the narrow window in time to see Meadow come round the corner. Then, out from behind the hedge, sloped a young hoodie on a pushbike. He couldn't have been more than fourteen. Harriet frowned. A KMA fan after an autograph? Some rock music wannabe from the town dropping off a demo tape for Declan? She craned her neck but whatever transaction was going on between them remained stubbornly out of sight. She could only surmise...

Just as well Mark was out of the way. He'd have had a meltdown if he'd seen it; jumped immediately to the obvious but not necessarily correct conclusion. Whereas Harriet was inclined to want corroboration before she assumed the worst. Brought up in the wrong way at the fortnightly house meeting, she could see it being a bit of a downer. Also, if she was honest, telling tales felt a teeny bit hypocritical. Hadn't they all sat round in the hot tub last night, drinking shots and smoking spliffs? Hair of the dog, Gary had called it and Harriet had giggled and joined in, ignoring Yvette's warning frown as she'd handed the joint to Declan, too intoxicated by the decadence of it all, to recall what Gary had told her of Declan's dodgy past – the urgent need for him to stay clean and sober. No, she needed to do a Sherlock; eliminate all the innocent explanations before assuming the worst.

She found Gary in the snug, watching the rough-cut of the KMA video on his computer. He patted the sofa next to him without taking his eyes off the screen. Harriet sat down, obediently, her thigh a decorous few inches from his. He disconnected the headphones, so she could join in the experience, but didn't restart the video. She watched for a while, tapping her fingers in time to the music, wondering if she'd have to sit through the whole thing before she dared start a conversation. She was very aware, suddenly, of their proximity. Her mouth was dry and even her smallest gestures, the crossing of her legs or touching of a lock of hair, seemed suddenly laden with meaning.

'Gaz ... ?' she ventured at last.

He paused the video with a slight air of exasperation and she moistened her lips nervously.

'I ... need to talk to you.'

Gary put aside the computer. He looked slightly grim.

'Yeah, actually, good thought ... I've been wanting to talk to you too ... '

He patted the back of her hand on the sofa, and then, as if realizing the inadequacy of the gesture, took it in his own, with all the enthusiasm as if it were a dead fish.

'The thing is, H ... what happened the other night ... Don't get me wrong, it was well nice and everything. Only ... '

'Oh, no, not about ... *that*,' Harriet said, in dismay, seeing the regretful look in his eye, 'that's just our little ... no, really, don't give that a second's thought. This is a practical matter.'

She tried to adopt a business-like tone, but her insides were falling away with mortification, with confusion. She'd been played for a mug. Here she was thinking they had a sophisticated understanding, a cool and mutual 'friendship with benefits' when really, she'd been just another groupie. And one he'd tired of at that. She heard her voice harden as she went on.

'It's about Declan.'

Was it her imagination or did he blanch a little at the mention of the name?

'What about him?'

'So ... you know you said he's had ... issues ... in the past with addiction and so forth, but now he's clean? Only ... I happened to be in the bathroom, you know, where we, er ... anyway yeah, *there*, and I happened to look out of the window, and who should I happen to see, but Meadow in a huddle with this dodgy-looking bloke and I know I've led a sheltered life and everything, but I couldn't help thinking he looked like he might be a ... '

But before she got any further Yvette burst into the room in a state of great agitation. She didn't even acknowledge Harriet; just handed her mobile phone to Gary.

'It's Janice, for you,' she said. 'It's about your mam.'

31

Gary

'I feel like shit.'

'It's grief, Gaz. That's what it feels like.'

Yvette checked her wing mirror and pulled out to overtake an articulated lorry that was zigzagging in the middle lane. She indicated and pulled back in a few metres ahead of it.

'Guilt more like. I can't believe I never even got to ...' Gary's voice grew thick with emotion. He watched his hand flex on the slub of his black trousers as if it belonged to somebody else. State of him. Look what he'd chosen to wear ... all the other blokes would be in their one good suit from Debenhams, but Mr Look at Me I'm a Rock Star was in bespoke Italian silk, like John Cooper Clarke on a bad hair day. What a dickhead. He took a deep breath and tried again.

'... I've been a terrible son.'

'You've not, Gaz. You're being too hard on your ...'

'... I have! I've been just up the road from her for the last four months and I've not been to see her once, and now she's dead.'

'You weren't to know. You've been working flat out; providing for your family. She'd understand that. It's only what your dad did, God rest his soul.'

'Don't bring him into it. He thought I was the biggest twat going. He'd rather I'd done anything than be a musician. He wanted me to get a proper job.'

'You've been a teacher. That's a proper job. Anyway, if the album takes off you'll earn more in two years than your dad did in all his time at Kellogg's. You'll be able to pay our Jade's fees up front. Help our Ruby out with the baby.'

'There's no money in album sales, anymore.' Gary could feel self-pity creeping in.

'What about the tour, though? That'll bring home the bacon,' Yvette pointed out. 'And there'll be another album, won't there, now you've got the bit between your teeth?'

Gary folded his hands between his thighs. It was getting on his nerves now, the pep talk. Or maybe it was the mention of the tour. It was one thing being on the road for three months with a bus full of beer and a dealer in every port, but this one was going to be more like a Methodist mission. No drugs or alcohol for Declan's sake and Little Miss Sunshine was coming along for the ride – their own on-board 'wellness guru'. Talk about killing the vibe. But why was he even thinking about the bloody tour? He was meant to be thinking about his mam.

'Do I look like a dickhead in this tie?'

Yvette glanced across.

'You can't *not* wear a tie.'

She was right. Yvette was always right. Her outfit was spot on, wouldn't you know. Navy pant suit; smart, low-heeled shoes. Respectful but not 'look at me'. She looked bloody good, as a matter of fact. She'd lost a bit of weight, or maybe she was just walking taller. Something had changed anyway.

'It says we come off here,' Yvette said, frowning at the sat nav.

Gary looked out of the window at flyovers and pedestrian bridges and low-level red-brick offices and thought he could have been anywhere, for all this place resembled the Manchester of his youth. They sat in the right-hand lane, waiting for the filter and Gary listened to the tick of the indicator and wondered who he was and where he was and what he was even for, and then Yvette took the corner and he saw the big old boarded-up pub where he and his mates used to get served at fourteen, and suddenly he knew to the yard where the bus shelter would come up on the left and at precisely what angle the branches of the horse chestnut trees would jut above the railings beyond and it could have been 1980 again. He'd never noticed the cemetery back then. It had just been the stop you got off at.

Yvette drove through the grand Victorian gateway, slowing the KA to a respectful ten miles per hour and Gary sank down in his seat, in case any of the black-clad mourners might be people he knew, or ought to know.

'There's your Auntie Pamela,' Yvette nudged him, 'talking to your mum's next-door neighbour. Shall I let you out while I go and park the...'

'No!' said Gary.

'OK, chill. We'll go together.'

Gary's eyes swam. He swiped the back of his hand across his nostril and nearly wiped it on his trousers, before he remembered he wasn't a kid anymore. He pulled the sun visor down and looked at himself in the vanity mirror. Blotchy as fuck. He reached into his jacket pocket for his sunglasses. Yvette wrinkled her nose.

'I wouldn't ... ' she said.

She swerved into a gap in the car park that wasn't really a proper space and a rosebush rattled against the passenger door.

'You'll have to get out my side.'

Gary stuffed his shades back in his jacket pocket and clambered over the gearstick arse-first, before straightening up. Yvette smoothed the shoulders of his jacket and took his hand.

'Ready?' she said.

The North Chapel was a hive of activity, the mourners from the previous funeral spilling out of its side door and into the rose garden, to the strains of Celine Dion, even as his crew gathered, apprehensively, under the portico at the front, waiting for their slot. All day, every day this must be going on, Gary thought – the cars drawing up, the curtains closing around the coffin, the chimney puffing smoke – a conveyor belt of death. He clutched Yvette's hand as they drew nearer. The people out front were starting to look vaguely familiar now, if not as individuals, then as a clan. A whole load of pale, short-arsed Taylors from his mam's side – the men balding, the women blonde or grey, punctuated by the occasional taller and more hirsute Kershaw. And now the names were starting to come back to him. There was his Auntie Eileen, who he'd assumed must be dead by now, but who didn't look any different from the last time he'd seen her, talking to his cousins Anthony and Tina. And the old witch from the Rawcroft Estate who'd dobbed him in to the police for graffitiing the garages – Mrs

Catterick, that was her. She'd got a nerve showing her face. There was a small delegation from the care home, including the nice black lady who'd shown him to his mam's room on the one day he'd condescended to visit. It was nearly all women, he noticed, middle-aged and elderly, for the most part; his mam's relatives, colleagues and friends; their husbands presumably either already dead from smoking and stress, or else skiving off down the pub. Here were brash and blowsy bingo players and dowdy church-women, co-workers from his mother's various jobs in factories and schools and call centres and only one conspicuous by her absence – the one he feared most.

'Where's Janice?' he murmured to Yvette.

'She'll be in the cortège,' she said, and Gary frowned, since he'd always thought that was a flower arrangement.

The chapel was lighter and brighter than he remembered, with a timbered roof like the hulk of a ship and sprays of flowers mounted at intervals on fluted columns. People were letting on now, nodding and saying 'hiya' but Gary could hardly meet their eyes – knowing himself to be the bad penny, the prodigal son. He tried to duck into the first vacant row, but Yvette dragged him up the aisle to the second pew from the front where he could feel eyes boring into the back of his neck. It wasn't hard to imagine what people were whispering to each other.

'That's him there; the one as thinks he's all that.'

He picked up the order of service. It had a photo of his mam on the front that he remembered from the big Quality Street tin that used to house the family archive. She was wearing a Fair Isle jumper that the girls would have given their eye teeth for and one of those wavy, shoulder length hair styles that all the women had back then. She looked sweet and shy and beautiful.

He ran his finger across the foiled script beneath her portrait.

Jean Irene Kershaw
1943-2018

He was about to look inside, when the piped organ music stopped. There was silence, then a shuffling of feet as everyone stood. Some old geezer at the back had a coughing fit and as that faded out, Samuel Barber's 'Adagio for Strings' faded in. Gary knew the piece well, not just as the kneejerk choice for every one-size-fits-all funeral, but as a key component of the GCSE music syllabus (time signatures). Yet if he'd thought its familiarity was proof against its power to move him, he was wrong. As the tense vibrato of the opening theme progressed stepwise from individual sorrow through collective mourning toward universal grief, he felt a weight of loss so heavy he could barely breathe. He could hear snivelling from the rest of the congregation and the creak of timber as people steadied themselves against their pews; then the dignified lockstep of the pallbearers' feet as they moved up the aisle towards him. Just as Gary feared he might actually sob out loud, the music faded out, and the casket was lowered onto a curtained bier just a foot or two ahead of where he stood. There she lay, his mam, probably not much bigger inside her fancy white casket than the spray of long-stemmed lilies that adorned it, almost within touching distance, yet forever, now, beyond his reach.

The chief mourners filed into the front pew – Gary's brother-in-law Alan, his nephew Stephen, niece Tamsin and finally, pale and dignified beneath a veiled pillbox hat, his sister

Janice. Yvette leaned forward and squeezed her sister-in-law's shoulder, and Janice half turned her head and acknowledged the gesture with a dignified smile. She didn't look at Gary.

A grey-haired woman in tortoiseshell-rimmed spectacles and a dog collar walked up to the lectern now and introduced herself as Ingrid, a lay preacher at the church Jean had sporadically attended. She was touched, she told them, to have been asked by Jean's family to officiate at what she intended to be as much a celebration of Jean's life, as a commemoration of her death. She had done her homework, had Ingrid. As well as offering her own personal tribute, she had mined friends and family for anecdotes, revealing, touching and laugh-out-loud funny. Gary found himself wishing he'd bothered to get to know Jean Irene Kershaw while he'd still had the chance – because according to Ingrid she'd been a proud mum and grandma who had doted on her son and daughter and sung their praises behind their backs. This, he imagined, must have come as even bigger news to Janice than it was to him. Jean had been a character apparently; a right laugh, a tough cookie with a heart of gold, whom everybody wanted on their team. Gary tried to square Ingrid's description of his mother with the dead-eyed old shrew who'd told him to fuck off when he'd visited her in the care home, and couldn't. But then he remembered how tenderly she used to sing 'Molly Malone' to him, and that sparked a cascade of suppressed childhood memories – the time she'd caught a bus to deliver his forgotten football kit to a key fixture, enabling him to come on in extra time and score the winner; the time she'd bawled out his head teacher for calling him a thief when a spate of dinner money thefts had seen him suspended on nothing more than the balance of probability (as it happened, he'd been guilty, but his mother's touching belief in his innocence had been a better corrective than any sanction the school could have imposed and he'd never thieved again). In her rough and ready way, he realized, with the tools she had available to her and the dodgy blueprint she'd been handed down by her own fierce and damaged parents, his mam had done the best job she knew how to do and, as she might have put it herself, you couldn't say fairer than that.

They said a prayer, then sang a hymn – 'The Day Though Gavest Lord Is Ended' – to which Gary was surprised to find he knew all the words, then Ingrid invited them to reflect quietly on everything Jean had meant to them and that was it. His mother's life, done and dusted in twenty-five minutes. Except it wasn't. As the muffled hydraulics started lowering the coffin beneath the closed curtains, the strident chords of an electric guitar rang out; the riff so plangent, so familiar to Gary at a gut level that at first, he thought his mother had chosen to leave this world to the strains of Jimi Hendrix. But then his own voice came in.

'*Yours was the first face that I seen*
You were my mam, you were my queen,
And where you come from, I ain't been
This is my song, my song for Jean.'

He frowned, and looked, in joyous astonishment, first at Yvette, whose sheepish smile and tear-filled eyes told him she had colluded in this, and then at Janice who turned now and looked him fully in the face, her smile of forgiveness tipping quickly into a grimace of mutual loss as they clung to each other across the wooden pew.

32

Mark

Mark was zigzagging his way across the concourse at Euston station when he saw it. He stopped frisking himself for his oyster card and gazed up, taking it in for a moment before his knees buckled. What. The. Fuck. It was a massive live advert for a new TV show called *Ethical Makeover* – maybe the biggest hoarding he'd seen outside of Piccadilly Circus. It wasn't the header that caught his eye, nor the Botoxed twenty-something influencer chattering mutely to the indifferent commuters. It was the animated logo, tiny by comparison with the rest of the screen, a mere foot or so across, but eye-catching all the same, not easily overlooked. A spinning green globe, the phrase 'sponsored by' writing itself out of cosmic dust around its equator, before the words 'Planet Beauty' appeared like a rainbow above it. Mark stood still, oblivious to the muttering of irritable commuters who had to side step him. He gazed open-mouthed, as it happened again and again. The spin, the squiggle, the rainbow; the spin, the squiggle, the rainbow. He glanced around guiltily, half expecting the station's surveillance cameras to swivel their lenses simultaneously towards him. He couldn't have felt more exposed if it had been a giant wanted poster with his mugshot on it.

Well, what else had he expected? He'd brought it on himself. The Planet Beauty contract was there plain as day in the company accounts. Well, not plain as day, perhaps... but discernible by any forensic auditor with a nose for bad smells. Technically speaking, a giant, strobing neon advert playing to – what? – fifty thousand commuters a day, didn't make Mark any guiltier of insider trading than if it had been a small classified ad in the *Macclesfield Advertiser* but it sure as hell made him *feel* guiltier. What had Ambrose been *thinking*? Mark couldn't have hinted any harder that he should drop Planet Beauty, and he'd thought the message had got through, but with Mark out of the way, Ambrose must have seen this as his chance to shine.

Mark stepped onto the escalator in a daze. He might as well have been descending into the bowels of hell. He stood on the right, gazing into space, turning his oyster card over and over in his pocket like a talisman. He emerged onto the southbound platform of the Northern line to the warm rubber-scented backdraught of a departing Tube train. He made his way towards the far end of the platform, and stood in the precise spot where years of commuting had taught him the doors of the rearmost, and therefore least congested carriage would open. He glanced up at the digital display. Four minutes till the next one. He smiled grimly. A four-minute warning. If only it were. If only he were about to be vaporized in a one-megaton nuclear explosion. He wouldn't even know it had happened. There'd be a blinding flash; a noise so deafening he wouldn't hear it and then his eyeballs would be welded to the back of his skull, his skeleton reduced to a radioactive sizzle. He'd be at peace.

God, those were the days. When Armageddon came in the shape of a cruise missile. Oh, to be vaporized. To not have to sit down with a fraud squad investigator and find out just how far he had inadvertently waded in shit. How far he would be personally liable; what the ramifications might be for his family. To not have to admit to Ollie that he'd been right all along – his father *was* a swindling, unprincipled dick-swinger. To not have to 'fess up to Jack ... oh God! *Jack*. Jack would be out on his ear once Deloitte's got wind of this. He'd probably get the old heave-ho from Trust Fund Maisie too. Mr Maisie wouldn't like the optics one bit; he might pay undernourished Cambodians poverty wages to manufacture multivitamins but he wouldn't marry his only daughter into a family of crooks. Even he was Mark's moral superior now.

Worse by far, though, than any of these horrid reckonings, was the thought of telling Harriet. Sweet, stalwart Harriet, who it had all been for. Harriet who had thought *she* was ethically compromised because her vaunting architectural ambition had put The Button Factory beyond the budget of the housing association from whom they themselves had ultimately bought it. Wait till she found out where the bail-out cash had come from ...

The train came in three minutes fifty-seven seconds, and Mark climbed aboard the half-empty carriage, sat down and stared at his reflection in the window, the pallor, the sunken eyes, the weak chin. A sharp suit could no longer camouflage the hollow man he'd always been.

His lawyer, Hannah Bannerman, was already installed in the reception area of the Serious Fraud Office sipping a coffee, when he got there. He didn't know whether to be pleased at her professionalism, or annoyed that he'd be footing the bill for her over-zealous punctuality.

'Mark, hi,' she said, half rising and offering her cool manicured hand for him to shake. She was so *young*. How could someone as young as her be 'the best in the business', as her boss Clive had insisted. Clive was an old university pal of Mark's, who had always turned out for him in person until now. He needn't have worried. They were in and out in five minutes. The suit who interviewed him was courtesy itself, softly spoken and almost apologetic. He explained that he was serving Mark with a Section 2 notice, which was the first stage in the process and compelled the provision of specified information and documents relating to a potential prosecution, a summons for which may be served in due course. It was like being shafted by the holy ghost.

It wasn't until Mark saw the cherry trees on Moorcroft Road, their bronze and yellow leaves against the cerulean blue of the autumn sky, that he really understood what he had lost. The peace, the deep unthinking banality of suburban life. They could have just carried on living here in quite considerable prosperity and comfort. He could have worked for another few years, then sold his controlling stake in the company and bought a little gîte in Brittany to whisk Harriet away to when being around Ollie got a bit much. Hell, he could have worked on his relationship with Ollie.

He reached number forty-five. The hedge looked a bit shaggy, and one of the venetian blinds was cockeyed, but otherwise it looked fairly respectable. There were no crates of empties outside, no syringes chucked in the flowerbeds. The wheelie bins were back in their corral. He took out his key and was about to put it in the lock when he thought better of it and rang the doorbell. His hand flexed on the handles of his laptop bag. He put one foot on the doorstep, decided that was too close, stepped back again. He swapped the bag to the other hand. At last, he saw a dark shape behind the stained glass and the door opened. Ollie seemed breathless, taken aback.

'Haven't you got your key?' he said.

'Oh no, yeah, I do only ... ' Mark shrugged, 'I didn't want to ... presume ... '

Ollie looked different. There was something wrong with his face. Mark leaned closer, but what had looked at first sight like a wound, turned out to be a small black cross between his eyes. Ollie stared back at him patiently.

'It's a tatt, Dad.'

'Oh-h— yeah, sorry. 'Course it is.'

'Do you want a cup of tea?'

Ollie walked down the hallway towards the kitchen and Mark followed, obediently. His son was stripped to the waist, his back a labyrinth of ink, his head still shaven. He looked thin.

The kitchen was much as Mark remembered it, but smelled of cauliflower and spices.

'Don't tell me you've been cooking ... ?'

He must stop defaulting to this condescending tone.

'I've gone vegan.'

Ollie finished filling the kettle before turning to Mark challengingly. 'Go on ... ' he said.

'Go on what ... ?'

'Take the piss.'

'No, I ... '

There was a pause while they regarded each other, then Ollie seemed to thaw.

'Sorry,' he said.

'No. You're fine. *I'm* sorry, I ... ' Mark took a deep breath and prepared to launch into the speech he'd prepared, but it seemed too formal; too fake. He grinned instead.

' ... *Vegan*, eh?'

He went over and sat in his customary seat at the kitchen table, surveying with interest a slew of A3 papers arrayed across it, but resisting the temptation to touch them.

'They're proofs ... ' Ollie said. He started gathering them up.

'Proofs ... ?' Mark said. 'So, what ... are you freelancing or something?'

Ollie looked cagey.

'It's OK, you don't have to tell me,' Mark said, trying to subdue his curiosity and mounting sense of optimism.

'They're mine,' Ollie said, handing one to Mark. He was blushing, Mark noticed. At a glance, the page resembled Ollie's tattooed back. It was covered in squiggly black-and-white graphics which on closer inspection proved to be a sequence of illustrated panels, with speech bubbles. It was rather accomplished, actually.

'You're drawing comics?' he said.

'It's a graphic novel. Sort of half sci-fi, half allegory.'

'And this is going to be *published*?'

Damn the incredulity in his tone. No wonder Ollie bridled.

'It is, yeah,' he said.

Mark looked back at the page in his hand.

A curse on you, allfather,
you have destroyed our planet and
betrayed your people

... a bare-chested, pointy-eared elf was saying to a bedraggled-looking warrior god.

Mark nodded and handed it back.

'That's ... amazing,' he said, 'I didn't know you could draw.'

Ollie shrugged.

'It was the only subject I got an A for at school.'

'You're right,' said Mark, 'I remember now. Maybe you should have gone to art college.'

Ollie's eyebrows shot up.

'Yeah, 'cos *that* would have gone down well.'

Mark smiled ruefully.

'You're a dark horse,' he said. 'Does anyone else know about this?'

Ollie shrugged.

'Jade,' he said, 'she helped me find where to send it.'

'*Jade* ... ' repeated Mark, pennies dropping all over the show, 'so are the two of you ... ? No, none of my business.'

Ollie's face was properly pink now. He squared off the papers into a tidy pile and shuffled it to the far end of the table.

'What happened to her Polish boyfriend...?' Mark said after a moment.

'He was Latvian. And he wasn't really her boyfriend. He had to go back. His mum got sick. He was all right, you know? He had it pretty tough.'

Mark watched his son slosh hot water onto a tea bag, then scoop the same bag into a second mug and repeat. He hooked them on the forefingers of one hand, opened the fridge with his other and took out a carton of milk. He closed it with his foot, set the mugs and carton on the table and sat down beside his father.

'So... you never said what you were down for?' Ollie said. Mark opened the carton and poured some milk into his mug to stave off the moment. He took a sip, then, closing his eyes briefly, set the mug down again.

'It's... complicated,' he said slowly, 'I've been meaning to tell someone...'

33

Yvette

The morning after the funeral, Yvette woke early. She left Gary snoring and went to make the tea. Shuffling in her mules and towelling robe, she was taken aback to find Harriet already perched at the kitchen island, working on her computer.

'Hiya,' Yvette said, trying to signal by her brisk tone that she wasn't really up for a chat.

'Oh, hi!' said Harriet, turning around, her face primped and pink and blooming; like she'd been up for hours. 'Don't mind me, I'm just making the most of the P&Q.'

Yvette jerked her chin in acknowledgement and made for the kettle.

'There's tea in the pot,' Harriet pointed out, 'here let me ...'

She bounded off her stool and reached for one of the red earthenware mugs she favoured. Yvette tried not to feel irritated. Her own blue-and-white china one retained the heat better, but Harriet had banished it to an inaccessible cupboard along with various other of Yvette's cherished possessions. She had tried to justify such high-handedness with some quote about not having anything in your home you didn't know to be useful or believe to be beautiful, but that was bullshit, because Yvette's plastic Salter scales were very useful indeed and they'd vanished off the face of the earth.

The tea wasn't hot enough and there wasn't enough left in the pot to take one to Gaz, but she'd have to sit and drink this one before she could make fresh without looking rude. God!

She perched on a stool next to Harriet sipping the tea politely. It was much too weak.

Harriet tapped the keyboard a few more times and then closed her laptop and pushed it away.

'So . . . ' she said folding her arms and raising her eyebrows significantly, 'what a night, eh?'

Yvette frowned.

'The gig!' Harriet said, as if it might have slipped Yvette's mind. Then she clapped a hand over her mouth and her eyes goggled with horror, 'Oh my God! I forgot. Oh, Yvette. Christ. What a . . . I'm so sorry! How was the funeral?'

Yvette smiled, won over in spite of herself, by Harriet's contrition.

'It was all right, as these things go,' she said. 'Short, but very moving, in the end. The wake was good. They know how to party, them Kershaws.'

'That's . . . nice,' said Harriet, dubiously, 'and Gaz held up OK?'

'Gaz got completely off his face and sang Beatles songs with his cousins, till I dragged him away.'

'Oh my God!' Harriet looked delighted. 'That's so Gaz.'

Yvette felt suddenly furious with her. How the hell did she know what was 'so Gaz'? And what made her think it was out of the ordinary anyway? It was just what happened at a wake.

She sloshed the dregs of her cold tea down the sink and filled the kettle again.

'Oh, by the way,' Harriet said, 'something came for you yesterday.'

Harriet slipped off her stool again and handed Yvette an A4 envelope from one of the tasteful pigeonholes to which, in Harriet's world, all things were assigned.

'Lucky you were here or I might never have found it,' said Yvette archly but she was too excited to stay even a little bit cross. She ripped it open, keenly aware of Harriet's eagle eyes.

'Strictly private and confidential,' Yvette murmured, her eye running anxiously to the next line. 'Great. I'm good to go. They've renewed my DBS certificate.'

'Good to go where? What does DBS stand for?'

'I'm not sure but it means I'm not a menace to the community. You have to have it to work with children.'

'Oh!' Harriet smiled happily. 'So you're getting a little job ...?'

Yvette closed her eyes and suppressed her mounting irritation.

'I'm going to do teacher training, yes.'

'*Teaching!*' said Harriet in surprise. 'How lovely. You'll be good at that.'

Yvette attempted a smile.

'Primary or secondary?'

'Primary.'

'Oh ... phew!' said Harriet. 'No, don't get me wrong, you'd be fab either way, but secondary's probably a bit ... intense, don't you think?'

Yvette felt her phone buzz in her dressing-gown pocket.

'Funnily enough, I've had some career news as well...'
Harriet prattled on happily. 'I had this email the other day
from Derbyshire Wildlife Trust...'

Yvette's phone buzzed again and this time she glanced at it.
It wasn't from Gary. It was a WhatsApp from Ruby.

Mum, I've had a bit of spotting.

'...I've been invited to bid for another...what's the matter?'
Yvette stared at Harriet, without taking in her words. Her
heart was thudding out of her chest, even before she had fully
absorbed the meaning of Ruby's words. Spotting. Blood. The
baby.

'What's the date?' she snapped at Harriet, who stared back
dumbly.

'I don't know. The eleventh? No, it must be the twelfth,
because the gig was on the...'

Yvette screwed up her eyes and calculated in her head. The
baby wasn't due for another four weeks. She started texting
madly with her thumb.

How do you mean a bit?

'...Actually, no, it's the thirteenth, because it's Maisie's birthday the day after tomorrow...'

Bubbles were appearing on Yvette's screen. She tuned out
Harriet's background prattle and watched, heart in mouth, as
the message appeared.

Not much. Hardly any. It's probably nothing.

'... And I made a note to get a card in the post. You don't think I should buy her a present, do you?'

'Can you give me a minute...?' Yvette snapped. Another message was arriving.

Don't worry I've got antenatal later.

'... Only once you start with that, where does it end?'

'I think our Ruby's miscarrying!'

Harriet's face seemed to crumple in slow motion. Only then did Yvette remember Harriet's own miscarriages. She felt a surge of pity, without yet quite losing the urge to slap her friend hard across the cheek. She'd *had* her babies. This was about Ruby. But Harriet had already swung into rescue mode.

'Send an ambulance!' she commanded.

'I can't remember her address!' wailed Yvette. It didn't even occur to her to look in her contacts. She just stood there, rendered mute and useless with shock.

'Ring her now and ask her. I'm ringing nine-nine-nine.'

The phone trembled in Yvette's hand.

After what seemed an age, she found Ruby's number in her favourites and stabbed the speed dial button. It rang and rang. Where *was* she? It wasn't like she could be tied up elsewhere, she'd been texting only moments ago...

Yvette cancelled and tried again, cancelled and tried again. She stared at Harriet, mutely shaking her head.

For what seemed an age they stood there, Harriet biting her lip, her eyes wide with anxiety, Yvette trying the number again and again, trying Jordan's number; getting nothing.

'I'm going down there!' Yvette said.

'To London? OK, then, go pack a bag,' Harriet scrolled on her phone. 'I'll drop you at the station. You'll struggle to make the ten to, but there's another one in an hour; change at Crewe. Should get you there by...'

'No! I can't be waiting around,' said Yvette, 'I'll get the ten to...'

34

Harriet

'Platform 2. You'll have to get a move on,' Harriet had barely got the words out before Yvette had thrown off her seatbelt and flung open the passenger door of Harriet's Mini Clubman. Harriet was about to pull the door shut, when Yvette ducked back into the car and embraced her. For a second Harriet's mouth and nose were full of Yvette's scent. She hugged her friend close, welling up with gratitude and shame, then, remembering Ruby, pushed her firmly away again.

'Run!' she commanded, and Yvette ran.

A taxi pulled up behind her and flashed its headlights. Harriet cast a last anxious glance in the direction of the London train, which was just starting to slide out of the station. She wondered whether to wait in case Yvette had missed it, but the taxi driver beeped impatiently, so with a muttered curse, she drove off.

She felt exhilarated by her race to the station, but fearful too. All her emotional investment in Ruby's reproductive destiny was now renewed. Even this tiny walk-on part in the drama had given her a stake in its outcome. It was an uneasy feeling; hope, laced with envy. She so wanted the best for Ruby and her baby, yet she was so very jealous of her. She was surprised at the visceral nature of it; had thought she'd moved on. She felt weepy and nerve-jangled and faintly sick; angry too. Irrationally, toweringly angry. But who or what with? Gary for humiliating her? Mark, for turning into a replicant? Or herself, for being foolish enough to think she could have the best of both worlds? She resolved, there and then, to do better. She would start by cooking supper. It was a small thing, but a symbolic one. Yes, she'd get some food on the go, and then spend the rest of the day on the Derbyshire water mill bid. Less chance, that way, of bumping into Gaz. Ever since their awkward little conversation in the snug had been interrupted by the news of his mother's death, she'd felt uneasy about how they'd left things. He had obviously got the wrong end of the stick and assumed she was coming on to him, when in fact she just meant to give him a heads-up about Meadow. Now the whole thing was such a mess, it seemed best avoided.

Harriet turned into the Waitrose car park. She was feeling better about herself already. She would show off her domestic side. Whip up something wholesome and tasty that would keep until whatever time Mark and Yvette got back from their respective London trips. Then, all being well, the four of them could reconnect. Kick back with a glass of wine, have a soak in the hot tub, enjoy a nice, bonding dinner together, like they used to.

She had grabbed a trolley and got as far as flicking through the free in-house magazine and choosing a recipe for spelt, fennel and kale stew, when, passing the sushi counter, she remembered that she hadn't had any breakfast. She popped a three-pack of sashimi in the trolley, but finding herself suddenly ravenous, prised it open and demolished a piece where she stood. One became two, which became three. They were delicious even without the addition of wasabi and soy sauce, which was too tricky to manage on the go. She did pluck out the pickled ginger with her fingernail, though. She'd forgotten how good the sushi was. She placed the empty pack conspicuously in the trolley to signal her intention to pay for it and then set about the rest of her shopping.

By the time she reached the checkout, her trolley was brimming. She'd bought the makings of a fruit cobbler to follow the kale and spelt thingummyjig, a large fromage frais, a sourdough loaf, two packets of ginger thins, a jar of gherkins, a bottle of Moët, because . . . well, why not? Also, thinking to put herself back at the top of Mark's 'to do' list, when he got back from London, a very expensive Bergamot and Jasmine body lotion and a black viscose slip, which was marked down and happened to catch her eye. At the checkout, just for the hell of it, she tossed in a bumper pack of M&Ms.

It wasn't until she had loaded her shopping on to the conveyor belt, requested a handful of carrier bags and was watching the items loom towards her one by one, that the telltale collection of starch and salt and sex and sweetness suddenly struck her, in combination with her seesawing emotions and slight nausea, as possibly more than coincidental. By the time the cashier asked for her loyalty card, Harriet could hardly hear her for the thud of blood in her temples.

'Sorry . . . what?'

'Have you got a Waitrose card?' the cashier repeated.

Harriet shook her head, and slotted her credit card into the reader with a trembling hand. It felt like some ritual she had once understood, but which had long ago ceased to have any meaning. The cashier looked away discreetly as she stabbed randomly at the numbers, getting the combination right at the last attempt, more by instinct than memory.

'Is there a chemist near here?' she said and her voice shook. The assistant frowned, remembering.

'There is yeah. Roberts. If you go out of the car park the back way, and through the ginnel, it comes up on your right. It's next to that new tapas ... oh, well, thank *you* very much too, madam ... '

'Slow down,' Harriet reminded herself. She was driving like a maniac, her foot juddering on the accelerator, partly with nerves, partly with eagerness to get home and find out if what she suspected was true. A traffic light turned amber twenty feet in front of her and she sped up to get through it, then lost her nerve and slammed her foot on the brake at the last minute so that the car jolted to a halt, halfway over the line. Harriet flumped back against the seat, with a little gasp, trying not to picture tiny atoms breaking apart inside her, before she'd ever have the chance to check if they were real.

A car tooted its horn and, realizing the lights had been green for some time, she moved off again, keeping the needle to a cautious twenty-nine and holding up a stream of traffic as she wound homewards. As the cars peeled off in various directions, the road narrowed and the hedgerows thickened, Harriet slowed to turn into The Button Factory courtyard. Glancing to her right she was dismayed to see two scrawls of fresh graffiti on the boundary wall; YUPPIES GO HOME rendered clumsily in white paint, and next to it, in much larger red capitals, SKAG HERE. Ordinarily she would have been mortified with shame and indignation, but right now all she could think of was the time bomb that she was ninety-nine per cent sure was ticking inside her.

She pulled up in her usual space and hauled the shopping from the boot. She was in survival mode now. It was just a question of keeping a lid on things... putting a brave face on it until she could be sure one way or the other. She had two bags in each hand and was shuffling toward the Button Factory entrance, trying to balance the urgency of her imminent task against the possible risk to her newly vulnerable back, when she noticed, through a ground-floor window, Declan and Gary sitting at a mixing desk, feet up, headphones on, the look on their faces either blissed out or spaced out or both, as they nodded along to the latest work of genius from The KMA. She wondered how Gary could focus on work when his grandchild's very survival was hanging in the balance, but that was men for you, she supposed. Certainly, he wasn't sufficiently engaged with the real world to notice Harriet's tentative smile of greeting, or the plea for assistance implicit in her beast of burden shoulder-shrug.

'Cheers,' she muttered bitterly, staggering onward to the main door and putting her bags down to punch in the code. By the time she had hauled her shopping up to the kitchen, she was tearful with exertion and stress, but most of all with anticipation. She dumped the shopping, dug out the candy-striped paper bag which the chemist had given her and hurried to the bathroom.

Harriet ripped open the packet, hauled down her pants and barely had time to put the little plastic stick in the way before her urine gushed sideways into the pan, like a burst dam, hardly wetting the test at all, but soaking her shirt sleeve instead. She waved the stick around frantically in the last few drips, hoping she'd done enough to get an accurate reading, and then set it down on top of the toilet roll holder to develop, while she washed her hands. By the time she turned back to it, she was starting to think she'd imagined the whole thing and was resigned to a negative result. The faint red line that would prove it had already started to appear in the slim rectangular window and that was right; that was good. She'd be forty-five in five weeks' time. She had two strapping sons and a rebooted career. If she *had* been pregnant, whilst the law of averages would have suggested Mark was the father, the outside chance it was Gary would have been the ultimate head-fuck. On top of all that, with Harriet's record, the chances of a viable baby at the end of it all were low, and yet she'd have had to go public. Lord knew what that would do to the already fraught atmosphere in The Button Factory. No. It was for the best. She was over it. No more.

She picked up the test, foot poised on the pedal of the bin, ready to discard it, and then stopped and peered at it more closely. Was it an hallucination? Double vision? No. A second line was appearing; faint, pink, narrow at first, but growing thicker and redder with every passing second.

35

Gary

'There's your bird,' Declan said, nudging Gary with a big spaced-out leer.

'Fuck off,' Gary said out of the corner of his mouth, trying to keep the tone light. If he could lay down one more good track before Declan lost the plot he'd be happy.

'Seriously. Mate. She's proper fluttering her eyelashes; giving you the whole damsel-in-distress vibe. Aren't you going to help her with her shopping, that's what she's after?'

'Fuck's sake, Dec, let it go, will you? Just make like you haven't seen her.'

'Hiya,' Declan mouthed to Harriet, stretching his lips in a fake smile, 'off you fuck. We're busy.'

He put his cans back on.

'You're all right,' he told Gary, 'she's gone now. Pass us them Rizlas, will you?'

'Mate. Come on,' Gary cajoled him, 'you promised you'd be a good lad, remember?'

'I *am* a good lad,' said Declan with a big slow sideways grin that told another story. 'I'm only after a fag, it's you that's after a shag. See what I did there? I'm a poet and I don't fucking know it.'

'Yeah, very droll. Only thing is, you're wrong on both counts. I'm *not* after a shag – not with her anyway – and *you're* not really after a fag, are you? You're after a fucking joint. At ten in the morning. How's that going to get the job done? Seriously, Dec, mate, it's a slippery slope.'

'Jesus, it's a little bit of puff to get the creative juices flowing, that's all. When did you turn into the world's biggest fucking killjoy?'

'About the time you got out of rehab, and said you was squeaky clean or nowt from that day fucking forward,' said Gary.

'Sorry, how is *this* not squeaky clean?' Declan turned to Gary and circled his face with his finger, so that his pinprick pupils, sunken eyes and unfocussed expression were plain to see.

'So, you're all right to smoke weed at ten a.m., then, are you?'

'Oh, come on, Goodie Two Shoes. A little bit of blow never hurt anyone, did it?'

'What happened to "I *will* always be an addict, Gary, but as long as I keep turning up to meetings…"'

'Yeah… it's about moderation,' said Declan huffily. 'All that abstinence stuff's for losers. Once you're six months clean you've reset the dial.'

'Is that what your live-in drug counsellor tells you?' said Gary. 'Because the last time I saw Meadow, she was in a fucking K-hole, so I'm not sure her…' he sketched speech marks in the air, 'programme's working out too well.'

But things were on the point of turning nasty and Gary wanted his breakbeat attending to, so with a sigh of resignation, he handed over the Rizlas and reached into the drawer for a bag of weed, pretending not to notice the clutter of spoons and tinfoil kicking around in there. Before the album launch, Declan's relapse would have felt like a disaster. The uncertainty of it all would have done Gary's head in and put paid to any chance of writing anything decent. But the reviews for *The Other Cheek* were starting to trickle in and so far, they were good. Better than good. The *NME* had called it 'gritty, witty and in places, downright trippy'. *Metacritic* had compared it favourably to The Stone Roses, which was not an accolade to be sniffed at. In addition, they'd already laid down six tracks for the new album. He'd just got to keep Declan on the straight and narrow for another week or two and then it'd be in the bag and they'd be done and dusted, as far as Gary was concerned.

Yeah, one more album; little tour; The John Peel stage at Glastonbury; he wasn't greedy. Then he'd be ready to knock it on the head; grow old gracefully; potter in his garage, be a grandad (God willing). Certainly, he'd be ready to call time on this whole fucking kibbutz set-up. It was turning out to be way more of an arse-ache than he'd anticipated. He could do without being ambushed by Harriet in a G-string every time he nipped out for a fag.

As a matter of fact, he'd already figured out an exit strategy. With what his mam had left him in her will, he'd only need to clear another hundred K or so from touring and album sales and then he and Yvette would have enough for a nice little semi in South Manchester. Maybe not Chorlton; that had gone through the roof, but Withington or Fallowfield, easy.

It was funny how differently he felt about the music business since his mam had passed. Not that he didn't still get off on performing. He definitely did. There was nothing like the rush you got from coming on stage; the buzz of knowing that a hundred or a thousand or ten thousand people had turned up just to see you. Only, ever since the funeral it had felt that bit less urgent; like the pressure was off. Which was weird because it wasn't like his mam had *wanted* him to do it. Quite the reverse; she'd much rather he'd been a used-car dealer, or a plumber or a computer programmer – was overjoyed when he'd knocked music on the head for a teaching career. And maybe that was it – maybe now she was gone, Gary no longer needed to prove to her that fronting a band had been a valid career choice. Maybe he no longer needed to rebel. He couldn't put his finger on exactly what had changed or when. Perhaps it was when he'd heard the first few notes of 'Song for Jean' at the end of the funeral, or when Janice had hugged him and he'd felt a weight lift off his shoulders. Perhaps it was watching Yvette get stuck in at the wake – handing round the ham barms, chatting to his batty old aunties; whispering the name of obscure second cousins into his ear at the crucial moment so he could say, 'Darren, how are you mate? . . . Lorraine, you don't look any different.'

That had been the other big change in recent months. Yvette. He didn't know if it was being back up North, or having the girls off her hands, but something was different. He'd always known she was smart, but, to use a musical analogy, she'd been one of life's bass guitarists; happier holding everything together in the background, than milking it in the limelight. Just lately, though, she'd come into her own – it might have been her new hairstyle, or that she'd learned a few tricks off Harriet, but she looked classier; fitter; more of a catch.

'This bit!' said Declan, through a cannabis haze, holding up his finger, to alert Gary to a guitar riff that he thought was slightly below par. Gary pretended to know what he was on about, but the truth was, he hadn't been listening.

'And you reckon *I'm* away with the fairies!' Declan scoffed. 'I tell you what you need . . . ' and he reached into his pocket and started cutting a line of coke right there on the mixing desk.

36

Mark

Getting off the train at Macclesfield, Mark decided a bit of Dutch courage was called for. The nearest pub was The Millstone, which was appropriate; the shame, the guilt, the sheer bloody mess of it all. It was an old school sort of joint; sticky carpet, fruit machines, one or two regulars propping up the bar. Walking in with his smart-casual jacket and his black backpack he might as well have had a neon sign over his head saying, SOFT SOUTHERNER.

'I'll have a pint of whatever you recommend,' he told the barman, with what he hoped was a winning smile. The guy shrugged and started pulling. 'And a double scotch,' Mark added recklessly.

He gave the bloke a twenty and didn't bother waiting for the change, just took his drinks over to a table and sat there like a condemned man, partaking of his last earthly pleasure. It was almost a relief, knowing it was over. Not that it *was* over yet, technically, nor would it be for some time. He'd have to come clean now. Hannah Bannerman seemed to think there was little doubt they'd prosecute, although she reckoned they stood a pretty good chance of getting a suspended sentence. He'd liked the way she'd said 'they', as if she'd be doing time in solidarity with him. They'd be wanting to make an example of him, asset-wise, she'd warned him, gravely. He couldn't be seen to have profited from his dodgy dealing, so they'd be after the spoils, and that meant his share of The Button Factory and probably Moorcroft Road as well. Jesus. He'd almost rather be in Wormwood Scrubs than endure the shame of moving Harriet to some tacky rental property. He imagined them watching telly in a trailer park somewhere and smiled bleakly to himself. The funny thing was, he could probably hack it. He'd only ever wanted the good things in life for her.

The pint was warm and the whisky coarse. He knocked it back with a shudder, then whacked down the empty glass and walked out feeling almost exhilarated.

Across the road, another train had just pulled in and the car park was thronged with commuters. The street lights were starting to come on and there was a nip in the air. Mark made a halfhearted dash for the taxi rank, just in time to see the last one commandeered by an attractive middle-aged woman with a shoulder bag. He'd just thrown up his hands in a gesture of 'why me?' despair, when its rear door flew open again.

'Mark!'

He stared. It was Yvette.

'That was lucky,' he said, 'I'd have been waiting ages.'

Yvette looked different; tired, like she'd had a tough day, but vibrant, too, somehow.

'Where've you been?' he remembered to ask. She didn't seem to have noticed she was travelling with a dead man.

'London, same as you. Our Ruby had a bit of a to-do with the baby.'

Ruby, yes. That was the daughter. And she was pregnant. Come on, Mark, get with the ...

'She's all right, though, is she? Sorry I forgot, when's it due again ...?'

She gave him a funny look.

'Not for another month, but they're going to do a Caesarean end of next week and she's on a monitor till then. I can't pretend I'm not worried sick, but ...'

' ... All's well that ends well,' said Mark.

Yvette frowned.

'And how about you?' she said.

'Me?' he said.

'How was your trip. Was it weird to be back?'

'God, yeah. Fucking weird!' said Mark feelingly.

'Did you see the twins?'

'Yeah, *that* part was good ...'

'So ... how are they liking Deptford?'

'Sorry?'

'Oh, no I just assumed you'd have seen ...'

' ... Jack? No, funnily enough I couldn't get hold of him. Kept going to answerphone. Couldn't get him at Deloitte's either. Hot-desking maybe ... But I did spend a lovely couple of hours with Ollie.'

He remembered their revelatory afternoon. The bonding and catharsis. The unexpected relief of spilling his guts to someone who had probably always known him better than he knew himself.

'He's only gone and got himself a book deal!'

'I know,' Yvette said smugly. She must have heard it from Jade, Mark supposed. Was he the last to know everything? God, he was tired. He could have done with this journey lasting forever. The thrum of the diesel engine, Yvette's pleasant, slightly astringent scent; the sporadic splash of orange across the upholstery as they passed another street lamp ...

' ... Mark, we'll be there in a minute.'

He jolted awake at Yvette's gentle nudge. She leaned forward and tapped on the taxi driver's screen.

'It's just coming up on the left,' then, as she was sitting back again, Yvette glanced through the window and did a double take.

'Uh-oh,' she said, 'Harriet won't like that.'

'What?' Mark asked, befuddled.

'More graffiti. We ought to get it cleaned off, really, or we'll get ourselves a reputation.'

'Bit late for that!' muttered Mark.

The taxi driver was offhand, bordering on rude. He set them down at the end of the drive so Mark didn't bother with a tip.

As they trudged towards The Button Factory, music was blaring from the roof terrace, its sound distorting in the wind like a calliope at the fairground. A burst of drunken laughter rent the air.

'You'd think the novelty might have worn off by now,' Yvette said, wearily. 'I don't know about you, but I might just opt for a cup of cocoa and an early night.'

Glancing upwards, Mark saw steam shimmering from the

hot tub and coloured fairy lights swinging hectically in the breeze.

'Sounds about right,' he agreed.

But as they climbed the stairs, a savoury smell drifted down to meet them and when they reached the kitchen, it became obvious that Harriet had made a homecoming supper.

There were six places set at the kitchen island, complete with cloth napkins and wine and water glasses. Mark's stomach lurched with dread. He wanted nothing so much as to lie down in a darkened room and never wake up again. Then again, it wasn't going to get any easier. He might as well make a clean breast of it while he still had alcohol coursing through his veins. In fact . . . he reached for an open gin bottle that was sitting next to a tray of melting ice cubes beside the fridge. After taking a long slug, he waved it at Yvette, but she shook her head, reaching for the kettle instead.

'D'you think Harriet'd mind if I ducked out of dinner?' she said, doubtfully.

Mark's felt his face crumple like an infant's. He hadn't realized how much Yvette's unflappable presence had been keeping him afloat.

'Hey!' she said now, seeing the strength of his reaction. 'Easy, partner. Don't worry I'll stick around if it means that much to you.'

She lifted the lid off the casserole.

'Mm, kale. Who could resist?'

The steps up to the roof might as well have led to the gallows. Mark and Yvette walked out onto the vast and chilly terrace like two spectres at the feast.

'I just can't believe someone as fundamendallee earthbound

as *you* did ball-a-ay, Harriet,' Meadow drawled, disinhibition exaggerating her Texan accent, and prompting a huge sycophantic laugh from her fellow bathers. Mark bridled on his wife's account.

Beside them in an ice bucket stood a bottle of champagne, as yet unopened. The atmosphere was weird – both strained and unbuttoned at the same time, as if everyone was trying to prove how happy and together and sorted they were – *sorted* being, perhaps, the operative word. Mark didn't know what they'd been taking, but whatever it was, he hoped to God there was some left.

'Mark, darling, you're back!' Harriet said, and he could tell by the staginess in her tone that she was neither as high, nor as chilled as she was making out. Something was up with her.

'Yvette!' she cried, clasping her cheeks, now, in a pantomime of guilty recollection. 'Oh my word! Ruby! I nearly forgot... How *was* she?'

Gary's head whipped round like a ventriloquist's dummy. He leaned out of the hot tub and silenced the music.

'Shit! Yeah, how's our kid? Is the baby OK?'

'They're both fine,' Yvette reassured them, 'the baby's small for dates, but they're keeping her in now, so...'

'I knew she'd pull through!' said Gary, complacently. 'I tell you what, though, I'm going down for the birth. Try and stop me. First grandchild!' He flexed his arm in a macho gesture and the others laughed.

'Oh, Yvette, I am *so* relieved,' Harriet said. 'Now we can have a *double* celebration. Open the fizz will you, Mark?' she indicated the bottle of Moët. 'The glasses are on the ledge there. Just a splash for me.'

The wind dropped for a moment, and the hot tub churned and cranked, its underwater lights flicking through the colour spectrum. Mark felt some rusty cavity clank open in his brain.

'Why, what else are we celebrating?' Yvette asked, with a wary smile.

'Well, I hardly dare tell you, 'cos I don't want to jinx it . . . ' Harriet's eyes shone.

Inside Mark's head, hinges creaked; cogs whirred.

'But here goes . . . I'm pregnant!'

A ball bearing dropped dully into a chamber somewhere.

Whooping, splashing, high-fiving. Five pairs of eyes were trained in his direction. Harriet gazed at him now, her expression searching his, full of hope, full of fear.

'Mark . . . ?'

'You can't be!'

Funny. His first instinct was to assume it was a genuine mistake. Not a betrayal; a mistake. That was how much he loved her, how much he wanted to believe her.

'I know it seems too good to be true, sweetheart, but I can assure you I am.'

The wind moaned. The coloured LEDs flicked through their sequence again.

'I did a test earlier today . . . it's downstairs if you don't believe me.'

She couldn't meet his eye. It was true then. Not another of her fantasies.

He could feel his body changing, swelling, as if a seed of rage that had been inside him the whole time had suddenly germinated, and was growing exponentially . . .

'So, who do I congratulate?' Mark pretended to look around him.

'What do you mean?' Harriet laughed nervously.

'Because it's not mine.'

'*Mark!*' Harriet chastised him. 'Of course it's yours. Why would you even say that?'

'Why?' Mark laughed bitterly. 'Because I've had a vasectomy, that's why.'

'Fuck!' muttered Gary, not quite inaudibly.

'You can't have done,' Harriet shook her head, still smiling, as though it was some sort of sick April fool. 'How could you have had a vasectomy without me knowing?'

'That residential course I went on in Harrogate ... '

'You had a vasectomy in *Harrogate*?' Harriet wailed.

'Well, technically I had it in York, but yeah ... '

'How could you do that behind my back?'

'How could I not? I couldn't bear it. What it was doing to us; to you. I was afraid.'

'Fuck!' muttered Gary again.

'Well, there you go,' Harriet said a little hysterically, 'you needn't have been. Because obviously it didn't work, I'm *pregnant*, Mark, and it can only be yours.' She half stood and reached out a placatory hand to him.

'It *did* fucking work!' he hissed, pulling his arm away so that she almost stumbled. 'They test you afterwards. I'm officially a sperm-free zone. I'm firing blanks. So, do you want to tell me whose baby you're fucking having? Or shall I guess ... ?'

He was almost relishing it now; enjoying the awareness that beside him, Yvette was reeling in shock, her eyes fixed incriminatingly on Gary, who seemed determined to tough it out, arms folded, face impassive.

Mark looked down at the bottle of champagne in his hand. He had forgotten how it had got there; what it was for ... ah, yes. He switched his grip from body to neck, lifted it to shoulder height and smashed it down on the edge of the tub, watching its contents discharge into the water. He saw limbs scrambling away from him, heard yelps and entreaties. Gary was staying put, though. Gary was going to be the big man. They faced off now, opposite each other – Gary jutting his chin, Mark brandishing the broken bottle. For the first time in weeks, months, *years*, Mark felt big; he felt real. He was going to prison anyway, might as well add GBH to the charge sheet. Might as well add murder. He jabbed the shard of broken glass experimentally at Gary, considering whether to go for the chest, the face, the jugular. Gary flinched in slow motion and then, just as he looked poised to strike back, the big man, the front man, the alpha male, his face changed. First a wince, then a grimace, then a frozen, comical mask of dismay. And now he was deflating like a popped balloon before Mark's eyes, sinking down into the water, recoiling, flailing...

The hot tub was deserted now. It nestled in the corner of the dark rooftop, the thrum of its pump competing with the low moan of the wind over the nearby Pennines and the discordant hee-haw of the retreating siren. The LEDs continued to cast their psychedelic glow through the churning water, red to purple to blue to green and back to red. Rocking gently at its bubbling centre, a bottle of Moët, its neck sheared off, only the label holding together shards which had unfolded on the surface of the water like a butterfly's wings.

PART III

TWO YEARS LATER

37

'Hey, Rubes, I think that was Rhianna!' Jordan nudged her, pointing through the rear window of the stretch limo, but by the time Ruby had turned round to check, the car had moved past the cluster of minders and press and was snaking slowly towards the VIP entrance of the O2 Arena.

Ever since the limo had collected them from Woolwich, Jordan had been in cheerleader mode, trying to jolly Yvette and Ruby along with jokes and compliments and celebrity gossip. He was busting a gut, poor love, but even the promise of a selfie with Stormzy wasn't going to do it for Ruby tonight. Sixteen months ago, when she'd still been a kid of thirty-two, maybe, but not anymore. Not now she was a mum and her dad was dead and the world had spun off its axis.

She indulged him all the same, pretending to be into the on-board cocktails and the tinted windows and the glamour. He was only doing his best; trying to take her out of herself, draw some kind of line in the sand, after all the shock and upset of the previous year.

The family had conspired to keep the distressing circumstances of Gary's death from Ruby until after Jeanie's birth. They'd even let her think his funeral had been delayed on her account, only admitting later that an inquest and an autopsy had been required before her dad could be laid to rest. They might as well have held the funeral without her anyway, because she couldn't remember a thing about it. Blanked it out, probably. And then it had been Christmas – the saddest and weirdest one she could recall with a Gary-shaped hole right at its heart. After that, she'd suffered six months of post-natal depression and Jordan's mum had moved in to help out. Then, just when it felt like they might be adjusting to some bleak new normal, *The Other Cheek* had been nominated for a Music Industry Best of British award, causing the whole scandal to resurface, with speculation in the media as to whether the album was a work of genius in its own right, or had racked up two hundred and thirty million streams because of the lurid circumstances surrounding its release.

And finally, this invitation to the MIBBs. Ruby's first instinct had been to turn it down, but Jordan had insisted they go – he'd mentioned the dread word 'closure' and cringy though that was, she had to admit, he had a point. Besides, in the unlikely event Gary won best single, her mum would have to go up on stage in front of all the lights and cameras and accept the gong on his behalf, so the least she and Jade could do was have her back.

Her poor mum. The look on her face, when the car had turned into their little cul-de-sac half an hour ago and Yvette had had to wave baby Jeanie bye-bye and hobble out to the limo in her high heels. She'd have been much happier gossiping with Rose on the sofa, taking turns to amuse her granddaughter, with the MIBBs on telly in the background. But it wasn't to be. As it was, Ruby had to sponge a little smear of baby sick off the green lurex dress that Yvette had kept spotless in polythene since she'd worn it to the Albert Hall in 1990. They'd marvelled that she could still get into it, thirty years on, although in all honesty it had been stress, not dieting that had taken the weight off – her mum had looked a whole lot better when she'd been a comfy size fourteen.

Considering her life had all but collapsed, though, Ruby had to admit Yvette had managed pretty well. Not 'well' as in pretending nothing had happened, in the fucked-up English way, but 'well' as in being at the end of a phone, twenty-four-seven, ready to listen and sympathize with her daughters' woes, despite the fact she had plenty of her own; 'well' as in not beating herself up too much about sinking all their money in a white elephant of a property up North, that now wouldn't shift. 'Well' as in not being deflected from her chosen career path, despite knowing literally no one in Macclesfield (except for Harriet, who, for some reason, she now wanted nothing to do with). And well, oh so very well, as in being offered an acting Deputy Head's job in some dodgy C of E primary school.

So, yes, Yvette had been a tower of strength, as no-nonsense Northern women so often were. Why then, Ruby wondered, as the limo slowed to a halt and a security guard opened the rear door, did she feel so *angry* with her?

Yvette blinked, momentarily blinded by a dazzle of flash-bulbs. Jordan had been right. There'd be no sneaking in the tradesman's entrance tonight. She stepped out onto, yes – an actual red carpet, albeit a nylon one, with some dodgy-looking stains. Now some young woman she vaguely recognized off the telly was waving a microphone in her face and her knickers were going up her bottom and Ruby and Jordan had disappeared and ... Oh God, Oh Jesus!

'Yvette Kershaw!' the woman said. 'Wife ... *widow*, I should say, of Gary Kershaw, the legendary lead singer of The KMA, sadly no longer with us. Our sincere condolences, Yvette. How does it feel to be here tonight, representing your late husband?'

She gently tugged Yvette round to face the camera and then held her elbow with an iron grip. Yvette winced as flashbulbs popped around her.

'It's ... well, yes, of course, it's ... er...'

'... Bittersweet, I imagine ... ?' the young woman prompted, tilting her head in fake empathy.

'Er ... yeah, kind of ... '

'... Especially as the new album's spent a record ten weeks in the download charts and Gary penned the title track which is up for best single ... ?'

Yvette noticed a bloke behind the camera making a 'wind it up' motion with his finger.

'... Heartbreaking, just heartbreaking. Have a great night!'

And that had been it, thank God. No tricky questions, no nudges or winks. No innuendo about the circumstances of Gary's death – orgies, sex games – the sort of sleaze the tabloids had hinted at six months ago when the album had come out. Though the truth would have kept them all happy, if it hadn't been so effectively hushed up. The truth would have been quite lurid enough.

Of the six who had been on the roof that night, Yvette was the only one at the O2 for the awards ceremony. She'd made sure of that before she accepted the invitation. Declan was in rehab, and Meadow had gone back to Texas, tail well and truly between her legs. Harriet and Mark hadn't been invited, but in any case, neither of them was currently available for jollies, Harriet being nose to the grindstone on some Derbyshire water mill conversion and Mark keeping a low profile after his suspended sentence.

Yvette was trying not to hate Mark; partly because she already hated Harriet with a vengeance, and there was only room for so much hate in one person's heart. Also because she could hardly blame him, in all conscience, for fronting up to Gaz that night. Who wouldn't take a pop at their best mate if they found out he'd been shagging their wife? Christ, she'd have slapped Gary around herself, if she hadn't been reeling from the shock. She'd stood by him, had his fucking baby, put her whole life on hold for him and he'd thanked her by knocking up her best mate, just as carelessly, thirty years on. How were you meant to get over a thing like that?

Only Mark knew whether he'd actually laid a finger on Gary – all Yvette could remember was the sound of smashing glass, followed by a blur of splashing and screaming and then sirens. According to the coroner, Gary had been a dead man walking. Coke in his bloodstream; arteries furred to buggery and the effect of immersion in hot water on a weak heart, a probable contributory factor. Verdict: misadventure.

You could say Mark had got off lightly. Or you could call a suspended prison sentence and his reputation in the gutter poetic justice. Him and Jack both, who'd have thought? Two felons together. Like father like son. Although according to Jade, Jack might actually do time. Possession with intent to supply. The blue-eyed boy had been dealing since college. She almost felt sorry for him, but not quite. Turned out Ollie was the only member of Harriet's family with any moral compass; which was ironic, since he was the one who looked most like a criminal. Still, he didn't look out of place at the O2 tonight, with his tatts and his crew cut and his book deal. He fitted right in.

'Here's your mum,' Ollie murmured in Jade's ear and he'd stood up gallantly and kissed Yvette on both cheeks, just like you were supposed to.

'Hello, love, how are you?' Yvette had said and Ollie had felt a surge of gratitude and relief. Jade had promised him Yvette would be OK with his being there, but it still felt weird, what with the rift between their families and everything.

Ruby and Jordan were next. They were nice to him too – but he'd not been so worried about them – they'd come to Ollie's book launch, after all, which was above and beyond, considering they had a little baby. She was a nice little thing, their kid, but he and Jade had agreed that if they stayed the distance, they'd probably not bother – babies seeming an awful lot of trouble, one way and another. Jordan gave Ollie a fist-bump-cum-hug and told him he looked sharp.

A waiter came over and recharged their glasses and they all raised them instinctively, and then looked blank, scarcely knowing, under the circumstances, who or what to toast.

'To ... Gaz, I guess ... ' said Yvette with an embarrassed shrug. There was a pause and then each of them took a sip and murmured his name, hardly able, it seemed, to swallow afterwards.

'We ought to go easy, really,' Ruby pointed out, as they sat back in their seats, 'it's nibbles only and it looks like being a long night.'

'Specially you, Yvette.' Jordan nudged her familiarly, in a way Ollie would never have dared. 'You might be going up there later.'

He indicated the stage, a daunting three-tiered affair, behind which giant screens now showed montages of past years' winners.

All credit to Yvette, she didn't look bothered. Anyway, he reckoned Gary was only shortlisted because he'd carked it and the winner was sure to be that earworm that had been the anthem of the summer. Then again, Ollie supposed, after the year she must have had, muffing an acceptance speech on the telly would be the least of her worries.

Ollie wondered if his mum would be watching, from her lonely eyrie in The Button Factory. He worried about her up there all on her own – had tried to persuade her to come back to Moorcroft Road, at least until the legal stuff went through, but she'd told him, in that brittle little voice of hers, that she'd be staying put while she finished the job she was working on. It was funny to think of the two women living in the same town and avoiding each other like the plague. Each sticking it out for what? Pride? Their careers? In Yvette's case he got it. He'd seen her in the classroom – had been the beneficiary of her empathy himself, all those years ago at Dale Road. She should always have been a teacher and he was glad she was finally going to be. But did Harriet really need to be in Macclesfield? Knowing nobody. Living in that draughty old warehouse on her own? It was as though she was the one in prison. Serving time on Jack's behalf maybe. Or maybe hanging on in The Button Factory, unable to cut the cord, hoping against hope that some new financial fix, some grant, some philanthropic repurposing might prevent her eviction and its eventual sale. He felt bad for her, bad for everyone; and guilty sometimes too. After all, he'd been the reason his mum and Yvette had made friends, all those years ago – he still remembered her and Jade coming round to the house, the fear of it; the thrill of it. And the two families had been solid ever since, until last year. It felt like they'd waited for him and Jade to figure out they were more than friends, and then imploded. He couldn't imagine what had been such a big deal that they were no longer speaking.

The lights dimmed now and the buzz of conversation gradually petered out. A disembodied tellyland voice boomed over the PA system.

'Good evening from the O2 Arena and welcome to the MIBBS 2020!'

Four huge, scary huffs of flame leaped like blowtorches at the front of the stage and a familiar dance track boomed out of the loudspeakers, as a troupe of acrobats dressed in luminous flower costumes started gyrating spectacularly in the pitch-black.

Once the proceedings got under way, time seemed to Yvette, both to collapse in on itself and stretch out forever. There were laser shows and dance numbers, guest appearances and speeches; so many speeches . . .

'...I never expected this...'

'...Last year these guys were supporting us on tour, this year...'

'...Keep it real!'

'...I'd like to thank my mum...'

'...Stay humble...'

Yvette reminded herself what she needed to say, in the unlikely event she'd be going up there, and then tried to put it out of her mind because she was pretty damn sure she *wouldn't* be going up there. She stared determinedly ahead, ignoring the curious glances of guests at nearby tables and the camera lens that was practically up her nose. Now the affable comedian dropped his voice to a portentous whisper.

'And the nominations are... L'il Ka for *In the Projects*, Aimee Dupree for *Dynamite*, Harry Binns for *Love Like it Oughtta Be* and The KMA for *The Other Cheek*...' He paused, looked into the camera, undid the envelope in slow motion and took out the card... 'And the winner is...'

Ruby was shaking Yvette's wrist. The audience was applauding, Macca's irresistible jangly guitar riff was pounding out of the speakers and Gary's voice, wry and beautiful and full of self-knowledge, was telling her what she had to do.

'*Turn the other cheek girl,*
You gotta turn the other cheek.
Well, I'm down on my knees and I'm begging you,
You gotta turn the other cheek.'

Yvette stood up and started to make her way towards the podium.

Acknowledgements

A big and heartfelt thank you to the following people:

My agent Sallyanne Sweeney for her enthusiasm, invaluable editorial input and all-round excellence. My editor Kate Mills for her unfailing instinct for pace, plot, character – the whole shebang.

My first readers and critics for their encouragement, support, B-S detection, adjective whittling and all-round bracing honesty: Julie Bull, Petrina Dorrington, Ken Frape, John Holland, Steven John, Jane Maitland, Kate O'Grady and Jan Turk Petrie.

My close-readers, amateur and professional, for dotting i's, crossing t's, removing howlers and helping me keep the balance between the local and the universal, the slangy and the downright obscure: Jon Appleton, Martha Everett, Thea Everett, Rebecca Jamieson, Kate Hulls and Polly Smith.

My musical mentors, Mark Radcliffe and Stuart Maconie of BBC 6 Music. Their warm and witty banter put this long-exiled Mancunian in touch with my roots, emboldened me to write from the point of view of a nineties Madchester muso, and provided the soundtrack, not just to the writing of this novel but to some of the most fun times of the last ten years.

My beloved husband Adam Goulcher for putting up with all the vacant stares and blank nods, the missed walks and cold dinners, for ploughing through every word of every sentence of every draft and always making it better.

ONE PLACE. MANY STORIES

Bold, innovative and
empowering publishing.

FOLLOW US ON:

@HQStories